Damaged Goods

Text copyright © 2015 Orange Publishing, LLC.
All rights reserved. Published by Orange Publishing, LLC.

Library of Congress Control Number: 2015902990

ISBN: 978-0-9887480-2-6 (paperback)
ISBN: 978-0-9887480-3-3 (eBook)

Printed in the U.S.A.
First Printing – March, 2015

Book Two of the Jack and Emily Series

Damaged Goods
By
Laura Strandt

Orange Publishing
Strasburg, PA

Thank You to those who made this possible...

To anyone and everyone who read "Crumbling Walls" ...
we owe a debt of gratitude to you that can never truly be re-paid ...
To those who have been diligent in their hassling of me to get 'Damaged
Goods' done (Chris, Kim, Abby, Mom, Dad, Marilyn, Aunt Carol, Hannah,
the other Hannah, Holly, StaciAshleySarah, Meadow, Hailey and a bunch
more whom I can't recall at the moment but love to bits and pieces just
the same).
To the kid, Abby, and the husband, Chris again for letting me write when I
wanted to and when I needed to ... you are awesome!!!
Forever thanks to Dave, the bestest cousin and editor and best friend a girl
could have ...
To everyone who helped with the cover: Jake Williams and Hannah Taylor,
who occupied a hammock in January and allowed us to nearly drop them
on the ground in order to get a good shot ... Chris for climbing the ladder
and photographing ... Kim for hair and posing ... Abby for keeping the dog
from photo bombing every shot ... Dave for the finished product ... and
myself for the hammock in the first place. 8^)
I love you all more than you'll ever know and am grateful to have each and
every one of you surrounding me ... don't stop hassling me ... ever.

About the Author

Laura's Version

I read … I draw … I write … I write some more … I work … I play … I color … I make dinner and feed my kid … I love my husband and my Abby … I adore my house … I enjoy my job … I play a mean game of Super Mario Bros. … my iPod is almost full and my gas tank is often on empty … I would rather sleep in a camper in the woods than spend a night in a fancy hotel … I've swam in the South Pacific Ocean … I've seen lava flows and flooded cities … I have fallen through holes in caves and climbed mountains where the air was so thin it was hard to breathe … I have accidently walked in on a boy in the bathroom … I understand how the Dewey Decimal System works … I believe in all sorts of crazy things except my ability to speak in front of crowds … I wish everyday that "The X-Files" was still on TV but am very glad to have found "Doctor Who" … I wonder often if aliens and/or God is watching me during the day and laughing hysterically … I have watched Dave lose his hair … I have accidently driven through bean fields … I make my own strawberry jam … I have been to entirely too many funerals in my life … I am 5 feet tall … my daughter once believed my middle name was pronounced 'Murray' instead of 'Marie' and I love it … I am Laura and this is my life :)

Dave's Version

What she said … except I haven't lost my hair. I know where every strand(t) has gone.

Prologue

Jack, who'd woken as soon as his mother had come in the room, opened his eyes, surprising them both with a groggy voice, "Can I go see her?"

Elizabeth tilted her head in his direction, sympathy clear, "She's had a really rough time."

"I just want to make sure she's okay."

Relenting, Elizabeth nodded slowly, "Be careful."

Upstairs in a silent instant, Jack stopped cold when he saw her lying there, and, kneeling down, he nearly toppled back in surprise when she opened her eyes to look at him. Now knowing what his parents must have felt when he did the same thing a minute earlier, he vowed never to do that again. Taking a deep breath, he whispered, "I thought you were asleep." Remaining silent, she simply stared at him, not blinking until he spoke again, "Do you want some company?"

This time he watched her nod twice, words being too much effort.

Settling in on the floor, he rested his head on the mattress, "I missed you."

Another nod.

"Do you want to talk about it?" Receiving a headshake of no, he let his eyes wander over her face, neck … any parts he could take in without moving a muscle. After his eyes adjusted to the dimly lit room, he realized something was different and asked her in a low voice, "Where's your hair?"

Whispering, "Cleveland," she shut her eyes again, her last thoughts being of the wonderfully dark, quiet place her mind was retreating to.

Chapter 1

Raising hell.

That was the order of business by the time everyone sat down for dinner on this mild March Sunday night. Will had argued that they should dole out their news slowly, not overload the kids' circuits with too much information at one time. Elizabeth, however, in a playfully feisty mood, grinned at him and shook her head, "Come on. How many times do we get the chance to render the seven of them speechless? Let's just tell it all at once and stand back."

Will gave his wife a raised eyebrow and a twinkling eye, "Sounds an awful lot like some psychology experiment. You're not trying to start a riot, are you?"

"Nope. I think, though, that it's all good news and everybody could use some of that right now, even if they don't know it yet."

Seeing her point, he nodded with a smile, "All right then. Let's go raise some hell."

During dinner a few hours later, Will waited until most of the food was eaten and the conversation had found a lull before he caught his wife's gaze, shrugged and sat back, allowing her to do the honors. With her own nonchalant little throat-clearing cough, "So, everybody, I'm pregnant."

There was a moment of dead silence where looks shot back and forth between the brothers with lightning speed, then the table exploded with activity: Jack calling for a due date, Dave wanting to know if it was a boy, Nate yelling 'not it' on future dirty diapers, Tucker cheering at the top of his lungs, hooting and hollering with a short chair dancing session occurring all at once. Sam couldn't keep himself contained and took off to run circles around the living room, ecstatic he'd finally have a person littler than him in the house.

Tim, however, raised an eyebrow in his parent's direction and called over the noise surrounding him, "Um, question … where, Dear Parents, do you plan on stashing this kid when it gets here? Or are you finally gonna sell one of us for money to build another room?"

Will smiled in his direction, "Well, since you're starting college in the fall, we were thinking that maybe you'd like to move into the loft over the garage? There's the bathroom downstairs and it's heated, so if you'd like it, we just need to clean it out and it's yours." Turning to Emily, "We were also wondering if you wouldn't mind giving up your room for the baby and moving down here? If you're not comfortable with being alone just yet, it's fine. We can figure something out easy enough."

Without hesitation, she nodded then opened her mouth to speak, but Tim's voice covered any sound she tried to make, "Seriously? You're gonna let me live out there? Alone? All by myself? With nobody else?"

Nodding his understanding in Emily's direction, Will then looked at his son, "Is that a 'yes' or an 'I don't want to be so far away from all you lovely people'?"

Giving his parents a grin, "When do we start cleaning?"

Will managed to get out a, 'we'll start after your party' before Sam, who'd been listening while still running in his circles, skidded to a stop and looked at Tim, "You'll still be my big brother if you move out, right?"

With a hint of a 'what an idiot' sigh, "Yes, Sam, I will still be your big brother."

"Can we stay over sometime?"

Gesturing out the back door in the direction of the garage, shoulders up in both annoyance and disbelief, "What the … ? Sam, it's thirty feet from the back door, and who is 'we'?"

This time it was Sam with the 'what an idiot' sigh, "Us. All of us. We can all come over and have a giant sleepover. Except Mom, 'cause she's gonna be too big to get up the stairs."

"Excuse me?"

Dave went instantly red as he shrugged at his mom, "We've shown him pictures of when you were pregnant before … and can I just say, you've never been the smallest of pregnant people."

She couldn't help her chuckle as she shut her eyes and nodded, "Very true."

Realizing that Tim never actually answered Sam's question, Emily stood and grabbed Sam's hands, swinging him around, distracting him, "You get to be a big brother for the first time!"

"And you get to be a big sister again!"

Before she could respond, Will cleared his throat and dropped bombshell number two, "Actually, Sam, that's exactly right and we have the paperwork to prove it." Holding an envelope out to Emily, "You are officially and undeniably, legally stuck with us from now on. Your guardianship papers came yesterday." Dropping Sam's hands, Emily's flew to cover her gaping mouth, staring at the envelope in Will's hands, but not taking it. He stood a moment later, walking it over to her, "You okay?"

Nodding, she whispered through her fingers, "What if I touch it and it disappears?"

"Then how about I put it over here," setting it on the mantle over the fireplace, "and you can take it when you're ready, okay?"

She nodded again, finally dropping her hands to her sides, both she and Sam returning to their seats amidst the unnatural silence that had fallen over the table.

Of course, the silence didn't last long. Nate, being the one to make them all jump when he proclaimed in a loud voice, "Two new people added to the family in under five minutes. I love it!"

And there went the silence.

Jack, however, who'd been mostly quiet next to Emily in the middle of the mayhem looked at her as the thought finally sank in, "Does this mean you're dating your brother now?"

Will overheard them, even through the insanity, "Nope. If we'd have adopted her, it would have gotten weird, but with guardianship, we legally take care of her, but she is not technically related to us."

Emily, eyes glued to the envelope across the room, "That would have gotten really, really weird."

Jack grinned, "Dex would have taken to calling us creepy."

She finally smiled, the left corner of her mouth curving upwards, "From him, that's a compliment."

Jack quickly kissed Emily's cheek, "Come on number seven, dish duty calls." Looking down the table at Elizabeth and raising his voice so she could hear him above the still more than lively chaos, "Unless there's more news to drop on us – Dad is now an astronaut and heading to Mars? You're moving us to Switzerland to teach us to ski? You've finally invented a way for all of us to use the bathroom at the same time, but never have to see each other naked?"

"Well, actually, there is one other thing," pausing for dramatic effect and then continuing, "your Uncle Bob and Aunt Jenny are moving here after school gets out."

It took a moment for this to process in Jack's already packed brain, but the moment it did, Elizabeth watched her son nearly drop the plate he'd just picked up, "Here?"

"Here."

Setting the plate down, he gripped his mother's upper arms, asking her, "Here, here, as in, 'down the street' here or 'two hours away with Grama and Grampa, but still in Pennsylvania' here?"

"Here as in not necessarily down the street, but much closer than Grama and Grampa."

Jack dug out his phone and dialed his cousin, Claire, without another word. When she answered, he said just one thing, "Seriously?"

"Seriously."

"Very cool."

"Exactly."

He then hung up, staring at his phone for a moment before looking around. The family stood in various positions, more amused than baffled at the swift conversation they'd just heard. Emily, however, asked in quiet confusion, "Um, what was that?"

Giving her a grin, "Just confirming."

Nate elbowed her, "Get used to it. That's how their conversations work. No one but them knows what in the world is going on."

"Thanks for the warning."

With all of the news out of the way, the family began their usual post-dinner cleanup, Emily moving to stand next to Jack. Beginning to stack plates, she shot a glance in his direction, "What did you mean by number seven?"

"You're the seventh kid added. You're here before the baby, but after Sam, so you get lucky number seven?"

"I'm lucky now, too?"

Recruiting Tucker to help with the chores by removing him from his chair with a headlock, "I have it on good authority that we're the lucky ones."

Tucker, being dragged along beside them, grinned up at her, "And now we get to wrestle you to the ground for the remote control."

"You couldn't do that before?"

"Naw, we had to be polite."

Emily loved her new family even more, "And now you're done with polite?"

After Jack released his brother and Tucker's face began returning to its normal color, "Yeah, you're part of the family now … and polite doesn't really work for us anyways." He then hopped on Jack's back, "Welcome to the family, Em."

♦ ♦ ♦

Lying in bed later that night, Sam snoring a few feet away, Jack began thinking, his mind turning over the idea of the envelope on the mantle. At first he was happy she was finally part of the family, although the whole marriage thing would have taken care of that in a few years anyway, but then he narrowed his focus …

… and this is where the problem arose. Those papers only existed because he'd killed her father. People said it was an accident. Emily knew it was an accident. He thought it was an accident.

The panic came quickly, squeezing his throat, causing his fingers to grip the rolled edges of his mattress while he tried his best to hang on in silence, his focusing thought being simply that he must not scare Sam.

He could not scare Sam.

He sure as hell better not scare Sam.

Ten minutes later, the sweat fresh on his face and his fingers numb, Jack finally opened his eyes. Staring at the ceiling, he loosened his handhold and felt his muscles uncoiling. Really wishing he could do some serious swearing, he ended up spending the next two hours awake, longing for sleep to find him before his alarm clock did.

♦ ♦ ♦

Jack's night panic and several small attacks after that at least had a fairly obvious trigger, Emily's guardianship paperwork. The smaller ones happened when he would catch sight of the papers on the mantle, but he managed to breathe through those, dealing with things himself yet again. It was the freak out that happened the following week that really annoyed him.

Dozing at the kitchen counter, waiting for his peanut butter and banana cupcakes, Nate's birthday dessert request, to finish cooking, Elizabeth dropped a plate. A simple breaking plate, which didn't have a damn thing to do with Emily, set him off. Luckily no one else was around at the time and Elizabeth could focus on talking him down as opposed to explaining things to worried children.

When Jack finally stopped clutching the kitchen table, Elizabeth stood to hand him one of the kitchen towels to mop the sweat off his face, "You okay?"

Feeling like he was about to throw up, Jack nodded slowly, "Where did that come from?"

"I don't know. The only thing I can think of is that when the plate dropped, you got scared, but what does a plate have to do with Emily? Were you having a dream about her or something?"

After resting his head on his arms, he stared at his mom through half open eyes, "I don't remember dreaming." He waited until the nausea had passed before sitting back up, "I'd really like this nonsense to stop. It's getting old."

Elizabeth couldn't help her smile, "This nonsense, as you call it, will get better, I promise."

Standing, he took a deep breath, "At least I know what this week's conversation with Amelia will be."

"You doing okay with her? I know you've only gone to her once but …"

Jack nodded, "She's nice. Ask me again after a few weeks, but for now, I like her."

Landing a kiss to the top of his head, "I will ask again, don't worry. Also let me know if I'm hovering too much. I'm going to hover a little, mind you, because I'm a mom and all, but if it gets to be overwhelming, just tell me, please."

She looked so worried that Jack gave her a nice, long hug, before pulling out the thankfully not burned-to-a-crisp cupcakes, "Promise."

Will took an even simpler approach. Twice a day, morning and night, Will gave his son a thumbs-up and asked, "Good?"

If he received a thumbs-up back and an echoed 'good', he carried on. He had not received a thumbs-down since he started, but Jack knew that if he needed to, he could give it and Will would be there.

Elizabeth had briefly told the boy that Jack was having a few problems and after that, Jack discovered he now had a pack of people keeping eyes on him. Luckily, once they realized he wasn't going to be growing a second head or breaking into torrential swearing fits, they, for the most part, forgot that anything was wrong and returned to their normal selves, which suited Jack just fine.

Dex, bless his soul, showed his concern on a whole other level. Instead of asking how things were going with Amelia or waiting for the torrent of swearing, Dex, at one of the cafeteria tables, box of Yoo-hoo in hand, pointed both box and straw directly at him, stating emphatically, "You pull that shit again and I'll kill you once I'm done peeing my pants." When Jack's smile appeared, Dex slapped a shocked look on his face, "Dude, you have teeth. Haven't seen those in a long ass time."

Wondering whether he'd either accidently or intentionally be squirted in the eye with Yoo-hoo, he raised an eyebrow, "Sorry to have deprived you of them."

"You haven't cracked a damn smile in the past God knows how many months. Usually it's furiously scowling Jack looking all pale and half-dead." Gesturing towards his friend's face, "You smiled. It was nice. I will not be commenting on it again."

"And why is that?"

"I'm not your girlfriend and I'm not in love with you, so I'm not gonna sit around and contemplate how pretty you may be when you smile, or the startlingly perfect straightness of your pearly white teeth." Standing, he leaned over Jack, pushing his head back and prying his mouth open to get a better look inside, "Damn. These things look better than those stupid posters at the dentists' office. You ought to go get yourself in some toothpaste commercials or something."

Jack pushed him away, shaking his head, but still grinning widely, "Get off me, you freak."

"Tooth fetishist. Get the name right next time."

Emily came up then, her eyebrow raised in curiosity, "Why was Dex in your mouth just now?"

In unison, "Don't ask."

And she didn't.

She also didn't ask about his trips to the 'psycho' lady, as Sam called her. She kissed him goodbye on Friday afternoons when he left for his appointment if she wasn't at work. If she was working, he'd stop by the Chinese place for a bowl of Wanton soup and a fortune cookie after the appointment. They talked about normal, everyday things, but never broached the subject of Amelia.

Chapter 2

On a semi-hot and humid mid-June day, Jack stood in the center of the yard, holding ropes in one hand and ground stakes in the other, "I can skip one session, Dad. You need my help and you know it."

"We'll be fine. You're more important than the party."

Tim, who managed to hear Will's reply over the whirring of Dave's weed whacker, looked towards them, "Thanks, Dad, glad you think this isn't important."

Not about to get into it when everyone was sweaty, tired, cranky and thirsty, he ignored Tim for the moment, taking the items from Jack, "Go wash a layer of dirt off before you go, please. Amelia doesn't need to see you doing your best imitation of Pigpen."

Giving in, he shrugged, "I could go in wearing a chicken suit and a wedding veil and she wouldn't even blink, but I'll try to scrape off some of the mud."

Will chuckled, then went to finish assembling the tent they'd borrowed from Dex's family. The canvas was every color of the rainbow and looked at least 80 years old, but it was sturdy and free, two qualities the Callaghans had learned never to argue against. Once Will had disappeared, Tim regarded Jack with narrow eyes, "You gonna bitch about me?"

"Not today. Your day was last week."

A quick smile leapt onto his face, "Whatever. Just remember this when I disappear in the middle of getting ready for your party next year."

"Push the devil down the stairs and I'll drive you to your therapy session myself."

Tim's smile faded slightly, "Too soon for jokes I take it?"

Realizing he was bringing Tim's mood down quickly, he smirked, his lips curling up slightly, "Maybe a week or two ahead of schedule, but that's it."

"Send out a memo when time's up, all right? I've got a good three, four dozen snarky comments waiting."

As Jack turned and headed over to Emily, he called over his shoulder to Tim, "Something to look forward to." Reaching her a few moments later, "I gotta go. I'll be back around five."

Looking up with dirt smeared across her face and sweat making her flyaway hairs stick to her cheeks, she left another smudge as she wiped her forehead and squinted towards him, "I'll still be here, fighting the weed bed that wouldn't die." Struggling to her feet, she kissed him lightly on the cheek, "Drive safely."

"I will. Make sure you don't let the weeds win. I like having you around." Turning before she could reply, he jogged into the house, intending to take exactly four minutes to scrub his face and change his shirt before disappearing downtown.

◆◆◆

Jack was in an air-conditioned office not much later, "Can I ask you a question about Emily?"

Amelia, who was intently sucking on one of the many lollipops scattered across her office, removed it before replying, "Of course. You know that."

He nodded towards the candy already making its way back into her mouth, "I like how you took that out to answer me."

"I'm a professional, remember?"

"I've got five brothers. None of them has ever answered a question without something in their mouth."

"Don't tempt me, Jack." Steering him back to the subject at hand, "What did you want to ask?"

He stood, picking up his own candy as he made his way to her window, taking his preferred perch against the windowsill as opposed to the too hard couch, "Do you think it's weird that we don't talk about my coming here? I mean, Tim will make sarcastic remarks, but still tell me to go get 'fixed.' Mom'll ask me how it went and, even though I only tell them that it went fine, she still asks each time. But Em, she's never once said a word about it, like she doesn't care, which I know is stupid because she's the one who made me tell my parents in the first place."

"From what I've heard, Emily is the last person in the world who wouldn't care." Not asking him to return to the couch, she simply shifted so she could see him better, pointing in his direction with her candy, "And I think I'd like to toss out there that maybe she's just not willing to pry. I imagine she'd talk to you if you let her know you were ready."

Letting that sink in, he crossed his ankles and hunched forward, nodding his head after a moment, "Makes sense, I guess."

"Do you ask her about her past, now that you know what happened to her? Do you talk about it?"

Having an enlightened moment, "No, I don't want to bug her. She tells me things when she's ready, and I guess … " wiggling his foot while he studied the carpet pattern, "I guess, when I look at it that way, it makes sense that she'd be doing the same thing for me."

"I'd bet my degree and, more preciously, my collection of Elvis memorabilia, that the moment you say, 'can I tell you about going to see Amelia?', she'll be more focused and intent than you've ever seen her."

Allowing himself to relax finally, realizing that sounded a lot more like his Emily, he glanced over at the therapist, "Always gotta be right, don't you?"

"It's a curse, let me tell you."

♦ ♦ ♦

Jack came home to find everyone, including Elizabeth and Will, lying on the back lawn, on both sides of the oscillating sprinkler, squeaking and jumping in amusement every time the cold water dropped on them. Standing on the edge of the deck, "Geez, the minute I leave, all y'all stop working. Can't do anything without me, can you?"

Emily answered for them all when she simply called out, "Shut up and lay down."

"Yes, ma'am." Out of his shoes and shirt in an instant, he wiggled between Emily and Sam, cursing quietly when the water hit him for the first time, "That's cold!"

This time it was Sam, "If it was heated, Jack, it would be stupid."

Holding up his hand towards his brother, "Nice comeback, little man. High five."

After the hand slapping, all remained quiet for another few minutes until suddenly, an impromptu wrestling match occurred, Dave and Tucker against Will and Nate. No one knew how it began, but it ended soon enough when Elizabeth, after struggling to stand up, turned the sprinkler directly on the group, "Break it up, people. I know I'm raising a bunch of savages, but there's no reason to ruin my lawn in the process."

Will, covered in mud and bits of grass, stood first, pulling a slippery Nate up with him, "Come on. Let's get cleaned off before your mother sells us to the gypsies, me included this time."

Sam looked up at his father, half-believing, "I didn't know gypsies bought people as old as you."

"Sam, my boy, even gypsies need someone to keep their books for them. They'll throw me in the corner with a slide rule and an abacus if necessary." Letting go of Nate's arm, he pulled Sam up next, "About face and shut your eyes. Your mother doesn't have the best aim sometimes."

13

✦✦✦

By that night, after the family had nearly depleted the water supply of the entire town with nine showers in a row and had eaten 21 ham and cheese sandwiches and two jars of pickles, Emily, Jack and Tim were the only ones still awake, the rest of the family having crashed face first into whatever bed happened to be closest to them at the time. Tim nudged Jack with his foot, "How was the shrink?"

"Her usual shrinking self."

"That'll work." He began to say more, but his phone vibrated across the kitchen table and, picking it up, he stood, heading into his room, calling goodnight in their direction before closing his bedroom door.

Jack looked over at Emily, "Sarah?"

"Who else would have him moving that fast?" Standing, she pulled him up, "I'm not tired yet. Wanna go sit on the front porch for awhile?"

"'Course." Once outside, however, he didn't follow Emily to the bench, but instead chose the same position he'd been in at Amelia's office earlier, leaning against the porch rail, legs crossed at the ankles, shoulder against the upright. In a way that he thought was casual, but to Emily seemed simply nervous, "Can I ask you something?"

"You can ask me anything, but I can't promise an answer that won't piss you off."

"I'm pretty sure that's Dex's response."

"He taught me well." Bringing her bare toes to rest over his, "What's wrong?"

Scrunching up his face, "How come you never ask me about Amelia or how I'm doing with all of this?"

Not as surprised by his question as some might have been, "You never demanded I tell you anything and I love you for that." With a slight shrug and a right-side smile, "I'm not about to do what I'm eternally grateful you

14

didn't do," Emily tapped his feet with hers, "but I'm not going anywhere and I do want to know everything, but at your speed, not mine."

"I'm pretty sure our speeds are the same right now."

Reaching forward, she pulled him towards her by his belt loops, shifting him so he sat down beside her, "Do you feel better?"

And they started to talk, neither realizing how much they hadn't said to each other in the past month. The conversation finally wound down around 2am. By then, Emily was lying across the swing, her head resting on Jack's thigh, his fingers playing with her ear and jawline as well as creeping down her neck to run absently across the scar at her hairline, "You never told me where this one came from."

He felt her shudder slightly as she told him quietly, "I don't think you want to know."

"Of course I do, but it's okay if you don't tell me."

She shrugged as best she could, "It kinda makes most of the others look tame."

He wanted to shudder some himself at that answer, but he held steady, "Do you mind me touching it or would you like me to stop?"

"I like it. Better a friendly hand than an unfriendly one." Reaching behind her head, she twisted her hair over her shoulder and out of his way, "Better?"

Shutting his eyes and tracing aimless patterns on her neck, "Was already perfect."

Chapter 3

Will was awake around 5:30am, but didn't come downstairs until after 6. Pulling open the front drapes, he was shocked to see the back of Jack's head over the top of the porch seat. Opening the door as quietly as he could, he stood against the railing, watching in silence for a minute, wondering fleetingly if he should just let them sleep. Problem was, he knew he couldn't and, hating himself, he reached out to shake Emily's shoulder, but Jack stopped him, "I'll wake her up."

"Jack?!"

"Whispering would be good here, Dad."

Bringing his voice down a notch, "How long have you been awake?"

Glancing at his watch, "'Bout a half-hour or so."

"Why didn't you come inside?"

Looking at him like he'd just asked the dumbest question in the world, "If you were me and Emily was sleeping on you, would you have gotten up?"

Point taken, "Very true, but you guys need to wake up. We've got a lot to do today and your mom feels like hell, so it's all on us."

"Define hell?"

"Bad enough to actually admit she feels like hell and, knowing your mom, that's pretty bad."

With a nod, he began stroking Emily's bare arm and playing with her fingers, "We'll be in in a minute."

Once Will had gone back inside, Jack moved his hand to her cheek, poking her lightly, "Em? Hey pretty girl, you've gotta wake up."

After a few seconds, she began shifting and then opened her eyes, "Jack?"

"Yeah?"

Her confused expression amused him, "We're on the porch."

"Never miss a detail, do you?" She sat up slowly, her wrinkled forehead moving him to laugh, "What? You fell asleep on the porch, what made you think you wouldn't wake up on the porch?"

Shaking the cobwebs from her brain, "I just didn't realize I'd fallen asleep."

With a smile, he kissed her, "Good morning."

Finally waking up, she kissed him back, "Thanks for last night."

Hanging his head for a moment, he looked at her out of the corner of his eye, "Thanks for listening."

Grinning over her shoulder as she walked inside, "Thanks for falling into the snapdragons."

◆◆◆

Jack was in the midst of furious mostaccioli making, with Nate's assistance, when Elizabeth came into the kitchen, stealing some already cooked noodles as she went by.

"Hey! No sampling."

"Rules do not apply to pregnant women who happen to be your mother."

Nate responded as he handed her several more noodles, "I thought you were upstairs puking your guts out?"

"Me and Junior here had a little talk," rubbing her hand over her already rounding belly, "and we've decided it would be a very good idea if I felt well today." Taking the big bowl of cleaned vegetables that Jack was holding out in her direction, "I also promised him copious amounts of ice cream if he settled down."

"Bribing before birth, you ought to write a parenting book." Jack gave her a toothy grin and handed her a knife, "But for now, can you cut those up for me?"

Elizabeth took the knife, settling down at the kitchen table, "You are very lucky there are no gypsies around at the moment."

"Mom, I'm beginning to believe the gypsy threat is an empty one."

Returning his smile, "Wanna bet?"

"Not at all."

♦ ♦ ♦

Once the party began, Emily met relative after relative. Jack tried to warn her of the talkers, the spitters, the space invaders and the cheek pinchers ahead of time, but some slipped by and after what seemed like days, she seriously thought she was going to scream. There were too many strange people in too small of a space for her nerves to settle even slightly, so, while Jack was occupied with a talker, she slipped unnoticed into the house.

Reaching the bathroom upstairs, she leaned over the sink, trying to slow the pounding of her heart. Forcing her muscles to relax, she couldn't believe how much effort it took to make a forced smile look somewhat natural. She massaged her cheekbones and the hinge of her jaw for a minute, wondering if she'd be able to hide upstairs for the rest of the day. Knowing that wasn't going to be possible, she took a deep breath and turned to leave.

Or tried to at any rate. Instead of an empty hall, she ran directly into a slightly taller girl with a head full of long spikes of spectrum colored hair and several eyebrow and lip piercings, "Oh God, sorry."

18

The girl's blue eyes twinkled, "S'okay. It's kind of nice not to be noticed for once."

Emily couldn't help but smile, "Jack's gonna go nuts when he finds out you're here."

"My reputation precedes me. Don't believe anything Tim tells you." Tilting her head in a knowing smirk, "Well, don't believe most of what Tim tells you, unless it involves me, a pound of hamburger and a parakeet, then it's totally true."

Her nerves began unraveling themselves, "I'll need to hear that story eventually and I'm pretty sure I'd recognize you anywhere. When did you get into town? Jack said you were running behind schedule and might not make it to the party."

"Well, the typical drive from Chicago to here is about 11 hours and we'd normally take a few breaks and maybe stay the night halfway here. This time, Allie started whining the minute we got in the car and Mom cranked up the radio, floored it and called my dad who was behind us to tell him we'd see him at the new house, then she was gone. I simply sat there and prayed I would die instantly should we hit anything."

Glad she could remember at least some of Claire's family, "Did Allie keep it up?"

"For about twenty minutes, then I threatened to make her sit up front within arm's reach of Mom. She shut up for awhile after that, but Mom never slowed down."

"Good Lord."

"Yeah. We got in last night and I opened the car door, kissed the ground in thanks for not having died en route, told Allie to shut the hell up for the 87th time and, yes, I counted, then Ester Ficklesworth jumped out of the car and took off like a bat out of hell. I can only assume she decided if Mom could drive like a maniac, she could run like one."

"Ester Ficklesworth?"

"The dog. Good as gold the whole trip, but even she knew she needed out of that car as soon as possible. Then I had to bribe everybody in the house to shut up about us getting here early. I wanted to surprise Jack today."

"He was getting nervous earlier that you wouldn't make it."

"Then my evil plan worked. Had to pay the siblings ten bucks each and promise dog poop patrol for a month to my dad to get them to keep quiet."

"Ten dollars isn't cheap."

"It's okay. I'll get it back when I force them to pay me to keep their dirty little secrets for them. Shouldn't take more than a week to get it all back, with interest if I can finagle it." Slipping around Emily and turning on the water in the sink, "Speaking of siblings, Ben sneezed on me on the way over here and I need to wash my hands." Scrubbing furiously, "I can't stand his boogers."

A sudden chuckle burst from her, "Um, just his? Everyone else's are okay?"

"Naw, just certain people. You know the saying 'you can pick your friends, you can pick your nose, but you can't pick your friend's nose'?" Emily nodded so Claire continued, "Well, I can pick my friends, I can pick my nose and, if necessary, I will indeed pick my friend's nose, given dire circumstances. Or, actually, if the mood so strikes me, I may stick my finger up there anyways, just for entertainment purposes." Drying her hands, she came back out and settled on the top step, "But Ben's not on that list."

She loved Claire already and, sitting down next to her, Emily lifted her head up, flaring her nostrils in Claire's direction, "What do you think?"

Leaning in, she studied them, "I'd go there."

"Cool." Wondering just how long she could keep Claire talking upstairs instead of having to go back to the party, "You know you're the first person today who hasn't hugged me?"

"We can rectify that if you want, but from the look on your face, I'd say I'm a shining beacon in a world of very touchy-feely people."

Emily nodded as she shrugged, "Although I guess a room full of people who are genuinely nice is better than a room full of awful ones."

"How do you know I'm not awful?"

"You don't make me feel like throwing up."

"You equate puking with grade of awfulness?"

Slipping just for a moment into her memories, "Something like that."

"Then thank you very much for not puking. I'll cherish it always." Pointing at her stomach, "So, changing the subject from snot and vomit, which is harder for me to do than you might imagine, when do we eat?"

"I've got to introduce you to Dex."

Claire grinned, "Why? Is he hungrier than I am?"

"Probably and he also enjoys his snot jokes. From what I can tell, he's you, just a little taller and a boy."

Before Claire could say anything, they heard Jack's voice drift through the downstairs hallway, "Em, you up there?" He came into view a second later, "Hey, you all right?"

"Yeah, just had to get away for a minute, trying to ward off a total freak-out."

"And she chose Queen Freak to assist her."

Jack turned to her in mock surprise, "Claire! I didn't see you."

"How the hell could you not see me? People in the next county can see me."

Jack held his serious face for as long as he could, then cracked into a grin, "How can you keep that straight face?"

"Years of practice."

Pulling her in for a bone-crushing hug, complete with pounding on the back and fake crying, "Good to have you back, cousin."

Returning the hug with a lung-crushing squeeze and trying not to knock them both down the stairs, "It's good to be back."

◆ ◆ ◆

Five minutes later, after some deep breathing and several humorous stories courtesy of Claire, Emily stood from her perch on the top step, "We should probably go back down."

Jack, sitting two steps below, looked up at her, "Feeling better?"

"A little. If I waited until I was all good, we'd be here a few more hours, so let's just do this before I go back to the bathroom until tomorrow."

Claire hefted herself up beside Emily, "Well, you've only really got my family to meet, then we can all go off in a corner and hide." She then tilted her head innocently in Jack's direction, eyebrows raised, "Unless ... maybe we can talk the boys into a game or two of volleyball."

As he began walking backwards down the steps, Jack let the sarcasm coat his response, "Remind me again, do they let you hit the ball yet?"

"Watch it, boy. I'm older and can kick your ass."

Jack turned and scurried down the stairs and out of sight as Emily touched Claire's arm lightly, "Why don't they let you hit the ball?"

"Oh, I completely suck at volleyball. I've actually had gym teachers ask me not to play out of fear for the other kids faces." They'd reached the edge of the kitchen by now and Claire turned to her with a smile, "But I like to play here 'cause my older sisters are really good and we usually beat the boys. As long as I promise not to touch the ball, I get to stand there looking like I'm in the game and then I get to share the bragging rights."

Jack popped up out of nowhere, "We might win this year. You never know."

"You lame-asses haven't won since we were 10."

"How do you know I haven't been practicing?"

"Have you been practicing?"

"No."

"Then shut up and get everyone ready."

"I thought you were hungry."

"Please, ass-whooping takes precedence over your chicken and mostaccioli."

With a grin, he once again disappeared as Emily flexed her hand, "I may not be much help to the cause. I just got my cast off a little while back."

"Well, stop if it hurts, but I'll make sure you can gloat with the rest of us … fair enough?"

Discovering that she was finally looking forward to joining the crowd in the backyard, she nodded, "Fair enough."

It turned out that the game was ridiculously easy to organize and soon, it was Tim, Jack, Nate, Dave, Tucker and another cousin, Ed, against Claire's two older sisters, Andi and Evie, her younger sister Allie, Claire, Tim's Sarah and Emily.

And what a sound whooping both games were. The boys took their losses gracefully, as boys generally do, by protesting and mumbling about cheating. The girls, for their part, kept the gloating and heckling to a minimum … mostly.

Jack, however, grabbed Emily by the waist and swung her around until she laughed in delight, "I didn't know you could play that well. I should have argued to keep you on our side."

Coming up beside them, Claire declared loudly, "Dude, you'd have lost that argument and just for future reference, she's ours from now on."

Emily had just finished filling her plate when Dex, who had arrived a minute earlier, caught her attention with a poke to the side, "Hey girl."

Turning, she smiled, always happy to see another familiar face, "Hey boy, I was beginning to wonder if you were going to make it."

"Yeah, sorry. Practice ran longer than I thought so I missed my bus and I just walked about 20 blocks with a saxophone and partial heat stroke." Looking around eagerly, "Can you point a guy in the direction of some form of cold liquid? A vat of ice? Sprinkler if need be?"

With a laugh, "Other side of the deck."

"You are a truly beautiful individual."

Convincing him to get a plate of food first, she headed to where a group of them were settled under the volleyball net. Sitting down beside Jack, "Dex is right behind me. He had to get something to drink."

With a mouthful of chicken, "Awesome."

Gesturing towards Dex, who was now only a few feet from them, she turned to Claire, "That's the one I said reminded me of you."

Claire looked towards him just as he stopped to stare at her, "Oh my god. You were playing the saxophone in the park last night. I forgot to hold onto Ester Ficklesworth and I had to chase her all over the neighborhood. I passed this park and you were there, playing."

Dex nodded as he gracelessly dropped to the ground beside her, "I saw you."

Honest as usual, "You missed a note."

Without pretense or embarrassment, "You distracted me for a second, I couldn't help it."

Claire went a vivid shade of red and, for the first time ever, turned slightly shy as she told him quietly, "I could have listened to you forever."

Dex, to his own shock, went speechless and Jack had to lean over, laughing as he hit him in the arm, "Wake up man and say thank you."

Instead, his normal grin returned and, looking Claire straight in the eye, "I think I love you."

Over her shyness, she fired back instantly, "We should probably go on a date or two first before starting to declare things."

"That's what I was thinking. I'm playing tomorrow at Higby's. Would you like to come? Maybe get some dinner with me beforehand?"

With a nod, "I think I'd like that."

And then the world started going again, except for the fact that their small crowd was staring at them in silence. Dex surveyed the bunch, "What? You've never seen a guy ask a girl out before?"

Tim aimed his fork full of chicken at Dex, "I totally thought you were gay."

Claire pitched her fork at Tim, "Don't make me come over there and kick you, Cousin."

Everyone was laughing at this point and Tim started to stand, but Claire waved him back down, "What'dya need? I've got to get another fork anyway."

"Just some more chicken."

"All right, back in a second."

Dex's eyes followed her every step until she hit the deck, then he stood as well, leaving his plate on the grass, "Um, I need to get a spoon. Don't eat my carrots."

As he disappeared across the yard in her wake, Jack looked over at Emily, "Em?"

"Yeah?"

"My best friend is gonna be making out with my cousin in about two minutes, isn't he?"

Reaching over, she squeezed his leg, "I give it a minute twenty at most," then eyeing Tim with a twinkle in her eye, "You realize you're not gonna get your chicken, right?"

Tim grumbled as he stood, "I know."

◆ ◆ ◆

Later that night, after a good portion of the people had left, Will lit the torches and Claire, sneaking out to her parents van for the second time that day, alone this time, retrieved her guitar. Settling on the grass, she tweaked a few things to get it in tune, then began playing, quietly singing, 'World Spins Madly On'.

Emily, who was already settled comfortably back against Jack in one of the deck chairs, "You realize the fact that she can both sing and play the guitar just might send Dex over the edge?"

Kissing the top of her head, he leaned down to whisper in her ear, "He's not that far from the edge as it is, Em, but for what it's worth, I didn't want to get his hopes up in case she gave it up or something."

Dex, who was sitting on the deck next to them, couldn't keep his eyes off of Claire. "You could have told me you have the hottest, most magnificent cousin ever."

With a grin, "Well, um, I prefer not to think of my relatives as hot. But at any rate, sorry ... I guess."

By the time Claire was finished with her first song, all who remained were sitting around her, on lawn chairs, blankets and the deck. With such a captive audience, "Any requests?"

Since most of the people there had done this before, they knew their favorites and were ready with them. Tim got in the first with his mom's

26

favorite, 'Leaving on a Jet Plane', then Claire's dad asked for anything by Billy Joel, to which he received 'Piano Man', after which Sam requested the Flintstones theme, to which everyone sang along.

In the following lull, Claire found Jack in the crowd, "I believe I feel a duet coming on."

"No, you don't."

"Yes, I do."

"I'm pretty sure you're mistaken."

By now Emily had turned to give him a look of total confusion, "You sing?"

"No, I don't."

Claire stood, "Don't make me spill the secret life of Jack Callaghan in front of all these nice people."

"Claire ... "

"Chemistry set."

With a muttered, 'son of a bitch', Jack shifted Emily to the side so he could stand up. Heading towards Claire and climbing over a few people in the process, he blew a raspberry in her direction then grinned, "You suck."

"Whatever." Pointing to the spot beside her, "Sit your ass down."

Cyndi Lauper had never sounded so off-key yet totally perfect until that very second. And four minutes later, Emily knew it would never sound the same again.

♦ ♦ ♦

They sang campfire songs and all kinds of familiar tunes before Claire finally called it a night with 'Good Riddance' by Green Day, which she beckoned Tim up to sing with her, which he did with a minimum of complaining, much to Emily's surprise, given she'd never known him to sing

27

more than 'Happy Birthday'. Putting her guitar back in its case, she flexed her stiff hands and Dex stood immediately, moving to Claire, taking her hands in his and massaging her fingers one by one while the family slowly moved around them, putting away chairs and casting amused glances in their direction.

Tim, now standing beside Jack, nodded towards Dex and Claire, "That didn't take long."

They amused Jack, "I wonder if their kids are gonna come out with normal hair?"

Emily grinned, "Doubtful."

"It's gonna get ugly when it doesn't last."

Jack gave Tim a confused look, "Claire is a pierced, boot-wearing musician with rainbow hair who swears like a sailor and can eat twice her weight in Butterfingers. She is, in essence, a female version of Dex. I think they'll be perfect."

Emily chimed in as well, "Don't forget she named her dog Ester Ficklesworth. His whole family will love her just for that."

Tim just shook his head, "We'll see."

After he walked away, Emily looked at Jack, "He's a happy little ray of sunshine, isn't he?"

Jack snorted, "Ignore him. Sarah just left and he's annoyed because Mom made him stay to clean up."

"This ought to be pleasant then."

Chapter 4

Only living about five minutes away by car and eleven minutes by bike, Claire became a regular at the Callaghan household, much as she had been when the two families lived in Chicago. She showed up unannounced, plunked herself down in the middle of dinner and joined the conversation without missing a beat, stealing bits off the plates of whomever she was sitting between, usually Emily and Sam, because, as she stated after her fourth carrot stick off Sam's plate, "They're easy pickings. They don't guard their food like the rest of you."

Emily simply sat back, grinning as she held her plate up to Claire's nose, "Take anything you like."

"I knew I was gonna love you," as she stole a potato using Emily's fork.

It didn't take long before Emily counted Claire as one of her best friends.

One Thursday, several weeks after Tim's party, Jack sequestered himself in his room for more studying after supper, his summer school classes bearing down on him. And given the rest of the boys were watching something bloody on TV, Claire and Emily chose to lounge on the back patio, sitting in the dark, laughing and talking about absolutely nothing, "So, how do you handle living with this many boys? The smell of feet alone would make me crazy."

Emily couldn't help the grin that overtook her, "I think you're pretty much crazy already."

"Just because I eat food from your plate does not make me crazy. And you need to start cutting your meat smaller. I nearly choked on that meatloaf tonight."

"You could just ask for your own plate, you know."

"But that's no fun. Besides, they're all used to me. I couldn't change things now, it'll just confuse them."

With an amused expression, Emily rested her head on the cushion, "I can see why Jack missed you so much."

"But the question is, what did he miss more? My charm, my wit, my good looks or my utter crappiness at Monopoly?"

"I think he missed his friend."

Claire shifted her weight and propped her feet up on the opposite end of the bench seat, "Yeah, well, I wasn't the greatest friend there for awhile."

"I don't think he cared."

The barest of smiles crept onto her lips, "He cared, but he always could take an awful lot of shit from me."

"Just make sure you don't give him too much more. He's got a lot going right now."

"How's this … ," she leaned over the arm of Emily's chair, "if I get all snarly and bitchy and sullen and angry and moody and thinking I'm all better than everybody else, you have my permission to sit on me and force feed me handfuls of mud until I come to my senses and realize I've got it pretty damn good."

"Claire?"

"Yeah?"

"He fed you mud?"

Her laughter echoed across the backyard, "That's just the tip of the iceberg, baby … how much time do you have?"

♦ ♦ ♦

It was just before midnight when they both turned to the sound of the sliding door moving, seeing the silhouette of Jack against the lone lamp that burned behind him. "Mind if I come out or should I leave you two to your girly-ness?"

Claire looked at Emily, "Do you think he can handle the amount of estrogen out here?"

"I don't know. We may have to paint his nails and try on eye shadow so he'll feel included."

Jack shut the door, coming over to them while shaking his head in Claire's direction, "You're tag-teaming me now?" Plunking himself down with a groan, "I don't know if I can handle two of you."

With a poke to his side, Emily astutely pointed out, "You were stuck with her, but you chose me, remember? You knew what you were getting into."

"Like I had any damn control over that; I was done the minute I rode past your house. Fate is not meant to be fought so, really, I'm actually stuck with both of you."

"Would you like me to leave?"

Leaning over and kissing Emily's smiling cheeks, "No … I'll keep you."

Chucking a flip-flop in Jack's direction, Claire asked, "What? Does that mean you want me to leave?"

"I'm not going to kiss you, but you can stay too." Raising an eyebrow in her direction, "The last time you left sucked enough. This time, you go nowhere young lady, understand?"

31

Knowing the truth when she heard it, she got up to retrieve her flip-flop from his chest, "I did apologize profusely for being a complete and total asshole, right?"

He gave her a look that she smiled at, "Profusely, prodigiously and profoundly."

Emily, amused by the interactions she now witnessed with regularity between the cousins, had to ask a fairly serious question, though, and this seemed to be the perfect segue, "Um, so, can I ask what exactly happened between you guys?" Aiming her thumb at Jack, who took it and shook it back and forth several times before keeping a hold of it against his leg, "I know bits and pieces of his end, but, I mean," stumbling with her words now that she had the full and attentive stare of Claire, "Or maybe I should just shut up?"

"Dude, never shut up when you have a question. I'll answer anything, which, probably sooner rather than later, you will come to live in fear of. But never shut up, alright? I hate shutting up."

Jack cut in, "And believe me, she will answer anything, and anything totally means anything."

Claire gave Emily a very serious expression, "Anything."

"Then what happened?"

"I love easy questions." Holding up a finger in their direction, "But let me call Mom first. I am supposed to be home in two minutes." It took two rings for someone to pick up the line, "Hey Ma, it's me … yes, I can tell time … yes, I'm here … yes, they're here too …no, I'm out on the porch with Emily and Jack … okay, Mom … Mom! … okay! Hang on …" Holding out the phone to Emily, "Can you tell her where I am, please." After re-assuring Claire's mom that Claire was indeed on the back porch with her, she handed the phone back and Claire finished up, "Yes, Mom … I'll be awhile longer, Emily just asked for my life story including footnotes and anecdotes … yes … no … yes … good Lord, I love you, too … bye." Hanging up, she grinned, "Sorry 'bout that."

"Did she really not believe you were here?"

"She knew, but likes to have me think she doesn't."

"And you're okay with this?"

"I don't mind having to call. Plus, when you know firsthand what will happen to you if you don't check in, it keeps you in line just a little bit more." Propping her feet back on the wooden table, "So, life story ... ready?"

"Yup."

"I'm a moron." Claire stopped, looking pretty much like that actually was the whole story. Emily waited a few moments, looked at Jack, who, amused, was just shaking his head. Finally Claire spoke again, "What? Did you want more? I thought that summed it up pretty well."

"Um, then there must be a damn long footnote coming."

Claire's burst of laughter got Jack going and it took another three or four minutes for the pair to get themselves under some semblance of control before she continued, "It's the mother of all footnotes."

In the next half-hour, Claire told of how she'd dumped Jack to hang out with some older kids at school, which quickly escalated into shaving her head, getting a homebrew tattoo, piercing things with an ice cube and needle, drinking some and smoking more, "I was not the model 14 year old your mother brags about."

"Holy shit, Claire. An ice cube?" Jack was wincing when he said the words, "What the hell were you on?"

"Nothing. Completely clear thinking decisions, every one of them. Well, possibly the tattoo was done while under the influence of Sharpies and Pucker shots, but hey, what's done is done." Turning her gaze to Jack, her eyes serious, but still twinkling, "And I like how, with that entire list I just gave you, you skim over the tattoo and the drinking and get stuck on the ice cube."

"But it's a hole in your head ... Several holes in your head ... With an ice cube ... And a needle ... an ice cube, Claire ... and a needle."

"Yes, I was there. I remember them well."

Claire continued through parts that Jack had been sketchy on and finally to parts that he hadn't heard at all, "And then I woke up in the hospital after the friend of somebody's brother's friend had loaded me up with Nyquil, of all things, and vodka and taken me for a drive a good twenty minutes outside the city, conveniently wrapping us around a tree before he had a chance to wrap himself around me."

This was definitely news to Jack, "Why didn't you tell me that? You called the next day and just said your friend was driving." Balling his fists in anger, "Tim and I'd have been up there to beat the crap out of that guy if you'd have told us."

"Which is exactly why I have waited until you were in therapy dealing with your anger issues before I mentioned it." Shifting, then standing, "You'd better tell this Amelia person that you're not getting your money's worth."

Jack studied her, "That was the first night you talked to me in almost a year."

"I needed a tree to knock some sense into my thick skull." Banging her forehead with her knuckles, "I'm a hard-headed pain in the ass, remember?"

"Just don't do that shit again or I'll be pissed, all right?"

"There you go with the anger issues again."

"Dude, I don't have anger issues ... well, not only anger issues ... and really, I'm not like the Hulk or something." Shrugging, he stood in front of his cousin, "But that's another story for another night."

Claire whispered at him, a hopeful look on her face, "Hulk smash?"

The grin was impossible to stop, "No Hulk smash."

Frowning for a moment in disappointment, she tweaked his nose, stuck out her tongue, then smirked as she reminded Emily of their sleepover the next day. Heading down the drive, she called good night, got in her car and began the drive, the unique clanging of her third-hand car letting them know loud and clear when she was at the end of the street and making her left to go home. Once the world was quiet again, Emily pulled Jack to a stop as he turned to head into the house, kissing him before he could say a word.

After their impromptu make-out session ended a few minutes later Jack asked, "Where did that come from?"

"Figured it was the best way to counteract any possible Hulk smash."

◆◆◆

Marking off the ninth day in a row on the calendar that Sam had hung on the wall to keep track of summer vacation, Jack couldn't help the smile that popped onto his face. It had been nine days since he'd last had a panic attack.

216 hours.

That was the longest he'd gone without one since beginning to see Amelia in the middle of May and, given it was the end of July, he honestly debated waking Emily up to celebrate. Then he remembered that she was at Claire's for the night, sleeping in an attic room, having her first ever girly-type sleepover. Figuring his news could wait until the morning, he gently rolled Sam over to stop the boy's snoring before climbing in his own bed, not exactly sleepy, but needing to stretch out and let his mind wander to points unknown.

He was snoring as well not five minutes later, sleeping through the myriad of texts that arrived at all hours of the night, thoroughly documenting the girls' evening together. The first one read, "Claire has a picture of you in a dress and heels riding a rocking horse with your finger up your nose and earrings on."

The second, an hour later, stated, "Headed to Wal-Mart. In my pajamas. And Claire's fuzzy bee slippers. To purchase zebra cakes and BBQ Fritos. I have been informed that this is what one does on a sleepover. Allie is amazed I have gotten this far in life without knowing these thing. Evie is driving. Claire says pray for us."

The third, arriving at 2am, "Allie fell asleep. In process of covering her body with magic marker drawings. I am beginning to think I have absolutely no idea what being a girl is like, but I'm having an awful lot of fun learning."

The fourth simply said, "She woke up. Hiding in bathtub with Claire."

The fifth arrived around 4:37am, "Back at Wal-Mart for bacon, ice cream and chicken nuggets. Apparently this will be our breakfast when we get back. I am pretty sure I am in love with your cousins."

He woke in time for Emily's next message, which came in the form of a chicken nugget wrapped in bacon waving under his nose. Feeling the mattress dip on one side, he sniffed a few times, then opened an eye in her general direction, the other opening to get a better view of her in a tank top and plaid shorts, hair piled on her head and a smile spread from ear to ear, "Are you awake?"

"No. Are you real or is this just a really good food dream?"

Bumping the nugget against his lips until he opened his mouth, she poked the chicken inside, "Real, but I gotta go. It appears we need to deliver some of these to Dex before we go back home." Emily stood, then leaned over, kissing his chewing mouth, "I feel like the bacon fairy."

And she was gone, skipping silently out the door, leaving Jack to grin, shake his head, swallow his early morning snack and roll over, going back to sleep for a good hour or more before getting up to begin his homework and chores, wondering idly if maybe it hadn't been a real smart idea on his part to get the two of them together. Then, still tasting the bacon on his lips, he realized, because of Claire, he got a bacon covered nugget and a chance to see Emily positively giggly. The bacon was good, but the radiant Emily was undeniably perfect.

Chapter 5

For the first time, Jack was glad Elizabeth had made him quit his job for the summer. He was beginning to feel the squeeze of summer school, especially English, when he found out he would be reading several big, fat tomes of literature dedicated to attempting to make him blind by using the smallest print known to man. On the rare occasions that he hung out with the family or with Emily and his friends, he found himself still having to read those damn books, eyes squinted to keep the sentences from mixing together as he moved from one row to the next.

Sometimes, sleep got the better of him and he'd wake up with his face squashed against his open Victor Hugo monstrosity, the pages beneath his mouth damp from escaped drool. He could roughly estimate how long he'd been asleep by how much Emily had drawn of him in her sketchbooks. She'd taken to drawing him as he "homeworked", using him as a perfect practice mannequin. Having finally given up her strict 'no one sees my work until it's done' rule, she sometimes had company while sketching, in the form of Sam coloring beside her or Claire transposing some song or even Elizabeth, who just liked to sit and watch her work. She filled an entire book with just pictures of him, some lifelike while others showed him as an alien or a three-eyed monster or, Elizabeth's favorite, the Scarecrow from *The Wizard of Oz*.

Jack didn't care. He was just happy that her hand seemed to have healed correctly and she could still work her magic with a pencil. He'd have read while standing on his head had she asked him to. Luckily, she did not.

Late one night, several hours after he'd said goodnight to Emily, he finally plowed his way through the end of *Hunchback of Notre Dame* and, throwing the book behind the couch in celebration, he stood, intent on tiptoeing into Emily's room, wanting to tickle her toes to wake her up so she'd watch some TV with him. He hadn't even made it out of the living room, however, when he heard low laughter and mumbled voices.

Barely lifting the curtain on the sliding door, he could see Tim and Sarah giggling and stumbling their way up the back part of the drive towards Tim's newly furnished, over-the-garage space. Jack snorted to himself, vaguely wondering if this was the first time he'd had her over there and if it would be for the whole night.

Jack watched them head up the outside steps, holding first to the railing, then leaning on the garage wall for support, trying not to fall back down to the cement below. He could have sworn they'd taken Sarah's car, but, with them clearly being drunk, he hoped they'd left it behind and gotten another ride. Sending a quick thanks upwards for letting the pair of idiots get home in one piece, he let the curtain drop and headed up to bed, not wanting to wake up Emily anymore, not wanting to have her find out Tim was wasted and entirely too close for comfort.

Jack was up by 7am and, choosing to eat his cereal on the back porch, he half hoped to catch Sarah sneaking out, but the garage apartment remained quiet, not a sound emerging until Elizabeth asked him to go make sure Tim was awake for work. Heading up the steps, Tim pulled the door open after his first knock, fairly annoyed, voice growling out of his throat, "What?"

Not having the opportunity to give the room a look, "Mom said to make sure you were up for work."

"God, when is she gonna realize I know how to use an alarm clock. I'm not the idiot everybody assumes I am." Continuing to tuck in his shirt, "But whatever, is there any breakfast in there?"

"Fend for ourselves day."

"Damn it." Tim pulled the door closed behind him, barreling down the stairs, not giving Jack the chance to see if anyone was still in the room, "Tell Mom I'm going out with Sarah tonight, would you?"

"You're supposed to be cutting the lawn tonight."

Tim waved him off, "There's at least six other people here who can do it. I'm sure it'll be fine."

He stood, teeth clenched, until Tim had taken off in his car, a brand-new, used purchase he'd made after graduation. Seething inwardly about his suddenly annoying morning, Jack slapped on a semi-smile and headed inside, hating his brother for making him messenger boy, a job that got really old, really fast in his world.

Later that afternoon, he heard the lawn mower fire up and, feeling bad about someone else having to do Tim's job for him, Jack looked out of his bedroom window, finding not Nate or Dave, but Emily leaning over the lawn mower. Her braid clipped up, the end sticking in the air much like a feather in a cap, Jack watched as she cut several nearly straight lines across the yard before he sat back down, tackling more homework while wishing with all his might that he could scream obscenities at Tim, then attach his hands to the mower handle with duct tape.

After what seemed like only a couple of minutes he heard the mower cut out. Getting back up, he saw Emily crouched over, cajoling something from the grass onto her finger. Standing a moment later, she carried the something to a nearby tree, waiting for it, he assumed, to crawl onto a branch. The smile lingering on her lips calmed him down, realizing that even though he hated her having to do it, she was perfectly fine cutting the lawn on a hot, sticky afternoon with the sun beating down on plenty of caterpillars or frogs that needed to be saved.

He had to admit, sometimes he thought she fit in there better than he did.

And he loved it.

◆◆◆

Intently attentive to his Biology book, he smelled her before he saw her. Still focused on his book, "You stink."

"Thanks a lot."

"You just spent an hour and a half behind a lawn mower. What did you expect?"

"You don't have to tell me about it though."

Half turning in his chair, he propped his head on his hand, looking at her sideways, "You look totally hot though, if that's any consolation."

Emily continued to stand in the middle of his bedroom, hands on hips, "Now you're gonna comment on how sweaty I am?"

"I'm just wishing it'd been me who'd made you all sweaty."

Her cheeks flushed and her head dropped shyly, but then she caught his eye, a small smile following, "Someday you will again."

Moving, he came to stand in front of her, leaning in to whisper quietly, "Just say when."

◆◆◆

As it usually does, time passed and Jack came back to the house one afternoon, threw his backpack in the closet and grabbed a banana from the fridge. Eating it en route to the hammocks, he was fast asleep within minutes. Elizabeth watched as he went by and, turning to Emily, who was laughing at him quietly, "I'm gonna go with it's the last day of class."

Amused to say the least, "You think?"

Jack slept right through dinner, so Emily tried to tempt him awake with dessert, specifically a bowl of chocolate ice cream, under his nose. When that didn't work, she turned to drastic measures, namely taking her own large spoonful, then kissing him with her ice cold, chocolaty lips. Laughing when his eyes popped open, "Damn, I was hoping that wouldn't work so I'd get to finish your bowl, too."

"I'm a sucker for ice cream. What can I say?"

"You can say you have room for me in there."

Immediately sliding over, he shifted wrong and instantly flipped onto the ground. Instead of getting up however, he lay there laughing while Emily just shook her head with a smile and finished his ice cream, one slow, cold spoonful at a time.

Sam found them still in their same positions a few minutes later, "Why are you on the ground?"

"Because I fell out of the hammock." Sam pondered this for roughly half a second before pouncing on his big brother, an impromptu wrestling match ensuing until Sam had to squeak out 'uncle', his face going purple from both laughing and lack of oxygen. Jack stopped immediately, rolling over to give Sam air and watching him return to normal color, "I'm in the mood for hide-and-seek. What do you say?"

Rejuvenated immediately, Sam hopped up, "Let me go get everybody."

As he disappeared into the house, Emily looked down at him, "In the dark? How do you find anybody?"

Jack stood up, brushing grass and dirt from his clothes, "That's the fun part."

Her stomach tightened in uneasiness at wandering around in the dark, having people hiding in the dark and them jumping at her from the dark, "Um, would you mind if I maybe stayed on the deck instead of playing?"

The nervousness in her voice told him what he needed to know, "'Course not. You can be home base on the steps."

"I just … "

He stopped her, "I know. It's okay." Taking her hand, he pulled her towards the house, where various family members were already piling out the door, "Just don't let Sam cheat. Don't think I don't know about you two."

"He runs a lot slower than the rest of you."

"Fine. Just don't let him cheat too much."

Jack ran off to unearth flashlights and batteries and soon, the boys were choosing who would be 'IT' first, by the wholly complicated procedure of all yelling 'not IT' as quick as possible, leaving one boy to muttering things under his breath as he turned and shut his eyes. This time, IT turned out to be Dave and, under strict orders from Jack, Emily had to make sure he remembered to count all the numbers. "We don't need another incident like 2011."

The boys nodded solemnly in agreement before scattering to all corners of the backyard, disappearing immediately into the shadows. Desperate to ask what the 'incident' was, she had to wait until Dave finished his counting before, "Dare I ask about 2011?"

As he turned around, already scanning the yard with squinted eyes, "Too painful. Wounds run deep, my friend."

Watching him creep off into the night, she grinned, wondering if this game would be just as rowdy as everything else the family seemed to play.

She was not disappointed. It appeared, as with most things they did, the boys had twisted the game to their own liking. 'IT' not only had to find a person in the dark, without using the flashlight, but then also had to flash them, yell their name out, grab who he'd found and hold them for five seconds, counting this out loud as well. If the caught boy, who'd basically been blinded by the flashlight, freed himself, by any means possible, then 'IT' was still 'IT'. If he couldn't get away, then the found boy was now 'IT' and the whole thing started again, everyone getting another thirty seconds to either switch hiding spots, dig in deeper or run for home.

There was also the option of whoever wasn't being held could yell 'HOME' and make a break for it during the counting, but only with the flashlight on, so the old 'IT' could dispense with both the counting and the holding and simply race after the one trying for home.

If caught, same rules applied, including the chance to wrestle themselves free.

Emily had no earthly idea how any of them made it out of the game in one piece. Apparently, as 'HOME', it became Emily's job to judge close calls and, on more than one occasion, barely get out of the way as two or more boys came flying at her, flashlights on and not being caught the only thing on their minds.

It was also her job to get Sam to 'HOME' without being tackled by boys double his size. He would give her a quick blink with the mini-LED keychain she'd slipped in his hand after his first loss, then when he stood to run home, she would move herself closer to him, 'HOME' relocating with her as she did.

Jack, amused, asked her the next time it was his turn to count, "Gonna keep cheating like that?"

"Until he gains another forty pounds, I sure am."

"Good. Makes it more interesting." Running off at top speed, it didn't take long for Nate's name to ring out and for Dave to come charging towards her, yelling HOME at the same time. Jack, however, had been messing with them and yelled Nate's name for no reason, bringing runners out of the woodwork and tripping Dave to the ground in the process. This sent his brother sprawling across the dirt, sliding a good foot or two with Jack's arms neatly wrapped around Dave's knees, holding him while counting loudly.

They played for another ten minutes until Emily realized she hadn't heard anything from Sam in awhile. Calling out Jack's name to get his attention, instead she got Tucker yelling HOME, Dave chasing him at top speed, Nate coming in from the opposite direction, all running and no one paying any kind of attention to their surroundings.

They all ended up in a painful pile, Emily at the bottom, with what felt like someone's elbow in her ribs and a knee dangerously close to her teeth.

"Em? You all right down there?"

"Sure." Grunting a few other words they couldn't hear, Tucker rolled off the heap, Nate following. Dave apologized for the elbow and Jack, nose bleeding, helped her up.

"Who's IT?"

Emily just shook her head, momentarily confused as to what in the world she'd been calling Jack's name for in the first place. A second later, "Nobody's IT right now. I wanted to know where Sam was."

Nate and Dave both hollered 'not IT' before Jack shushed them, "Sam?" Turning around and looking into the near pitch-black backyard, "Sam? Hey, Sam? Come on out for a minute. We need to regroup. We're in time out so it's okay."

He didn't appear like he should have and Emily tried, "Hey Sam? Honest, we're in a time out. I just want to see you for a second."

A small voice traveled from somewhere higher up and to the right, "Emily?"

There was something nervous in his tone that made her worry, "Yeah? You all right?"

"Um, I can't get down."

The five of them looked at each other, Jack asking, "Where can't you get down from?"

"Up here."

"Dude, where is 'up here'?" They were already walking towards the sound, flashlights pointed up, "Are you up in the tree?"

"I was. Now I'm up on the roof and I can't get back down."

The younger two burst out laughing, with Jack grinning as well as he headed to the side of the garage, "Hang on a few, kid. I gotta find the ladder."

"I've been hanging on for forever already."

Emily called up to him, letting Jack get the garage door open, "How far up are you?"

"I'm sitting on the top pointy part."

"Sam."

"Yeah?"

"I love you."

"I love you, too, Emily. Are you telling me that because you can't get me down?"

Jack was already setting the ladder against the wall, "Don't worry, buddy, I'm on my way up."

Soon, both were back on solid ground, the beams of four flashlights from the ground getting them safely to the edge of the roof and onto the ladder.

Jack, still holding onto his hand, "Sam?"

Hoping he wasn't going to get yelled at, he screwed up his face, figuring it was inevitable, "Yeah?"

"That was the best hiding spot ever."

"But I can't use it again, can I?"

"We'd prefer not."

"Okay. Are you going to tell Mom and Dad?"

Before anyone could answer, Will called from the porch, "I think we'll keep this one from your mom for now. No roofs again, though, understand?"

Everyone, including Emily, called in their 'okay' as they filed past Will and went into the house.

Jack, grinning at his dad, leaned forward towards Emily, "How'd you like your first game of hide-and-seek in the dark ... otherwise known as flashlight tag?"

Heading to the kitchen to grab him a wad of paper towel, which she held up to his nose, "I think I'm surprised this is the only blood to show for it."

"You totally have to play our version of Twister then."

◆ ◆ ◆

45

The next two weeks passed quickly, with Jack still unemployed as per Elizabeth's instructions. He spent those weeks mowing the lawn, weeding, cleaning and painting the patio furniture.

He also received in the mail his letter from the school informing him that he had passed his summer classes and would be moving up to 12th grade with the rest of his class. Jack did a little dance by the mailbox when he read this, happy to have it in writing and signed by Phil himself. Heading into the house, he handed the letter to Elizabeth, "I am officially a senior in high school."

Elizabeth turned over the envelope, looking at the address, "This was meant for me, dear son."

He bumped hips with her, slinging his arm over her shoulders, "Will you forgive me for opening it?"

"Just this once." Squeezing his waist in a side hug, "Congratulations."

"Let's hope I never have to look at another 1000 page classic ever again. 750 I can handle, but 1000 is pushing it."

"You have British Literature this year ... I'd let the hope go."

With a groan, he left the room, muttering about doorstops and going blind from the miniscule print.

Instead of dwelling on school, however, he instead chose to have marathon 'X-Files' sessions that went well into the early morning hours. More than once Will found both Jack and Emily, along with Dave, Dex and Claire, asleep on the living room floor at 5 in the morning.

On the final day of summer vacation, Will found them all tangled up in a pile of stocking feet and pillows. Never one to turn down a prime opportunity, he retrieved his camera and took a priceless shot of Dex's enormous feet propped on his son's chest.

Sometimes waking up at 6am really did pay off ...

Chapter 6

Finally, with school starting the next day, Emily was just about to slip off to sleep when she heard the telltale squeak of the wood floor just inside her door. She then heard a small shuffle and a muffled curse as his head caught the leg of her nightstand. Emily held in the smile as she shifted and, hanging her head over the side of the bed, studied him in the moonlight, "Can I help you?"

Jack, non-plussed, "Did you know that nothing rhymes with the word orange?"

"You snuck all the way down here just to tell me that?"

"Well, I mean, it's interesting. How the hell can there be nothing that rhymes with it? I mean, absolutely nothing."

"We've got to get up early for school, Jack."

"I know." He lay there in silence for another minute or two, until, "Did you know they don't make green Pixy Stix anymore? They were my favorites too, those and the purple ones. The orange ones too actually and the red weren't bad either."

Still more than half-asleep, Emily asked in a voice muffled by both pillow and hand, "What about the blue ones?"

"Oh, the blue ones are just disgusting. They're a complete mockery to the candy industry and the bastard stepchild of the originals. I mean, does everything have to come in blue now? And really, have you ever seen a blue-raspberry anyway? Plus, they taste like Hawaiian Punch. Why the hell would blue taste like Hawaiian Punch, which is red?"

By now, Emily had reached over the side of the bed and, putting her fingers lightly over his lips, "Do you know you ramble when you're nervous?"

Kissing her fingertips, "Who says I'm nervous?"

"Did you hear your diatribe on blue candy?"

Jack smiled to himself, moving her hand down to his chest, "Sorry about that."

Shifting so she could comfortably look down at him, the moonlight casting a hazy light through the room, "So, what's up?"

Rubbing her middle knuckle, "What if I get to school tomorrow and completely freak out?"

"Then you'll find me and we'll work it out, but why do you think something will happen?"

Jack shrugged, "I don't know. I pretty much sleepwalked through the last quarter and I got in more than a few arguments with people. What if they're still pissed?"

The fights were news to her, but she didn't ask, "Well, apologize if you need to, explain if you want and if that doesn't work, move on. Besides, Amelia is only a text away, right? And you see her again on Friday."

"Amelia won't be there to hide behind when Marcus Sayers remembers I told him he was full of month-old horseshit." The chuckle snuck out involuntarily and Jack immediately pulled her off the bed, sheets and all. Laughing, he tickled her ribs, "Marcus Sayers is not funny."

"No, but what you said to him was."

Loving the heaviness of her on top of him, he kissed her nose, "True, but he might still kick my ass."

Leaning forward, she whispered in his ear, "No one touches that ass but me."

"I would give up a winning lotto ticket for a condom right now." After twisting his head, his lips caught hers and their tongues began roaming, as did Jack's hands, up the back of her shirt to rub along her scars and spine.

Marveling at the fact that his hands never made her flinch or shy away, she pushed herself up from him momentarily in order to pull her tank top off. Leaning on her hands over him, "There's plenty we can do without one."

"You're awfully forward tonight, Miss Ward."

"I think it was all the Pixy Stix talk."

♦♦♦

A good hour later, Jack was sliding under the covers of his bed upstairs, wide awake and amazed at the beautiful girl exactly 44 steps away. He thought about her so much, in fact, that within ten minutes, he was sleeping peacefully on her floor.

As she listened to him breathe, she slipped her hand once again from under the covers and laying it against his cheek, slept as well.

♦♦♦

Will found them there around 6:30 the next morning and after clearing his throat several times, then unsuccessfully nudging Jack with his foot, he finally shook him by the shoulder, "Hey, school starts today and if you get up right now, I may forget I found you sprawled on the floor."

Jack's eyes finally opened and he stood fast, swaying at the sudden equilibrium change, "I'm up ... I think."

Catching his son by the shoulder, he steadied him, "I thought we had this talk already, remember? The one about how you don't sleep in her room."

Given he was still asleep, he spoke before thinking, "God, Dad, it was one night and I was on the floor. Calm down."

49

"Excuse me?"

His brain registered and his eyes opened wide, "Shit … sorry … I didn't …"

Stopping him with a hand in the air, "Kitchen. Now." Once in the kitchen, Will stood in front of Jack, hands in pockets, "It may have been one night and you may have been on the floor, but we've discussed this. No bedrooms. Do I make myself clear or would you like to have a louder talk and get your mother involved as well?"

Jack knew when to leave well-enough alone so he backed up just slightly and conceded, "Sorry. I was nervous about going back to school and it helped me fall asleep."

Glancing over Jack's shoulder, he saw Emily standing tousle-haired in her doorway, "No more room sharing. Either of you." Not sure what had happened, but knowing when to keep her mouth shut, she just nodded and watched Will cast a long look at his son before softening, "Have a good day, okay? It won't be as bad as you think."

After nodding, he watched his dad head towards the front door, then turned to Emily, "That was a fun way to start the day."

They could hear feet coming down the stairs so she just shrugged, "I think I'm glad I stayed asleep."

He gave her a quick kiss, then turned her around to face her room, "I'm thinking you should go get dressed before Mom gets down here and we have a much scarier second act."

◆ ◆ ◆

School began as usual and Marcus Sayers walked right by Jack without a second glance. Emily heard him sigh in relief and giving his hand a quick squeeze, "I told you it'd be fine." Dex showed up a few minutes later, grumbling and being generally 'first day Dex', with Emily commenting, "Hey boy, angry at the world already?"

"Blar." Stuffing his saxophone into his locker, "And roar."

"How can you already be annoyed? School doesn't officially start for another five minutes."

"I'm just practicing for later on when Phil asks me why I've done something."

"What have you done?"

"Nothing. That's why I'd better start practicing." Noticing Dave quietly standing next to them, "First day, huh?"

Nodding, "Yeah."

"Don't take any shit, understand?"

Dave cracked his first smile of the day, "Okay."

"Good luck then." With a grimace, "Bye girl, bye girl's boy, bye girl's boy's brother."

Emily grinned, "We have names, Dex."

As he headed down the hall, "Mere formality ... British Lit awaits."

All three watched his now blazing purple head disappear down the hallway, then Emily turned to Dave, "Now, expanding on Dex's advice, pay attention to the notes I wrote and for the love of all things dry, avoid the front row in Fenton's class. You'll be soaked five minutes in." After he nodded, she moved on, "Do not eat the chili or the roast beast and make sure that if you need anything, you find me or Jack or Dex, okay?"

Dave nodded for a third time, "Thanks."

Jack clapped him on the arm, "And steer clear of Marcus Sayers. He may want to enact a bit of revenge on me by proxy."

"Which one's Marcus?"

Jack discreetly pointed towards a rather rotund 6-footer, "Him."

"Gotcha."

The four-minute warning bell rang, "Have fun."

As Dave disappeared into the crowd, "I'll try."

♦ ♦ ♦

They'd all had Calculus together that morning, but didn't actually get a chance to talk until lunch. Dex snagged one of the smaller tables and was already digging in by the time the other two showed up. Jack looked at him in amusement, "Hungry?"

A piece of ham swung from the edge of his sandwich as he ignored the question and indicated to the other side of the cafeteria, where Dave was surrounded by a small group of laughing students, a pretty girl next to him, "He doesn't waste much time, does he?"

Jack could only stare at his brother as Emily leaned towards him, "He does work faster than you, doesn't he?"

Dex, his mouth moving quicker than his brain, "Jack's just lucky I let him have you or he'd still be working." He got the stink-eye from Emily for this and back-pedaled immediately, "Loaned you to him permanently? Turned you over to him without a word ..." By now, both were smiling, "Supported you in making your own decision and now couldn't be more gleefully happy for you two even if I was a small, blonde Austrian girl running through a field of daisies with a puppy at my side, the wind in my hair and Julie Andrews singing the soundtrack of my life?"

"Bingo."

"Thank God. I didn't want to have to break into a Bette Midler song."

"We all thank God for that, Dex."

Jack just shook his head and turned to whisper in her ear, "You didn't want me working fast last night."

Her cheeks instantly flamed red, "I never said fast was necessarily good."

Well, now that Jack wouldn't be able to stand for a few minutes and Emily knew it from the look on his face, she pointed over her shoulder, "You need anything to drink?"

Digging enough change out of his pocket for the both of them, "Yeah, thanks."

With a grin, she took Dex's order as well, then walked away, leaving the two boys, who gossiped just as well as a pack of girls, "Do I even want to know what happened last night?"

Jack, with brute force honesty, "Let's just say the more I think about it, the longer I'll be forced to sit here, hidden from view under the table."

And, of course, being a guy, he understood immediately. After laughing loudly for a minute, he calmed enough to ask, "You want to talk baseball or Shakespeare?"

Chapter 7

Within a few weeks, Jack discovered something. In the franticness of summer school, he had learned how to study. He seemed to be picking up things at a faster pace, he remembered more and actually enjoyed doing his homework. Mentioning this to Emily one day during lunch, Dex overheard and knocked him on the head with his bag of cut carrots, "You shall now shut up about such things or suffer the consequences."

Emily grinned, "So, aiming for all A's this time around?"

Jack, first stealing, then eating one of the aforementioned carrots, "Not so much aiming as accidentally achieving." Given he didn't want to jinx himself, he changed the subject, "Hey Dex, you gonna take Claire to homecoming?" Knowing this would send Dex off on a diatribe about ritualistic high school brainwashing and herd references, Jack let him ramble for a good five minutes before he interrupted, "Yeah, but are you gonna take Claire?"

With a giant Dex smirk, "Of course."

◆ ◆ ◆

Once home and both diligently plowing through homework, Jack popped his head through Emily's open doorway, "Hey."

"What's up?"

"You want to go to homecoming with Dex and Claire?"

"Shouldn't Dex and Claire be asking that? Besides, I'd feel awkward on a date with them while you sat at home."

Jack gave her an appreciative look, "Nice comeback. You're getting faster."

"Like I have a choice in this family." Grinning at him, "Now rephrase your question, please."

"Would you like to go to homecoming with me? If yes, you and I can go as a couple together with Dex and Claire as a couple, thus making it a double date. Specific enough for you?"

"Yes to homecoming. Yes to Dex and Claire. Yes to specificity. And you totally just want to see if Dex's head'll explode when he realizes he's at a dance, don't you?"

"Kind of. Plus, you look extremely hot in a dress."

Despite Jack's many compliments, they still caught her off-guard, "You think I look hot in a dress?"

Still holding onto the doorframe, he swung into her room and, kissing her, "You look hot in anything, but you look particularly hot in dresses."

Kissing him back, "Problem is, I don't have a dress and I don't think I have the money to get one."

"Well, how 'bout you wear the dress you wore to the wedding last winter and I'll pay for the tickets?"

Elizabeth, who could hear the conversation from the kitchen, came up behind Jack, "Or how about you let me buy you a dress and Jack gets the tickets and you get him out of my hair for one night? Pretty good deal from where I sit."

Suddenly self-conscious, "I couldn't have you do that. You already let me live here for free and feed me, I don't need you to spend more on me."

"One," pointing over to the mantle, "you're officially part of the family, remember? And two, I've been dying to go shopping with you for I don't know how long. Granted, you look good in Nate's hand-me-downs, but I've always wanted to go dress shopping and Jack just refuses to try one on."

Without missing a beat, Jack put on his hangdog face, "Do you really want your boyfriend to run around in a dress? I mean, I will to make my mother happy, but can you imagine the backlash?"

"I would prefer you not ever wear a dress, thank you very much," and turning to Elizabeth, she grinned, "I'd love to go shopping with you, although I'm not really sure how to do the girl shopping thing."

Elizabeth's face lit up and she chuckled, "Neither do I. I haven't done it since I was in high school, but we'll figure it out."

◆ ◆ ◆

It was very clear once they entered the mall that neither of them had any idea what they were doing. The first clue came as they entered J.C. Penney and Elizabeth walked them directly to the boys department. Emily followed, wondering what exactly they were doing. It took a good ten seconds of standing amongst the size 10 pants and skateboarding t-shirts for Elizabeth to turn a slow circle, her eyes eventually stopping on Emily, "Yeah, we're not gonna find a dress in this section, are we?"

"I hope not."

Elizabeth began to grin, "Well, there has to be a teenage girl dress section around here somewhere." Find it they did and looking through some of the racks, Elizabeth let out a low whistle, "I might not be as entirely in touch with trendy fashions as I used to be when I was your age, but I'm pretty sure these outfits do not have enough fabric on them to cover even the most essential parts."

Emily gave Elizabeth a nervous smile, "If they all look like this, I don't think I can even go to the dance. I have more than essentials that need to be covered up."

Giving her a one armed hug around the shoulders, "We'll find something, I promise."

Emily began to doubt this promise as they entered their fourth store. She wasn't used to clothes shopping. It used to consist mostly of Salvation Army stores and clearance rack necessities and now it usually consisted of

56

Salvation Army stores, clearance rack necessities and an expanded
collection of Nate's hand-me-downs. The dresses they kept finding were
either entirely too sparkly and attention grabbing or cut to share her scars
with the world; others were so expensive that the prices made her eyeballs
spin in horror. Her winter dress from the wedding last year had been a
hidden gem in the new arrivals section at the Army and, about to suggest
to Elizabeth that they just go there in order to save both Elizabeth's wallet
and her own head from exploding, she happened to catch sight of
something dark blue at the back of a rack of sequined nightmares.
Checking that it was her size, she pulled it out to show Elizabeth, who,
having learned in about three seconds what Emily's tastes were, realized it
was perfect. Smiling at her, "Hurry up and go try it on."

With fingers crossed, she went to the changing room and Elizabeth sat in
one of the chairs to get off her feet. Once Emily slid the dress over her
head, however, she discovered a very ugly problem that made tears well
up for just a second. She couldn't reach the zipper in the back, no matter
how many contorted, twisting attempts she made. In order to get
completely dressed, she realized, she was going to need someone to help
her. The thought of having to show her scars to anyone again, nearly made
her pull the dress off, put it back on the hanger and give up on the whole
damn dress shopping experience.

Before she could decide, though, Elizabeth's voice drifted into the changing
room, "You okay in there? Need any help with zippers or anything?" When
no reply came, she stood and tapped lightly on Emily's closed door, "What's
wrong?"

Emily simply unlatched the door and let Elizabeth in. Swallowing her pride,
her worry and her fear, she turned away from Elizabeth, head dropping
down as she pulled her hair over her shoulder to reveal the open zipper
and the scars. Without a word, Elizabeth closed up the back of the dress,
then, tilting Emily's head up to look in the mirror, put her own head beside
Emily's, "You look way better than Jack would in this dress."

She couldn't bring herself to smile quite yet, asking instead, "Will you help
me again when I get dressed for the dance?"

"I will help you whenever you need it. You do know, though, that any one
of us could zip this zipper and no one would say a word."

Raising an eyebrow at Elizabeth's reflection, "Really? You think Sam would just let it go without one question?"

Thinking for a moment, "Sam would probably go all 'angry ninja' as the boys call it, demanding he get to go hit whoever did that to you."

"'Angry ninja' seems to run in the family."

Elizabeth gave her a small smile, "We're just very protective of the people we love and I think I'd rather have a few 'angry ninjas' than a family full of people who didn't care."

"We should get the boys t-shirts declaring the ninja thing."

By now, Emily had finally given into a smile and Elizabeth hugged her tightly, "I will definitely be there to help you get dressed and remember, you get to go at your own speed in telling people things, okay? Just promise me you won't let how you look or your past get in the way of living your life ever again. Please?"

After nodding, Emily blushed, "I almost came out to tell you that the dress didn't fit and we should just forget this whole shopping thing."

"Like I would let that happen. I've finally got a daughter to dress up and, having missed her first 17 years, I am not about to miss anything else at this point, even if it means dragging you all over creation to find an absolutely stunning dress." Turning her by the shoulders, Elizabeth looked Emily up and down, from her pink cheeks and bright eyes to her ratty tennis shoes, "And I hate to break it to you, but the shopping is not over yet."

The look on Emily's face was priceless, "What? We have the dress already."

"My dear, I would be voted world's worst mother if I let you out of the house wearing those shoes."

"But I have my black flat shoes back at home."

"I'm sorry to break this to you as well, but those are not 'going to homecoming, gotta live up to the dress I just bought and make my mother proud' type of shoes."

"They have those type of shoes out there?"

"Yes. Yes they do."

"I had no idea."

Turning Emily back around and unzipping her, Elizabeth slipped out of the cubicle, shutting the door behind her, "By the way, I'm pretty sure my son is going to overheat when he sees you in that dress."

"Overheat?"

Amused to say the least, "Or have a minor heart attack. You seem to have that effect on him."

"Should I apologize for that?"

Stepping back as Emily emerged, having changed quicker than Elizabeth thought possible, "Only apologize if he actually does collapse. Everything else, I expect."

Sticking out her untied shoes, "Do we really need shoes?"

"Yes, dear, we really need shoes. Then lunch. I'm starving."

Shoe buying seemed to go much faster with Emily commenting on how the homecoming gods must have felt sorry for her, giving her a good pair of strappy, slightly heeled dark blue shoes that matched her dress perfectly. Elizabeth retorted that it was more likely that the food gods didn't want her getting 'hangry' in the middle of the mall.

Either way they were soon in the food court, Emily weaving through the tables balancing the tray of food and drinks, Elizabeth following behind with their two bags.

Finally sitting down, Elizabeth let out a sigh, "These kids are gonna make me immobile by Thanksgiving, I can feel it."

Emily stopped dead, straw half unwrapped, "Kids?"

Looking surprised at herself, "Well, I let the cat out of the bag on that one, didn't I?"

Still holding her pose, "You're having twins?"

Nodding happily, "Yeah. Found out about them yesterday. It seems that one's been hiding behind the other for some time now."

"Do you know if they're boys or girls?"

"They seem to be hiding that as well. It'll just have to be a surprise."

Finally putting her straw down, she got up and hugged her, "This is so cool. The boys're gonna flip."

Returning the hug, "Don't say anything when we get home. I want to wait until I can get everybody together tonight at dinner."

"I think I can manage to keep a secret for a few hours."

"Good girl."

♦ ♦ ♦

Once they got home, but before they went into the house, Emily stopped Elizabeth, "Thank you."

"You've already thanked me more than enough, but you're welcome."

"I meant for the day in general. This is about as close to ... ," feeling shy all of a sudden, "well, I mean, I got to ... I got to spend a day with my mom. I've never had that before and it was ... it was perfect."

Elizabeth teared up instantly and hugged her tight, "There's plenty more days like this to come, I promise."

The boys did indeed flip. There was a lot of hooting and hollering, general mayhem and wagering on the sex of each baby. Both money and chores were bet and Nate, knowing how his brothers sometimes liked to remember their own version of the truth, made sure to write everything down. Giving the list to Will for safe keeping when he finished, "You're the only one who can be trusted with this, Dad, keep it safe."

Trying so hard to be serious and nearly succeeding, "I will, Son."

The rest of them burst out laughing and after another burst of excitement, went about their chores before movie night began. Jack went back to drying the dishes Emily had just washed and, finishing quickly, "Want to come upstairs for a little while? Found some new music you might like."

"Don't feel like a movie?"

"I don't really want to watch *The Mummy*, but I will if you want to."

"Just make sure it's okay with Will that we're upstairs and I'm all yours."

Will was fine with it. So, soon, they were settled on Jack's bed, iPod in front of them. Before he turned it on, "So, I hear you found a dress."

"Yup."

"Gonna let me see it?"

"Nope."

"Aw, come on. Just a little hint?"

"Nope."

With a grin, he slid his arm under hers, "It's gonna kill me, isn't it?"

"Sure is. Your mom figures you'll have a heart attack."

Willing himself to calm down, "You have no idea what you're doing to me."

Knowing exactly what she was doing to him, "You only have to wait until Friday."

With a quick kiss to the side of her head, he hit the play button, "That's six days too long."

◆ ◆ ◆

Sam woke her up a few hours later by shaking her shoulder, "Hey Emily. Dad says it's time to go downstairs."

She opened her eyes slowly, finding Sam only inches from her, "What?"

"Dad said to tell you to come downstairs. I need to go to bed."

"Oh." Sitting up and dislodging Jack's hand from her hip, "Yeah, um, I'll be out of here in a second." After untangling herself from the earphones, she moved the player to the nightstand and, leaning over, gave Jack a kiss, then gave one to Sam on his cheek, "G'night."

Sam, who secretly loved Emily's kisses, looked at her with slightly starry eyes, "G'night."

Once she was back downstairs, she found Will cleaning up a few things in the kitchen, "Ah, Em. I see Sam found you."

With a yawn, she nodded, "Yeah and if you don't need anything, I think I'll go back to sleep."

"Go ahead. I'm all set. Also, thanks for asking before you went upstairs."

"You're welcome."

"Good night."

"'Night."

◆ ◆ ◆

Friday finally arrived. Dex showed up with Claire, his purple hair matched her dress and Claire's hair was dyed the exact shade of fire engine red as Dex's leather Doc Martens. Tucker nodded his approval, "You gotta show me how to do that, Claire."

Grabbing him playfully around the neck, she twisted in order to whisper in his ear, "Two packages of Kool-Aid, a dark towel, an old shirt and your parents gone for at least two hours."

"I can swing that."

"Cool beans. Give me a call." Letting him go, they both chuckled at the look Elizabeth was giving them and Claire shrugged lightly, "What? Can't I give my favorite cousin named Tucker a hug?"

Jack had some snide comment prepared, but just then Emily appeared in the room and he once again, as happened fairly frequently in her presence, forgot English. Her hair, pinned on the sides, curled down her back in that way that only girls knew how to do and the beaded necklace she wore fell perfectly against what he thought was the most kissable neck in the world. But it was the dress that made him catch his breath.

Standing still in front of him, she asked in a small voice, "Do I look okay?"

"I didn't think you could get any better."

As she ducked her head, "Glad you like it."

By now, he had come out of his trance, "I like you in ratty jeans and Nate's Luigi shirt, but I'm glad you chose this instead."

Elizabeth stepped in here, telling them, "As my mother likes to say, 'break it up and make room for Jesus'. Now go stand over by the couch so Dave can get pictures."

Dave, having opted not to go to the dance, had been unanimously elected, by himself, to take photos of the four, and decided to play up his role to the best of his ability. The next five minutes were spent with him jumping up on furniture, lying on the floor, speaking in an atrociously bad French accent and muttering, 'beautiful, just beautiful' under his breath a lot.

Once he'd gotten the photos, he handed the camera back to his mom, "I cannot work with these people. They are giving me nothing." He then walked away, shaking his head in dismay, as everyone else began applauding. Waving his hand over his shoulder, he disappeared around the corner, "No applause necessary."

Will looked at his wife, "That is definitely your child."

"I can handle that." Turning back to Jack and Emily, she informed them that curfew had been lifted for the evening, "Just don't get into too much trouble."

"Dude, why didn't you tell me that last week? I work in the morning 'cause I thought I had to be home by midnight."

Looking at her son with an eyebrow raised to near her hairline, "Dude?"

He had to give her two hugs and a bag of M&Ms from his backpack in apology before she let them go. The dance itself was fun, once everyone finally stopped staring at Dex and Claire. At first, the heads turned because of how they were dressed, then Jack overheard someone comment that it looked like Dex wasn't gay after all. Laughing when Jack passed this one along, Dex grinned and, looking over at the gossiping group, grabbed Claire, kissing her full on the lips for a good 10 seconds.

Phil, of course, came over to break them up and Dex smiled at the Principal, "Just letting people know I'm not gay, Sir. Won't happen again."

Claire, not caring about Phil or his rules, laid another on Dex then and there.

All in all, both were having a very good time.

Jack kept his arms wrapped around Emily most of the evening, only letting go when Dex stole her away for a few dances. Jack, odd as it felt, asked Claire if she wanted to dance. "Sure, as long as you keep your hands to yourself."

"God, Claire, could you give me any more of a gross mental picture?"

"Your parents having sex."

Jack just shook his head, "Nope. That doesn't actually bother me."

Claire made a face, "And you say I'm the gross one?"

"It's not like I sit around picturing it. I just say, if they enjoy it, why not?"

"You're more twisted than I ever thought."

Twirling her around suddenly, she laughed and he dipped her so low the tips of her hair spikes hit the ground, "And I learned it all from you."

By the end of the evening, all four were exhausted and grinning like fools. Dex and Claire had to leave immediately after dropping Jack and Emily off so that they could reach Claire's house in time for her curfew. After watching Dex's car disappear around the corner, Jack turned to Emily, "So ..."

"So ..."

"So, I'm thinking that we should take full advantage of this no curfew thing."

Already liking the idea, "Advantage how?"

"Well, we could go catch a really late, really bad movie at the dollar theater."

Emily wrinkled her nose, "Naw, too nice a night for that."

"'Kay ... we could hit Fred's and eat ice cream 'til we explode."

She shook her head, "Not hungry."

Raising a finger In the air and shaking it, "Got it."

"What?"

Doing his best impression of over-exaggerated sneaking, he beckoned her to the backyard, where he first retrieved several old quilts his mom kept in plastic storage bins on the deck, then stage-whispered, "I can hear the hammock calling. It misses us."

Smiling, "It told you that?"

"Well, I miss it and I like to think the feeling's mutual."

◆ ◆ ◆

Not three minutes later, they were all tucked in, cozy against the late-September, Indian summer night, "Okay?"

Nestled comfortably against him, "Perfect."

"Good." Resting his lips against her hair, "We should have just skipped the dance and stayed out here all night."

"Didn't you have fun?"

"Oh, I had a blast, but I was just thinking how nice it would be to have spent the last six hours listening to you breathe."

"I think you might have gotten bored after an hour."

Pushing a strand of hair out of the way with his nose so he could kiss her forehead, "I think it would take a good 240 years to get bored, give or take."

Unbuttoning one of the buttons of his shirt, she slid her hand in and settled it on his stomach, the tip of her finger resting lightly in his belly button. They sat in silence for quite awhile until, "Jack, you still awake?"

"Of course."

"Would you go to the Winter Formal with me?"

"You totally just want to see me in a suit and tie again, don't you?"

Snuggling in closer to him, "Do I really have to answer that question?"

"Not at all."

"And did you notice Dex's head is still intact?"

He would have answered her, but they heard a car pull into the driveway, a door shut and within moments, saw Tim stumble slightly as he headed towards the garage and up to his apartment. Emily nearly called out a 'hey,' but Jack stopped her with a finger to her lips, "Sshhh." Emily, to her credit, remained quiet until Tim closed his door and Jack moved his finger, "I think he's drunk and I don't want him bothering us."

"Tim drinks?"

Waiting until he heard the mysterious car drive off, Jack nodded, knowing it was time she knew, "Apparently he does now. I saw him pretty much the same way around the beginning of August."

"He was drunk?"

"Him and Sarah. They eventually made it up to his place."

"Why didn't you tell me?"

Tracing the outline of her lips, "Because I didn't want to worry you."

"Did you tell Elizabeth or Will?"

"No. It's been a good month and a half since the first time. Maybe he's just being stupid because he's in college. I think he'll be fine, but if you think we should tell somebody, we can."

Waiting a few moments and not getting the scared feeling she thought she might, she shook her head, "If you think we should stay quiet, it's okay with me."

Not really wanting to think about Tim at the moment, he mumbled into her neck, "I'll keep an eye on him."

Emily's temperature rose what felt like 1000 degrees and she pushed Tim to the back of her mind.

♦ ♦ ♦

Jack woke up abruptly and for the life of him, couldn't figure out why he was outside. It was the warmth of Emily next to him that jogged his memory.

Which prompted a smile.

Which prompted him to rub his eyes a bit to wake up so he could see her better.

Which gave him a clear view of his watch.

Which showed him he only had 15 minutes to get to the diner.

Damn him and his 8 to 8 shift.

He tried his best to get out of the hammock undetected, but as anyone who has ever tried to get out of a hammock undetected knows, he failed miserably. As he sent the thing violently swinging, Emily's eyes opened with the same confusion as Jack's had a minute earlier. Body on automatic pilot, she began windmilling her arms, her legs going first directly in the air, then coming down on one side of the hammock, balance shot to hell. Jack lunged to catch the hammock, succeeding in grabbing the edge but not before Emily took a face plant in the grass, missing a sticking up tree root by roughly half an inch and taking a wad of dandelion fluff right up her left nostril. Jack, in turn, had to jump over her in order not to step on her, his momentum carrying the hammock forward and landing him in the dirt perpendicular to her, half covered in the quilt.

Both lay there stunned for a few moments before Emily broke the quiet with first one sneeze, then two more in quick succession. Will, upstairs to wake Jack for work and finding the bed empty, happen to look out the back window to see the scene play out. Pushing the window open further, he called down to them once Emily had stopped sneezing, "You two should charge money for your show. You'd probably make millions."

68

Emily sneezed a response while Jack stood up, brushing dirt from his pants, before slipping his hands firmly under Emily's armpits and hefting her back to her feet, keeping her upright as she swayed, "I don't think we could be this amusing if we actually tried to be."

Will laughed, "Morning Em. How're you doing?"

Several blades of grass sticking to her forehead, she looked up at Will, "I am discovering that I should probably avoid hammocks in dresses from now on."

"I think I'd kind of like to see that hammock in a dress."

"Really, Dad? Grammar jokes this early?"

By now Sam was standing on a chair so he could look out next to his father and he called down as well, "Why are we yelling out the window?"

Beginning to grin as she brushed the grass off of herself carefully so as not to pull any of the sequins with her hand, "Because the neighbors don't think we're noisy enough as it is."

"But Miss Delilah is a grama and she won't mind grama jokes."

His unexpected play on words took a moment to register with them, then Emily turned and blew Sam a kiss, "Good morning, Sam."

"Morning."

◆ ◆ ◆

Jack raced into the house, now really late and really hungry. He was back through the front door three minutes later, dressed for work. Elizabeth only had time to hand him his Pop-Tart before he was gone, leaving her shaking her head and smiling as she turned to find Emily coming through the sliding door in the living room. Looking in at her from the kitchen, "What was all the yelling about?"

"Your son dumped me out of the hammock when he realized he had to be at work in ten minutes." Stealing a donut hole from Nate's hand two inches before he ate it, she smiled and whispered her thanks at him as she continued to head towards her room to change, "I also discovered that one should not attempt to breathe dandelion and that Will and Sam make fairly good, punny grammar jokes."

The three boys at the table and Elizabeth looked at her in confused silence until Elizabeth shrugged her shoulders with a smile, "You people are all certifiable."

"We prefer nuts, Ma. Or just plain crazy."

"Dave?"

"Yeah, Ma?"

"You people are all nuts."

"Thank you."

Once Emily returned to the kitchen, fancy dress exchanged for shorts and a t-shirt, she made herself some cereal while Elizabeth impatiently waited beside her, staring as she poured the milk. Emily contained her grin until she couldn't take it anymore and turned to the older woman, "You want details, don't you?"

"Good Lord, yes!!"

Emily liked having a mother.

♦♦♦

Jack came home a little after eight that night and crashed, literally, on the living room floor. He would have fallen asleep, but for the boys poking him with their toes and rolling him with their feet. Finally giving up, he stood and went to the kitchen to find some dinner. Tim was there, rummaging in the fridge, "Hey little brother."

"Grab me something, would you?"

After Tim re-emerged with several bowls balanced in his arms, "You two have a good time last night?"

"Yeah, and from the look of it, so did you?"

Looking up from the counter, "Huh?"

"We were out in the hammock when you stumbled your way up the driveway."

Tim reddened slightly, "Oh."

Jack's voice went low and serious for a moment, "Don't do it around Emily, okay? She doesn't need that."

"Geez, calm down. It was one night."

Opting not to mention the first time he'd seen him, "I'm just asking, that's all."

Handing his still empty plate to his brother, "You know what? I'm not hungry." Walking to the mud room door, "And careful who you judge."

Jack just stood there a few moments, confused by the last statement, before he put the plate down and followed. Catching up to him halfway across the yard, "Tim."

"What?"

"I didn't judge you."

"You sure as hell did."

"All I asked was that you not drink around her."

"I didn't know you were out here."

"Point taken, but I'm just asking, okay?"

Tim deflated slightly and nodded, "Okay."

They stood quietly staring at each other for a minute, "I didn't think I was judging you."

"You judge everybody who crosses her path whether you realize it or not."

♦ ♦ ♦

Jack headed back inside, made his plate, ate his dinner and excused himself. He half-slept with his iPod playing quietly in his ears and only vaguely remembered Sam crawling into his own bed. He didn't stay asleep long though and when he opened his eyes, the clock told him it was a little after 11. Sliding out of bed, he went downstairs to say goodnight to Emily. With a quick glance in her room, he found it empty, so he proceeded to the living room, where she was just polishing off a peanut butter sandwich, her hair still wet from the shower.

Seeing him, "Hey, I thought you were already asleep."

"I was, but I wanted to say goodnight so I woke back up." Laying on the floor by her feet, "And I missed you."

"Missed me? After only 16 hours? Impressive."

"I always miss you."

Resting her feet on his chest, "Do you have more Pixy Stix facts to share?"

Both loving and hating the fact that she could read him so easily, "I'm not really that transparent, am I?"

After licking the stray peanut butter from her fingers, she moved to lay opposite him, pillow under her head and feet by his ear, "What's on your mind, Jack?"

"Am I too protective of you?"

"What?"

"Tim said I judge everyone who crosses your path."

Giving him a stern look, "Tim has no idea how we work so the next time he opens his mouth, tell him to stick it."

He couldn't help the chuckle that escaped, her words chasing away his annoyance with Tim, "Yes ma'am."

Chapter 8

September rolled into October and very soon, three birthdays were looming on the horizon. Tim would be eighteen, Jack and Emily seventeen and, given that all was right with the world, Emily would be joining in her very first public birthday party.

Early one morning, a week or so beforehand, Elizabeth asked, "So, Miss Emily, who would you like to invite over for the party?"

"Just Dex and Claire really."

"Jack? What about you?"

"Those two cover me as well and Tim said to tell you that Sarah'll be there."

Elizabeth, growing more enormous by the second, was sitting at the kitchen table, her feet already up at 8am, "That'll be easy enough, but if you don't mind, at least this year," patting her belly, "no big dinner or anything. Probably just hot dogs and cake."

Jack grinned at her, "That's tantamount to neglect and it'll take me awhile to deal with the abandonment issues, but I think I'll be able to function in society eventually. Amelia and I'll discuss it, it'll be fine."

Emily cuffed him lightly on the back of the head, "Shut it, boy." Looking at Elizabeth for approval, "Did I do it right or should I have flicked my wrist more?"

Laughing too hard to respond at first, "Honey, that was perfect, thank you. I may hire you to do that on all the boys. It's nice to know I have a stand-in."

Jack just poked his mom's belly and addressed the two babies inside, "Y'all better watch it when you get here. You've got two women to deal with now. It could get real ugly, real quick."

Emily, with one eyebrow raised, "I could always leave, you know. Get out of your hair?"

Ignoring the fact that his mother was two feet away, he pulled her into a kiss, "You're not going anywhere, young lady, not if I can help it." Elizabeth dutifully looked down, divvying up the weekend chores for everyone until she heard Jack laugh, "Sorry. You probably didn't really want to see that."

"I see nothing but the kitchen table, I promise."

Leaning over, he kissed her quickly on the cheek, "I love you, Mom."

As Nate came tearing in, followed closely by Sam, who was chasing him with a swinging pillow and shouting something about pirate attacks, Elizabeth pushed him away, "Go make sure they don't break too much, would you?"

"The things I do for pregnant chicks."

♦ ♦ ♦

The party went smoothly and soon, Emily got to hear her name mashed in with Tim and Jack's during the 'Birthday Song'. It made her absurdly happy and, noticing the smile, Jack slipped around to stand behind her, hands on her waist. When the sixth verse had finally been sung, Elizabeth, with camera aimed, "Ready?"

All three leaned in and on the count of four, Elizabeth snapped the picture while Tim and Emily huffed and puffed to get all 52 candles out in one breath.

Yes, Elizabeth had managed to jam 52 candles in the cake, a full set for each of them. She'd commented on this earlier, "It's a fun idea in theory, but next time, I'm just gonna find those number candles; much less of a fire hazard."

After the cake and ice cream were eaten, gifts were opened, ranging from a box of crayons from Sam to Emily to Tim's and Jack's laptops. Explaining the last two were also a good portion of their upcoming Christmas gift, the two boys realized just how much their parents had spent and looked at each other in complete awe.

Emily's gift, however, seemed to be the best of all, at least by her standards; two heavy boxes containing 'ready-to-assemble' bookshelves. Giving an uncharacteristic squeal of delight, she hugged both Elizabeth and Will at once, "I love them. Thank you so much."

Dex, as usual, had to rib her a bit, "Geez, girl, there're laptops everywhere and you get excited over a pile of wood."

"Dude, you got me books."

With his flash of a grin, "And they better be the first ones on those shelves or I may never speak to you again."

"You mean that's all it'll take?"

"I'll return them, I swear."

Leaning up on her toes, she kissed his cheek, "Thanks, Dex."

With a disdaining swipe to his cheek, "Ugh, girl kisses."

♦ ♦ ♦

It was almost 11 by the time Jack and Will had the shelves put together and bolted proudly against the wall where all her old milk crates had been. Standing up creakily, Will squeezed Emily's shoulder lightly, "I'm heading to bed. Don't stay up too late."

Emily hugged him, "Thanks again, I couldn't have asked for a better birthday."

Once Will was gone, Jack turned to her, "Should we fill them up?" The eagerness in her eyes made him smile, "I'll take that as a yes."

Nodding enthusiastically, "Yes!"

It only took about 15 minutes to organize all the books and, soon after that, they were sitting with backs against the bed, staring at the half-full shelves, "Looks like you need to go shopping."

Thinking of the gift card she'd gotten collectively from Nate, Tucker and Dave that was already burning a hole in her wallet, "That'll be next weekend's mission." Sliding her head onto his shoulder, "Can I ask you something?"

"Sure."

"Why didn't you blow out any of your candles?"

"Did you really want a third person spitting on the cake?"

"You're not gonna answer me, are you?"

After a shrug, "Well, given you never had a birthday party that you can remember and last year's was one measly little candle in a leftover piece of cake, I figured I'd let you have my wish, too. Make up for a few of the ones you missed, but next year, watch out 'cause I'm a hell of a candle-putter-outer."

"Candle-putter-outer?"

"Fine. I'm full of hot air. Happy now?"

Turning, she swung her leg over and settled on his lap, facing him. Pushing a strand of disheveled hair from his forehead, "Very."

Jack stumbled silently upstairs awhile later, grinning at both the thought of the bruise his lips had left behind her ear and that luckily her hair would hide it.

♦ ♦ ♦

She did indeed come to breakfast the next morning with her hair loose. It went unnoticed for the most part and the boys cleared out for chores, leaving Emily alone with Elizabeth, who came to stand behind her. Without a word, Elizabeth gathered up Emily's hair and moved it first to one side, then the other, "Ahh, there it is."

Emily blushed to the roots of the hair in question, "Um … "

She let the handful of hair fall back in place, "Am I going to have to start supervising bed time around here?"

Turning in her chair, "I'm sorry."

Putting her hand gently on Emily's cheek, "Just promise me you'll be careful." Now looking her straight in the eye, "I don't really think either of us could do with another scare like the last one."

Her stomach dropped to her knees, "What?"

Just then, Will came in from the garage with Nate and Dave, and taking one look at Emily's face, "What's wrong?"

Elizabeth just took Emily's hand and walked her to her room, "Just a little girl talk. We'll be out in a while."

After the door was shut, Emily asked again, "You know?"

"I found the pregnancy test in the garbage."

"But we took that bag out so you wouldn't find it."

"And I wouldn't have, but Dave thought he threw away his retainer so I had to go digging."

Still standing in the middle of the room, "You weren't supposed to find out."

"Will you tell me what happened?" The look Emily shot her was almost comical, "Not that part. I have a pretty good idea how that part works. I meant when you thought you were." Emily finally sat down on the bed and, with some difficulty, Elizabeth settled in beside her, "I'm not mad, I promise. I'd just like to know the whole story."

Realizing that she didn't have a choice, Emily settled in and began, "It was the beginning of last May … "

♦ ♦ ♦

Previous May:

"Jack, I need to talk to you."

He hadn't slept the night before, as usual, but to top it off, he had a sore throat and a headache, "Can we do this later? I feel like hell and I've got a history test tomorrow that I'm about 40 years behind on." Pulling his textbook from his bag and dropping it with a thud on the bed, "Although how the reign of Alexander the Great affects me, I don't know and don't really care."

Emily just stood quietly in the doorway during his rant, then slipped down the hallway, calling a quiet, "all right" over her shoulder.

Jack, who really just wanted to hug her and take a nap, immediately felt guilty and climbed to his feet to follow. Poking his head into her room, "I'm sorry. I didn't sleep too great last night and I believe I'm what my mom likes to call cranky."

She couldn't help but smile at his apology, "It's all right. I just wish you felt better."

"Well, I will once you tell me what's on your mind so I don't have to sit here and think I'm in trouble. It doesn't help with the studying at all."

"It's fine. You're not in trouble," already moving to get him back to his room, "but you need to pass your test, so get out."

79

Hearing the anxiety in her voice and catching her by the arm, careful to avoid her cast, "Hey, what's wrong?"

"Jack ..."

Closing the door while still holding her elbow, "Em, what's wrong?"

Her eyes now also held a hint of panic, but keeping her voice steady, "Remember our night at the hotel?"

Mental images racing immediately through his mind, "Of course."

"I'm beginning to wonder if I was wrong about the whole 'no condom' thing."

It took a minute for this to re-write itself in his brain to mean, 'I think I might be pregnant.' "But what about when you were in the hospital? Don't they usually check for that before x-rays and stuff?"

"I don't think I would have even been pregnant at that point. It takes a few days for everything to organize itself." With a shrug, "I don't know how these things work any more than you do."

Jack finally let go of her arm, "I take it you haven't started your period yet?"

Shaking her head, "I'm about a month late and I'm starting to freak out a little."

Not knowing what to do, he hugged her tightly.

◆ ◆ ◆

They had to wait until two days later when the house was empty again before Jack could open the pregnancy test he'd stashed in his drawer. Soon Emily was out of the bathroom and the longest, most silent five minutes of their lives ensued.

◆ ◆ ◆

The grin Emily had when she returned to the bedroom was enough to allow Jack his first deep breath in 48 hours. She almost laughed at the look on his face, "You okay there?"

Taking another deep breath, "I just re-discovered oxygen so you'll have to give me a minute."

Coming to stand in front of him and feeling fairly awkward, "I think I can spare the time."

Noticing the awkwardness, "Hey, come here." With his arms wrapped firmly around her, he whispered in her ear, "I wouldn't have been angry. I wouldn't have left and I sure as hell wouldn't have turned into him. I'd have loved this kid more than anything. I'm just glad we don't have to think about it right now."

With that, a few tears of relief rolled down her cheeks, "How'd you know what I needed to hear?"

As he kissed the top of her head, "'Cause I know you better than you think."

◆ ◆ ◆

Elizabeth continued to sit in silence once the story ended and Emily, mortified at the whole truth she'd just spilled, "I'm sorry."

Sliding her arm around Emily's shoulders, "It's all right. Just promise me you've been careful."

"We haven't done that since, I swear."

"Good, because I don't know that I could handle having my children and my grandchild sharing a crib." Leaning her head over to rest on Emily's, "He's not your father, Em, and he never will be. Trust me on that."

"I'm still not very good with the trust thing, am I?"

Elizabeth smiled, "You're getting there. It takes time."

"Do we have to tell Will? I don't want him looking at me differently."

"You know he'd adore you regardless."

"Well, I'd prefer not to put that theory to the test."

"We can keep it to ourselves, then." Still hugging her, "You know you can tell me anything, right? I may yell some and look terrifying for awhile, but at the end of the day, I'll still love you, okay?"

Emily pulled away slightly, "You love me?"

"How could I not?"

♦♦♦

Jack showed up later that evening just as the younger boys were doing the supper dishes. Struggling through the front door, he gently set down a brown-paper wrapped object, flat and from the sound of it, made of glass, "Oopphhhh ... "

"What's that?"

Looking around, "Birthday gift. Where's Em?"

At the sound of her name, she came around the corner, "Right here. What's up?"

"Happy Birthday." The look on her face made him smile, "What? I told you I couldn't pick up your gift 'til today. Did you think I was just trying to weasel my way out of getting you something?"

Turning bright red, "No, I just wasn't expecting anything quite that large." Suddenly, the dimensions of the package triggered something, "You didn't, did you?"

Jack held his grin, "This just proves I really do listen to you."

Ripping into the paper, Emily found what she expected, but it still made her catch her breath. Jack had heard her say months back that she wished she had the money to custom-frame the shoe drawing from last year's art class, but since she didn't, her drawing remained safely tucked away. Running her fingers lightly over the wood frame and smooth, cool glass, "This cost a fortune, Jack."

"Then we are all very lucky that Dale hired me back."

Again, "It's too much."

"It's never too much, Em."

Suddenly, her eyes lit up and she caught him in a kiss, "And I love it."

The younger boys groaned while Will came over to look at the gift, "Any idea where you want to hang it?"

Emily turned immediately towards her room, "I know right where … " she stopped suddenly, "oh my God."

"What?"

"I have the bookshelves now. I don't think there's room on my walls."

Jack picked up the picture and walked past her, "It'll fit." Boy, was he wrong. Standing in the middle of her small room, "Dad, next time we need to coordinate better."

Elizabeth, now leaning in the doorway, "Couldn't you move the shelves?"

Rubbing his forehead, Will answered, "We bolted them to the wall and besides, we can't move them anywhere else really. I kinda bought them for where they are. With the window, the dresser and mirror and the doorway, there's not enough wall anywhere for it."

Hatching a plan, Elizabeth turned to Emily, "Honey, would you mind if I suggest something in the meantime?"

"'Course not. What're you thinking?"

Leading the way into the living room, she motioned for Jack to put the picture on the mantle. After moving several objects, pictures and various birthday cards, he centered it as best he could then stood back, "Can't argue that the thing isn't meant to go here. If I didn't know any better, I'd say she drew it to go here and only here."

"Then here it stays, if that's all right with you, Em?"

Emily could only nod to Elizabeth's question, an odd feeling settling at the back of her brain; an idea that had to grow a little before she tried to figure out what it was.

Luckily it didn't take too long.

Later that evening, with only Elizabeth, Will, Jack, Emily and Dave left downstairs, Emily, who had been lying on the carpet most of the evening, pillow stuffed under her head, suddenly stood up. Jack, half-asleep beside her on his own pillow, opened his eyes when he felt her move, "You okay?"

Moving to stand in front of the mantle, she first studied the picture for another moment or two, then reaching behind it, pulled out the envelope with the custody papers Will had put there the previous May. Opening it up in silence, she read the papers, ran her fingers lightly over the words, then read them a second time before turning to look at the people staring intently in her direction. Her eyes squinted for a moment, as if studying the objects of her next art project, then she smiled at them, her cheeks glowing pink in happiness, "I drew this before anything happened and when I drew it, I already knew I wanted to be yours." Her revelation seemed to floor her, but she recovered with a shake of her head, her smile getting wider, "And these papers prove that I am yours. I'm seriously, completely, legally, happily yours."

Dave gave a look of confusion that just amused her more, "But that envelope's been up there for six months."

"I know." Nearly laughing at this point, "It just took this long to sink in." Repeating, simply because she could, "I'm seriously, completely, legally, happily yours."

Jack popped up so fast Emily took a step back, nearly falling over the hearth, "Then we need to celebrate the fact that you are seriously, completely, legally, happily ours." Taking the papers from her, he set them back on the mantle, then pulled her out of the living room by her hand, calling over his shoulder that they'd be back by graduation.

Emily just let him lead, her shoes hastily pulled on, but not tied, her sweatshirt pulled over her head inside out, keys forgotten. A few blocks from home she finally made him stop, laughing as she did, "Hey, can I at least tie my shoes? I'm gonna fall and break myself if I don't."

Jack just grinned, hopping from foot to foot in his impatience, trying to keep warm given he'd remembered Emily's sweatshirt, but not his own.

Once her shoes were attached properly to her feet, they moved on, ending up in Grant Park, which, as Emily had told him over a year ago, had the best swings in the world. Without a word, she sat down in one of the swings and began pumping her feet, free flying hair brushing the woodchips as she leaned back on the upswing, her feet aimed at the deep, blue night sky. Jack swung next to her for a few minutes, but then moved to lean against the post, perfectly content to watch her fly until the end of time.

As they were walking home, Emily remembered her talk with Elizabeth from earlier, "Can we stop for a minute?"

Figuring they had about five spare minutes, he came to a halt, still holding her hand, "What's up?"

"I meant to tell you before and don't get mad and I don't want to ruin a perfect night but, um … I had to tell Elizabeth about the pregnancy test. She saw my neck after you left for work and," stopping when Jack took on a horrified look, "you okay?"

"Um, yeah … just …" his head stopped spinning after a moment, "you told my mom that we thought you might be pregnant? Good lord, I'm glad I missed that conversation."

"She found the test in the trash when she went looking for Dave's retainer. She didn't mention it then, but when she saw me this morning, she took me into my room and basically made me spill the beans."

"Damn Dave and his crooked teeth." Rubbing his hand across his forehead, he gave her a sheepish grin, "And I gotta say, better your conversation than mine."

Emily grinned at him, pushing him lightly on the shoulder, "Are you mad I told her?"

"Naw. I'm surprised she didn't smack me when she first found out though. I wonder why she didn't?"

"You could always ask her."

Giving her a second horrified look, "Are you insane?" He started walking back home again, "Let's hope we never have to discuss our sex life ever again with either of my parents."

They skirted back through the front door just before midnight, apologizing profusely to Will, who had stayed up to let them back in the house since Jack had forgotten his keys as well. Will, given he really didn't mind waiting up for them in the first place, motioned for the pair to follow. Once they reached the living room, Emily noticed first and immediately turned into the hug Will had been hoping for. Jack just grinned, arms crossed and body relaxed. The picture Emily had drawn wasn't just resting on the mantle anymore, but was hanging on the bricks above, permanently affixed for years to come. Below, crowded in with various other mementos and pictures that had been put back in their places, was the envelope, tucked neatly beneath the picture frame that held the drawing of one girl's feet squished among her six boys.

Chapter 9

It was toward the end of October and Emily couldn't help but notice him. He was about 5' 10", completely bald and feverishly spinning the combination on the locker four down from the door of her second class and apparently having absolutely no success whatsoever. The swarms of students ignored him, trying to get to their own classes on time. Emily, without another thought, slid in beside him and put her hand over his to stop the spinning, "Breathe."

"Do I have to?"

"It usually helps in the whole 'keeping alive' equation."

He took what may have been his first deep breath of the morning and she removed her hand. Looking away for a second, he then re-focused on her, a half-smile on his lips, "I'm Matt and yes, breathing is a good thing. Thanks for reminding me."

With her own friendly smile, "I'm Emily and from experience, these lockers can't be rushed. The minute they sense you're in a hurry, they jam right up." Reaching out to take the scrap of paper with the combination on it, "Let me try." She had it in one shot and, giving him back the paper, "I've discovered that the best way is to have most of the numbers already done so you'll only have to do the last number when you come back." The bell rang just then, "Gotta go. Good luck."

She was gone before he could ask where in the world his next class might be, but, at least, he thought, he would remember one face today, if nothing else; the face of the girl who managed to get him into his locker. Doing as told with his combination, he turned a full circle before remembering his hallway map was still in his locker. Praying the last number thing worked, he grinned when it did. He'd have to find that girl and buy her a donut in thanks.

♦ ♦ ♦

He didn't see her again until lunch and with a boldness borne from depths unknown, he set his tray down next to hers at the otherwise empty table, "Um, mind if I sit down?"

Emily turned to him, both curious and confused until she saw his face, "Matt, right? Sure, sit down."

Sitting as told, he opened his mouth to thank her for that morning when her face suddenly and inexplicably disappeared behind some brown-haired head. Hearing the unmistakable sound of a kiss happening, he immediately swung his head in the other direction, only to come face to face with a blue head of hair intently inspecting his lunch tray, "Dude, you've got to be new." All he could do was nod, because once blue hair lifted his head to speak, Matt was confronted with a glinting eyebrow ring and half a ham sandwich in mid-chew. "Em, you're slacking. Newbie here isn't fully versed in cafeteria cuisine."

As brown-hair sat down and blue-hair continued to chew in his ear, Emily reached over, shoving blue-hair back with a push to his forehead, "Would you stop chewing in his face please? He doesn't love you enough for that yet."

Brown hair muttered loudly, "I don't think I love him enough yet for that."

Blue-hair grinned and retreated some as Emily turned to him, "Matt," waving her hand in Dex's direction, "Dex. Dex, Matt."

Dex shook his hand, "Nice to meet you, Matt. Welcome to hell."

"Dexter Grenden, do not make me come over there."

Matt watched in fascination as Dex twisted his face into an apologetic, penchant pout, "Sorry, Miss. Won't happen again."

88

As a bit of ham from Dex's sandwich hit her square in the cheek, she continued unphased, although the smile on her face betrayed her amusement, "And this is Jack. Jack, Matt."

Instead of a handshake, which only Dex could pull off without question, Jack gave a friendly nod, "I hear she found you fighting with your locker this morning."

"Yeah. It would've won if she'd been thirty-seconds later."

"She's good like that."

That said, they continued on with lunch. Emily did, however, stop Matt with a hand on his arm as he went to eat a spoonful of the chili, "Dex is right. Don't eat that."

Frozen with the spoon midway to his mouth, "Why?"

Dex chimed in before she could, "It doth not take well to the intestinal regions and prefereth to make a hasty exit."

Jack, eyeing Emily's hand on Matt's arm, kept his voice light as he translated Dex's poetic statement, "He means you'll be shitting in minutes."

Putting the spoon down swiftly, "Oh."

Emily handed him part of her lunch, "Exactly. Ready for a few Cavendish High vital life lessons?"

Glancing warily at the steaming chili, Matt nodded slowly, "Yes, please."

◆ ◆ ◆

By the end of lunch, Matt had the major rules down, including the minutia of cafeteria life as only Dex could describe. The three of them, in turn, discovered he'd moved from Arizona, had two sisters, including his twin, both of whom went to private school and that he loved all things music and baseball.

Dex had perked up instantly when he mentioned music, "Do you play an instrument or just like to listen?"

"I listen. I had a friend whose family owns a bunch of used record stores. We found all kinds of weird crap in there and I ended up liking most of it. Now I listen to everything and we had to pay the moving company extra to move my record collection."

"Wait. Honest-to-God records? As in vinyl and record player needles and smooth Jazz grooves?"

"More alternative and punk than Jazz, but yeah."

"I may kiss you sometime in the future, just as a warning. Claire will be fine with it, by the way, once she hears you have vinyl." Dex aimed a bony finger in Matt's direction, "And speaking of Claire, where do your sisters go to school?"

"Some guy's name. D. … something. Why?"

"D. Jeffries? Claire goes there." Raising the pierced eyebrow at him, "Why don't you go there?"

Matt shrugged, "I tried the whole private school thing back home, but I wasn't a big fan. Can't stand the uniforms and the rules and all that, which reminds me, can we wear hats around this place? My head is cold as all hell." Rubbing his hand fast over his scalp several times, "Having no hair works in Arizona, but here, not so much."

"It'll grow back in a few weeks, won't it?"

Looking at Emily, "I'm keeping it short. The longer my hair is the puffier it gets." Holding his hand several inches off his head, "Which would you choose, puffy hair or freezing scalp?"

Before Emily could answer, Dex leaned back in his chair, "Give me your hat and few minutes with Phil and we'll see what we can do."

"Who's Phil?"

Emily laughed, "The principal and when necessary, Dex's best friend."

"Seriously?"

Dex pulled him up from his chair, "I shall use the last five minutes of lunch to argue your case. Follow me."

Looking at Emily in confusion, she simply pointed out the door, "You'd better go before he changes his mind."

While Matt hurried to get his things, Emily stood as well, giving Jack a quick kiss, "Can you take my books to class for me? I'd rather not take them to the bathroom."

After he nodded, he watched both Emily and Matt disappear down the hall, his jealousy bubbling under the surface. Matt was new, he needed some friends and if he stuck around through ten minutes with Dex, there was a good chance he was a halfway decent guy. Deciding to reserve judgment, he stood up as well, dumped the remaining trash from the table and headed towards their next class together.

◆◆◆

Dex waited for Matt to get his hat from his locker, then, seeing the hat, grinned and grabbed it, "This is gonna be fun."

Walking into the office, Dex asked the secretary, or June as he got away with calling her, "Mr. Tangelo please, June."

Phil, who had been having a rough day, with a fight in the hall, a broken leg in freshman gym and two exploding toilets, heard him through the open door of his office. Coming to stand in the doorframe, "Whatever it is, no."

"Dude ..."

Knowing the 'dude' only led to his inevitably saying yes, "Oh, God, fine ... as long as there are no drugs, police, alcohol, sex or vandalism involved, consider it legal and allowable and get out."

"You, sir, are totally awesome." Turning to June, "You know this man is totally awesome, right? You need to write to somebody to have him given a legal holiday or at least a free lunch or two. He puts up with a lot of crap from us kids."

June fought the smile and lost, "Yes, Dex, I'll get right on that."

"Thank you." Turning Matt around and pulling the winter hat down on his head, Dex called over his shoulder, "I love you, Mr. Tangelo."

Even Phil, for some reason, felt a little better than he had three minutes earlier, "Get out!" Once the two had left, Phil turned to the witnesses around him, "Any idea what I just agreed to?"

Pointing out the windows into the hall at Dex, who was now waving Matt's hand back and forth enthusiastically, gesturing at Matt's hat and giving Phil a thumbs up with the other hand, "Pretty sure that kid'll be wearing that hat the rest of the winter."

Phil took stock of the Marvin the Martian stocking cap the boy was wearing and sighed, "It could have been worse. Make a note, please, June, to announce that during the winter months, hats may be worn during school hours, but I or any teacher reserve the right to remove said article of clothing if deemed inappropriate, at our discretion."

Back in the hall, "Mission accomplished. Now, where do you go next?"

Matt, exhausted by the last three minutes of his life, shook his head, "I have no idea."

"Dude, preparation is the mother of getting to shit on time. Give me your schedule." Taking it a moment later, "Easy. Torrey. History. You're with the three of us. Follow along."

Following as ordered yet again, Matt decided Pennsylvania might not be so bad after all.

Rushing into class at the last second, Matt headed to the teacher while Dex saluted to both Jack and Emily while striding to his seat.

"Hi. I'm Matt. Just started today."

"Welcome to American history." Pointing up towards Matt's hat, "And for future reference, no hats in class, okay?"

Dex called from his desk, "Mr. Torrey. I'd be expecting an announcement soon or by tomorrow at the latest reneging on that rule."

Moving only his eyes towards Dex, then up to the hat and finally back around to Dex, "If you ever run for President, Mr. Grendan, I will no doubt be casting my vote for you out of fear that if I didn't, you'd show up on my doorstep and talk me into it."

"Grendan, 2028. Bring me a baby and I'll kiss it."

It took another few minutes for the class to calm down enough to begin working.

Matt had no idea if he would make it to the end of the day.

♦ ♦ ♦

Since this was their last class together for the day and he had to work right after school, Jack caught Emily outside the classroom, "I'll see you at home."

"Wake me up if I'm asleep."

Already heading down the hall, "Love you."

She didn't answer because he was too far away. Turning, she ran right into Matt, "So, where do you go next?"

"Mathers. Um, oh, study hall."

Pointing down the hall, "Three doors to your left," she turned in the other direction, "have fun with Dex."

Sighing to himself, he moved to his last class of the day. Dex waved a lazy hello to the teacher and lightly shoved Matt up towards the large desk,

"Mrs. Mathers, this here is Matt Quatermass. He's new and I want to know if I can steal him to help me move chairs in the music room?"

Mrs. Mathers, like most of the teachers, felt she should be annoyed with Dex, but, for some reason, could never work up to it. Pointing her attendance book towards the door, "Welcome, Mr. Quatermass, now get out."

Matt, not knowing what the hell was going on, didn't argue, but instead followed Dex into the hallway. With the classroom door shut firmly behind them, "Um, Dex? Am I really going to move chairs for the next hour?"

"Well, given I know we don't have any history homework and that's the only book you have with you, I figured you'd rather help me than sit picking your nose for the afternoon."

Seeing his point, "So, do you get out of study hall a lot?"

"Only when necessary. Remember, if you abuse the system, it'll abuse you."

With a smirk and a shake of his head, "Haven't you pushed the system enough today and just how often is necessary?"

Flashing a grin, "90% of the time. There are always other things that need to be done and I figure I might as well be the one doing them."

Once they reached the music room, Dex waved to Mr. Sylvester in his office before heading to the stacks of chairs that needed to be set out.

For the first time since he met him, Dex wasn't talking so Matt broke the silence, "Dex?"

"Yeah?"

"How long have Jack and Emily been going out?"

"Little over ten months and I wouldn't go there."

Not to be dissuaded, "Are they that serious?"

Dex stopped his chair placement to look Matt square in the face, "New guy needs to move on."

"Sorry, just curious."

"Curiosity killed the cat and will get the cat dug back up and beaten a second time just for fun. She's extremely incredible, but extremely off the market."

Knowing when he was beaten, "I'm just asking because after class, he told her he'd see her at home and she said to wake her up if she was asleep. How does that work?"

Shoving a few more chairs in place before answering, "She lives with him."

Matt nearly dropped the chair he was moving, "Are you kidding?"

"Along with his five brothers and his parents and two more kids on the way."

He stood in confusion, "She lives with her boyfriend's family. That must be awfully convenient at 3am."

Dex was by him instantly, "I like you and you're new so I'm not going to kick you in the balls, but if Jack heard you, his foot would be so far up your ass, you'd have sock lint in your throat."

Given Dex was towering over him at this point, "Um, how about I just stop assuming things and you back the hell off a little bit."

Not moving just yet, but shifting his tone to below 'I'm going to melt you with the fire from my eyeballs', he continued, "Emily is one of a kind and there are things that you don't know that make you wholly unqualified to even begin to assess that relationship. So, how about we just decide that she is Jack's and Jack is hers." Stepping back finally, "That's the end of your lessons for today."

Matt now wondered if it was safe to be in a room with someone this obviously unstable.

Dex could see this clearly and he grinned, "Hey, we are some very uniquely awesome people. I think you just might fit in, given your ability to roll with whatever is thrown at you and the fact that you haven't run screaming back to study hall yet."

"Grendan, 2028? Bring him your baby and he'll kiss it?"

Dex laughed and started in on the chairs again, "There is totally hope for you yet."

A few minutes later, just before they finished setting up, the subject of Claire came up. Dex stopped mid-chair shove and pulled his wallet out of his pocket, digging up the picture he had of her from the birthday party, "Your sister will probably know her if you ask. She's not one you forget easily."

"She looks perfect for you. She also looks disturbingly like Jack."

Pocketing the picture once again, "She's his cousin."

"Nothing like keeping it in the family."

Smirking at Matt, "You amuse me."

"Just no hitting on anybody, right?"

"Hallelujah, he can be taught. Now," turning in a circle to survey the room, "the real fun begins."

"Why? Are we gonna be re-grouting the locker room next?"

"Hell no. I'm not about to go anywhere near where Marcus Sayer's feet have been." Pulling open one of the doors along the back wall and unearthing his saxophone case, "I plan on practicing while you either take a nap or be entranced by my musical prowess. Either way, we don't have to be quiet and waste an hour trying not to get in trouble for falling asleep in study hall." Pointing at the closest chair, "Sit and be amazed."

Matt sat and did indeed enjoy the show, deciding after about 15 seconds that he might like to keep this character as his friend, along with Emily.

Jack, he didn't know about yet, but figured they were a package deal, so it would be a good idea to befriend them all. Besides, he figured, Jack was only acting the way most any boyfriend would. And, at the very least, he figured, Jack couldn't be as nuts as the musical genius before him.

Chapter 10

Thanksgiving snuck up on everyone that year. Usually, Elizabeth had everything organized, assigned and timed to the letter. This year, however, given her burgeoning condition and the unexpected wallop of the flu that confined Will to his bed, dinner fell mostly on Jack and whoever he wrangled into assistance. Luckily, Elizabeth could still direct from the kitchen table with her feet up, "Jack, if you don't think you can do it, it's fine. We don't have to have everything we usually do."

Jack, his body half-wedged into the corner cabinet digging for pans, called out, his voice sounding hollow given his positioning, "I will not be defeated by one stinking Thanksgiving dinner." Backing out, he smacked his head on the edge of the door and, swearing, collapsed onto the kitchen floor, face against the linoleum.

Emily bit her tongue, but Dave, who was perched on the counter tearing up loaves of bread, refused to let this pass, "Depends on how you define defeat?"

"I define it as not having everything on that table by 3 o'clock tomorrow afternoon." He stood carefully, shaking his head while rubbing the sore spot, "Why the hell did they build a cupboard in the corner anyway? Some sadistic architect's idea of a good time?"

His mother tilted her head in sympathy, having been knocked around by that very cabinet several times in the past, "It's really okay, Jack. We'll get done what we get done." Turning to Emily, "Would you mind going to check on Will for me? He should still be asleep from the Nyquil, but could you go see?"

Nodding, Emily ran upstairs, then returned almost immediately, "He's still snoring … loudly."

Elizabeth nodded, "Thanks, hon." She now surveyed the three in the kitchen and the three other boys hovering around the door, "From here on out, you listen to Jack and any griping gets an answer from me, understood?"

All heads nodded and Jack grinned, rubbing his hands together in glee, "I can already feel my power growing."

♦ ♦ ♦

It was after 11pm and they were just beginning the pies when Jack dismissed the boys with a wave of his chopping knife, "Get out before you fall asleep in the filling." Gladly they obeyed, helping Elizabeth up the stairs before collapsing in their rooms. Jack looked over at Emily, who was covered in flour and apple pie remnants, "You look like you're about to crash land in your bowl."

"Naw, just getting started."

Her yawn declared otherwise and he chuckled, "Go. I could do these in my sleep."

Emily shook her head, "I'll stay. Just don't yell at me if you see me sneaking apples as I go."

Turning back to the counter, he stopped his dough-making about ten minutes later when the front door opened. It had to be Tim, but he looked over his shoulder anyway, "Tim?"

He walked into the kitchen, "Who'd you expect? Sam coming in from some late night mailbox baseball?"

"No, actually I thought it was Tucker with the strippers he promised."

Tim rolled his eyes at his brother, "You don't bring the strippers home, idiot, you go there to see them."

99

Jack, being too annoyed not to be drawn in to the ridiculous argument, "Strippers make house calls, too, dumbass."

"How would you know?"

Emily's lip curled in disgust when she realized that Tim might actually have been at a strip club that evening. Jack, seeing Emily's expression, thought the same thing, and asked hesitantly, "You didn't actually go … to a strip club, did you?"

"I was at work, moron." Stealing a large piece of sugar-coated apple from Emily's bowl, "Besides, I have Sarah for that." After licking his fingers clean and ignoring the still disgusted look on Emily's face, "Why are you cooking all this stuff tonight? Why aren't you and Dad doing it tomorrow?"

Jack had that steaming look about his face, so Emily answered quickly, "Will's got the flu, remember? So Jack's in charge of dinner. You gonna be around to help?"

Turning towards the refrigerator for something to eat before heading out to his apartment, "Nope. Eating over at Sarah's, then going to a party." After surveying and finding nothing appealing, he grabbed a 2-liter then shut the door, "So have fun."

"Are you kidding me?"

He looked at his little brother, "What?"

"You're seriously blowing us off for Thanksgiving? Mom's gonna kill you."

"Mom doesn't care. It's not like there aren't enough of you to fill up the table without me." Heading towards the back door, "Anyway, I'm over there at 11 tomorrow. Tell Mom for me."

Emily, putting her hand on Jack's arm and stopping him from throwing an unpeeled apple at his brother's head, whispered in his ear, "Don't."

With a clenched-jaw, "Why not?"

She tightened her grip on him, "Because if you do anything, Elizabeth'll be down here, she'll make him stay tomorrow and it will suck for everybody because he'll be whining about it the whole time."

Giving in, he slipped his hand from hers and returned to his crusts, "I also love how I get to tell Mom he won't be there. Really nice of him, wasn't it?"

Not knowing what to say at this point, she just picked up her knife, "I'm almost done here … you ready for filling yet?"

"I have half a mind to …"

"I know you do. But I need the non-pissed part of you to stay here; help me get these done so we can go to bed and get up early tomorrow to have a fun, happy Thanksgiving."

Looking sideways at her, he saw the determined set of her mouth and her tired eyes. Deflating with a slow nod, he held his hand out to her, "Give me pie plates, would you?"

After midnight, Emily abandoned Jack for her nice, soft pillow, under strict orders to go to bed before she fell down. She heard the quiet clinking of dishes in the sink and the soft thud of the cupboards closing as Jack put everything away after drying. Taking her pillow with her, she situated her head at the foot of the bed. Laying just right and at a slightly awkward angle, she could see him standing at the kitchen sink, body relaxed and hunched slightly to reach the far side of the counter with his washcloth.

Or, she thought fleetingly before closing her eyes, not relaxed at all; bent over instead because he seemed to carry the self-imposed weight of the world on his shoulders.

♦ ♦ ♦

Jack had the sense to be up before everyone else, to catch Elizabeth when she was still half-asleep. Telling her about Tim while handing her a steaming cup of tea and a still warm Pop-tart seemed, to him, the best way to deliver the news. Apparently it was, given she nodded only once, "Well, at least he let someone know." After taking several sips and her first bite, she looked around the still quiet kitchen, "He's just enjoying his freedom.

He'll realize he misses all of us eventually." Jack could only shrug at that so she let the subject drop and gave her son a smile, "What would you like me to do for you?"

After they exchanged the bare minimum of awkwardness, he smirked, "You can open up the green beans, if you can still reach past your stomach."

"Don't make me waddle over there and …" her threat ran out of steam and she dropped her hands to her lap, "oh hell, bring over the cans and I'll see what I can do." Emily stumbled into the kitchen a few minutes later to find Elizabeth with a can of green beans resting on her stomach while she twisted the can opener. Elizabeth, beating Emily to any smart remark she might be thinking, "Yes, I am using my belly as a table. Yes, I am opening a can of beans on the heads of my unborn babies. Yes, it probably does look hilarious and yes, if you must, you may make your comment now."

She did, however, say it with a twinkle in her eye and Emily only grinned, "Just wanted to say g'morning."

Everyone but Will followed down within the next half-hour and soon, the place was hopping. True to his word, he had the food ready for the table a little after 3, "It's not exact, but if Nate hadn't decided to try to crush his finger in the oven door, I would've made it."

Nate just sat there, tear streaks still evident on his face, but wearing his commonplace smile, dimples showing, "If you hadn't slammed it in there, I'd be fine."

"Dude, you should have gotten out of the way." Jack tossed a biscuit to him, "Sorry about that."

The dinner was boisterous and rowdy and chaotic as usual, food falling, utensils dropping and jokes being told for the sole purpose of seeing who would be the first to shoot milk out of their nose.

Jack, having been the one to fire his milk, had to go to his room to change. Returning dry, he found a truly unnerving sight; everyone was quietly sitting at their own spot, using their own utensils, wiping their mouths with their, swear to God, own napkins instead of each other's shirt sleeves. Sam was using his fork to eat his turkey, Tucker said 'excuse me' when a small burp escaped, Dave said thank you when someone handed him something. "What the hell did you people do?"

Elizabeth looked innocently up at him, "Whatever do you mean?"

"Okay. Am I gonna find, like, an entire salt shaker mixed into my potatoes? Did somebody lick all my carrots?"

Looking aghast, his mother took a small bite of green beans, "Dear, you shouldn't be so paranoid. We are trying to show good manners in front of the one who cooked such a wonderful meal."

"I'm dying, aren't I?" Moving towards his chair, "You could have at least told me after dessert."

Emily gave him a smile and patted lightly near his plate, "You're not dying. Now sit and eat before it gets cold."

With his finger, he prodded his potatoes and turkey, "Well, not frozen or scalding." Still wary, he sat down.

And the chair broke under him, dropping him on the ground. He only let out a muffled, "Shit!" then lay on the ground while everyone stood and stared at him in awe. Looking up at his family, "I can take a joke as well as the next guy, but breaking a chair just to see me fall is fairly destructive, don't you think?"

Elizabeth was the first to laugh, everyone else following suit quickly. Between wiping her tears and turning a scarlet red color, "Oh ... oh, God ... we didn't break the chair at all. That wasn't us."

It took a moment to sink in, then Jack, laying amidst the wreckage, joined in the laughter as well, "Then you guys actually were just using manners and crap like that?"

As Emily pulled him up, getting out the words as best she could while trying to breathe, "No. Nate licked all your carrots and Sam mixed a load of salt in your potatoes. I tied your napkin to the tablecloth and your mom ate your Jello."

"Holy ... I am a damn good guesser."

"Yes, you are."

"So the chair just chose right then to break? You really had nothing to do with it?"

Elizabeth looked at him, "Do you really think I'd ruin furniture for a prank?"

"You let Nate lick my carrots."

"Still way better than sawing through the leg of your chair."

Pushing the pieces of chair away with his foot, he went to grab the kitchen stool to sit on, "Very true. Anyways, dear mother, how was eating my Jello a prank?"

"It wasn't. I just wanted more Jello and your plate was closer than the bowl."

He saw the logic in this and taking a mouthful of carrots, he stopped after three or four chews because everyone was looking at him, "What?"

"Um, I licked all those."

Shrugging at his brother, "Like it matters."

Dinner continued once again.

♦ ♦ ♦

Afterwards, when Jack started moving dishes to the sink and opening the dishwasher, Elizabeth waved him away, "Go sit down, do nothing for awhile. I'll spearhead the cleanup in here."

"You sure?"

"Get out before I change my mind."

He did as ordered, settling himself happily on the couch while the rest of them stashed the leftovers, then piled into the living room to watch TV and attempt to digest the three pounds of food each of them had just eaten. Just as Jack was about to fall asleep against Emily's shoulder, Will appeared around the corner, "Hey."

Everyone stopped and looked at once, with Elizabeth struggling to stand immediately. Once Dave helped her with a friendly shove, she urged her husband to sit, "Hey yourself. What're you doing down here? Did you need anything?"

Will shook his head weakly, "I just got tired of laying down, although the trip downstairs has got me doubting my decision to travel this far."

Jack was up by now. Pulling Emily with him, he cleared Nate onto the floor at the same time before saying to his dad, "Then lay back down 'cause you look like you're about to drop."

With a nod, Will settled in, "Anything left over that might sit okay in my stomach?"

Sam, being Sam, didn't stop to think that he shouldn't be describing all the food in detail to his dad's still unsettled stomach and begin he did. "The dark meat was the best. It was still slippery and greasy when Jack cut it off the turkey, just the way you like it. I bet if we put in the microwave with some butter it would be good again. Oooh, and the green beans were really good, too. Emily put some bacon in with them and the soup was extra chunky because Jack had her put in more mushrooms. It looked just like what I threw up when I was sick last week. Are you still throwing up chunks, Dad?"

Everybody groaned at this comment and Will held up a hand immediately, "On second thought, don't tell me, okay? I'm not that hungry after all."

With the couch now occupied by a curled up Will, his feet on his wife's lap, and the floor packed with overfilled brothers, Jack took hold of Emily's hand, "I could use some sleep. Feel like heading upstairs so we can slip into a nice, quiet turkey coma together?"

A half-smile curled her lips, "A nap could work right about now."

Clearing it with Elizabeth, he was about to lead her upstairs when his phone vibrated in his pocket. Pulling to a stop at the bottom of the stairs, he read the text to her, "Dude, sister at friend's with Caleb, parents have given me the house while they sleep off their deep-fried Thanksgiving upstairs. Cards await. Claire's here … can you get Matt? Sucker doesn't have a car right now."

Emily looked up at him, "You wanna go? We'd have to ask first."

"I'd feel kinda bad about it, though. Aren't we doing what we're pissed at Tim for doing?"

She turned him towards the living room once again, "No, because we were here for dinner and we're going to ask and if she says no, we won't throw a fit."

After asking and receiving permission, Jack and Emily took Will's car to pick up Matt. They found both him and his sister standing on the front porch. Jack leaned out his window, "Why the hell are you outside? It's like 12 degrees."

Matt started for the car, a decidedly grumpy look on his face, "It's a stupid story that ends up with both me and," indicating to the girl still standing on the porch, "Corrine locked out until at least 11 tonight." He opened the door and started to climb in the backseat, then stopped, calling back to his sister, "You sure Grunge is picking you up?"

Corrine, the look of annoyance reading loud and clear on her face, "His name is Granger. How many times do I have to tell you?"

"Granger, Grunger, Grunge, … who cares what his name is … is he gonna get you off our porch sometime tonight?"

"Yes, he is. He's on his way now."

"He's been on his way for 25 minutes." Drawing in a deep breath, "You sure you don't want to come with us? At least it'll be warm."

This just seemed to harden the girl's face more, "He'll be here."

"Whatever." Matt climbed the rest of the way in and shut the door behind him, "Idiot's gonna freeze before he finally gets here, that is, if he can find the house." Catching Jack's eye in the rearview mirror, he shrugged, "She said no so let's go."

Jack raised an eyebrow as he backed out of the drive, "Can he really not find the house?"

"No, he'll find it … and become just another in the long parade of jackasses my sister chooses to use for her amusement." Heaving a heavy sigh, he knocked Jack lightly on the shoulder, "Can we go around the block, then park so we can see the house? I want to make sure she doesn't stand out there all night."

Emily moved Matt up another notch on the decent guy scale while Jack asked, "How long are we staying?"

"I give our winner 10 minutes, then I'll go stuff her in the car."

After sending a text to Dex telling of the delay, they sat and wasted a few minutes until a semi-decent car rolled past them, then proceeded to the house. All three watched Corrine get in the car, but not before she looked directly at them, then waved ever so slightly with her fingers. Matt chuckled, "All right, we can go."

"She knew you were here?"

Switching his gaze from his sister to Emily, "It's a game we play … she pretends that I'm annoying as piss … I know she's a pain in the ass … she knows I'm watching her … I pretend I don't care …"

"So she's actually nice?"

"Not at all, but she knows and I know that I won't leave her on the porch." Settling back into the seat, he changed the subject, "So, how much is Dex's house going to scare me? Is he a product of his house or is the house a product of him?"

"It's more like Dex is a product of his parents who were a product of their parents who enjoyed the '60's." Laughing at his expression, Emily reached back and patted Matt's knee, "You'll be fine … probably."

♦ ♦ ♦

Pulling up to the house, everything seemed fairly normal, but Matt elbowed Emily in the side anyway, "Why do I have that feeling you get before you go into the funhouse at an amusement park?"

Jack just shook his head while Emily pulled at his coat sleeve, repeating, "You'll be fine."

"Are you taking me into hell? 'Cause Mom'll be thoroughly pissed."

Once inside the dark blue door, everything changed. The front hall was painted a cobalt blue and the color carried into the front room. Beyond that, Matt could see a blazingly bright yellow kitchen and an equally bright purple living room. All the furniture looked like it had once been new, but was now broken in and perfect for flopping, dropping and jumping on should the proper mood strike. There was a pile of boots by the front door, a mess of colors and ranges of worn. The carpet, where there was any, seemed to be of the shaggy variety and a deep shade of red that somehow managed to match whatever wall it was up against.

Dex met them in the hall before Matt could take in anything else, "Dudes, welcome to life after Thanksgiving. Claire's got the cards out and the fireplace going. Tonight's specials are s'mores and flaming turkey." Matt seemed rooted to the spot by the colorful assault on his senses and Dex grinned, "What? Did you expect me to live in a boring brown house with .5 siblings and a 1.5 car garage or something?"

Matt blinked a few times, then let half his mouth curve upwards, "I just … I've never in my life seen a paint job quite like this," then he shrugged, "although I totally would have been more shocked had you lived in a boring brown house with .5 siblings and a 1.5 car garage, so in the end, it works."

"Damn right it works. You should see my room. Bright green and black leopard spotted."

108

"Seriously?"

"Dude, I never joke about leopard print."

"Dude, I believe it."

Jack threw his arm over Matt's shoulders, realizing he was once just as amazed by Dex's house, "Come on. Claire doesn't usually let s'mores sit around for too long. You gotta get there early or you're screwed."

Soon, everyone was settled comfortably in the back room, surrounded by TV, more comfortable furniture and a piano against the wall. Claire was lounging next to a large, low table in the center of the room, beanbag chairs all around it, also in a multitude of colors. Already chewing, she waved the empty graham cracker package at them, "I just ate the last s'more so ya'll are gonna have to make more."

◆◆◆

The evening was a success by the group's standards. The leftover turkey had been flambéed to perfection in the fireplace, the box of graham crackers and bag of marshmallows had been devoured, and Jack taught them the card game Nertz. Explaining, "It's basically like competitive Solitaire. Everyone has their own deck of cards and you play like normal Solitaire, except you have a Nertz pile you have to clear, the aces are in the middle and are communal and whoever is fastest wins, meaning we have had jammed fingers, wrestling matches and blood by the end of a round."

Dex began hunting down four decks of cards, declaring the violence should begin immediately. As Dex was looking for cards, Emily looked at Claire, "Blood? Seriously?"

"Long fingernails are both a blessing and a curse in this game."
"Does your family know how to do anything peacefully?"

Both Jack and Claire feigned hysterical laughter for a few moments, then turned deadly serious and with straight faces, "No."

Emily just shook her head, chuckling to herself and wondering what exactly she had gotten herself into with these people.

Almost two hours later, after a copious amount of swearing, threats and loud, frustrated growling on Jack's part, Dex was the only one of them in need of a band-aid. Declaring this a successful, yet tame game, Jack said he'd have to get the rest of his family playing with them in order to see how a true Nertz game is played.

Dex held up his now bandaged finger, "I shall bring Neosporin and gauze."

By this point it was getting late and, if she left right then, Claire would be making it home before curfew with a whole thirty seconds to spare, so she tore out of there immediately, calling goodbye as she pulled the front door shut behind her. Dex looked longingly after her for a moment, then rubbed his head, "We have got to do something about that curfew thing."

"Hoping for later?"

"No. The earlier she goes home, the earlier I get to sit and stare at the wall, braiding my hair and hoping against hope that there's a Gilligan's Island re-re-re-re-re-re-re-rerun somewhere on TV." Smacking Jack on the back of the head, "Yes, hoping for later."

Jack grinned, "Just messing with you."

Dex shoved his shoulder, "Sorry for smacking you. Reflex action in response to dumb questions."

"I thought there were no dumb questions?"

"You wish." Giving him a very large, very surprising hug, "But I love you anyways, no matter what you ask me. Now, get out. I'm tired and have very important things to do tomorrow."

Matt, leaning over to pull on his boots, "Work?"

"Nope. Gotta take a nap before I sit and play Legos with Caleb all afternoon."

"Taxing day."

"Naw, my sister managed to produce cute and amusing offspring. If he was ugly and obnoxious, then it would be a taxing day."

Once they'd dropped Matt off and waited for him to bang on the door for his mother to let him in, Jack and Emily continued home. After hanging up their coats and shoving both pairs of shoes into a corner Jack looked at her, "You know what?"

Emily looked through the neck hole of the sweatshirt she was in the process of pulling over her head, "What?"

"I'm not tired."

"Well, I'll make you a deal, free me from this, then we'll go see what kind of crappy television they show at midnight. Bet you we find a horrendous amount of 'Law and Order' on."

After he'd gotten her out of her fleecy prison, both changed into pajamas and met on the couch. Emily trailed in a minute after Jack, prompting him to question, "Were you brushing your teeth?"

Baring her teeth in his direction, "I've had turkey strings jammed in my gums all night."

"How pleasant."

Settling quickly, Jack gave his first snore within two minutes and Emily, covering them both with one of the well-worn and well-used afghans, let him sleep, choosing to channel surf until she landed on the Food Network, watching a heated Iron Chef battle until she, too, shut her eyes.

The creak of the front door woke Jack first and as he moved to sit up, Emily slid down the back of the couch, her face hitting the cushion before being jarred awake. Both, however, heard a thump in the kitchen, which was followed by a groan.

"What was that?"

Knowing that groan from years of living with Tim and his inability to cross their bedroom in the dark without banging into something, "It's Tim. He probably bumped the cabinet." Kneeling on the couch, he looked over the top of the counter, "Tim? That you?"

His question was answered with a slurred, "Yeah."

Both walked into the kitchen to find him slumped against the cupboards, "What the hell are you doing on the floor?"

Tilting his head slightly, his eyes rolled, "I'm on the floor?"

With a disgusted sigh, "Yes, jackass, you're on the floor."

"This isn't my floor. How'd I get here?"

Already reaching down to pull him up, Jack mumbled, "I assume you forgot you didn't live here anymore, numb nuts." Glancing back at Emily as he struggled with his brother, he saw she hadn't moved from the kitchen doorway. Not wanting her anywhere near Tim, Jack suggested, "Why don't you go to bed? I'll take him up to his place and watch him for awhile."

Tim, drooling slightly, looked at both of them, "Hey, don't let me keep you from doing … whatever you want. I'll just sit here quiet until you're done." That said, he giggled and hiccupped at the same time.

With a twinge of fear in her eyes, she ignored Tim and turned to Jack, "Will you be able to get him there yourself?"

Kicking in his reserve power, he practically dragged Tim to the back door, telling him to shut up several times during the short trip, before, "We'll be fine. Lock the door behind me. I'll use Tim's key to get back in."

Emily locked as instructed and watched their progress across the yard through the curtains.

♦♦♦

The next morning, noticing Jack was not in his bed, Will figured he'd find both of them sacked out in the living room. Finding the couch also empty sent him immediately and angrily towards Emily's room. Looking through the half-open door, he stopped short when all he saw was Emily, asleep in her bed.

The door creaked, however, and she opened her eyes immediately, "Jack?"

"No, it's me. Sorry to wake you, but um, do you know where Jack is?"

Forcing her brain awake and suddenly remembering the night before, she answered in a gravelly voice, "I think he slept over with Tim."

"Oh, okay." Something in her eyes, though, caught his attention, "You all right?"

"Yeah, I'm fine." Sitting up, her hair in a tangled knot hanging over one shoulder, "Just waking up. What time is it anyway?"

"Little after 7. When do you work?"

"Noon, but Jack works at 8."

"Guess I'd better go wake him up then." Will turned to leave, but just then, both heard the garage door open and close again.

Making a bee-line for Emily's room, Jack slowed when he saw his dad in her doorway. With a deep breath, he put on a face that he hoped made him look like he just woke up, "Hey Dad, thought I was in there, didn't you?"

With a guilty grin, "Wouldn't be the first time."

"I decided to crash with Tim. We were watching TV and I fell asleep."

"I'm glad you're not still annoyed with him for skipping dinner, although you look exhausted. You sure you got any sleep over there?"

Biting his lip in order not to tell his dad the entire truth about the night, he shrugged, then, "Guess that ratty old couch isn't as comfortable as it looks."

Will, ruffling his hair as he passed back into the kitchen, "Well, since I feel better than I did yesterday, I'm going to go find myself some breakfast. You want anything or are you gonna be late?"

"I'll be out in a second." Once Will was out of earshot, he turned to Emily, "Tim puked all over his bed, twice, before passing out around 3."

Her face wrinkled in disgust, then reformed into a sympathetic head tilt, "Did you leave him sleeping in it?"

"I wish, but for some stupid reason I keep cleaning up after him ... I'm beginning to wonder when I finally won't give a shit."

Running a finger along the familiar scar on his chin, "Do you really think that'll ever happen?"

"He keeps this up and sure as hell it'll happen." With a low growl, a headshake and a face-scrubbing with his hands, he stood back up to his full height, "But whatever ... you want to come out and get some breakfast with us?"

With a gentle shove out the door, she started closing it behind him, "Out in a second, just let me change."

Jack raced out the front door minutes later, Pop-Tart hanging from his mouth and apple juice in hand, leaving Will and Emily at the kitchen table, still working through bowls of cereal. Realizing this might be the only time she could get him alone today, "Um, can I ask something?"

Relishing in the ability to enjoy solid food again, he gathered up another spoonful and, pausing before eating, he nodded at her, "Fire away."

The idea had been niggling at the back of her mind for a while, but last night clenched the deal for her, "Do you think, maybe, I could get a lock for my door?"

Will chewed thoughtfully for a moment, then swallowed, "Do you mind if I ask why?"

Already having her reasons laid out, she stuck as close to the truth as possible, "Well, Sam and Tucker, but especially Sam, have a habit of just walking in. Luckily I was only doing my homework last time, but if he had been five minutes later, he would have seen me changing." Hoping this would be enough to convince him, she shrugged, "I wouldn't lock it most of the time, just when I need to."

"I'll run it by Elizabeth and I think we need to have a discussion with both Sam and Tucker, but I don't see a problem with it, and there'll have to be some rules regarding you and Jack and the locked door."

She knew this would be the case and answered accordingly, "We'll keep the same rules as now. Door open if we're in there unless you or Elizabeth are home and even then, only if we need the quiet for school." Relieved she didn't have to actually lie about anything, "Right?"

"Right. I'll see what I can do about it this weekend, okay?"

"Thanks."

Will returned to his breakfast and the morning paper. Emily relished in the fact that she hadn't had to tell him, in all seriousness, Sam wasn't as much of a concern as was his oldest son, who had been scaring her to death recently.

Jack, however, was much harder to convince. Telling him that night, the first question out of his mouth was simply, "Is this about the boys or about Tim?"

Afraid that telling him it was about Tim would lead down a dangerous path she didn't want either of them to have to go on, she simply shook her head, lying to him and dying inside at the same time, "It's about the boys. I normally wouldn't care, but like I said, last week Tucker would have seen me totally naked and Sam just cannot understand why he can't just come in. I'd rather him learn with a locked door than with a naked me."

Jack wanted to push the subject, knowing there was more to it, but just then, Sam burst through the half open door, "Emily! Want to play Battleship? Hi Jack." Skidding to a stop, he suddenly looked guilty, "Oops. I forgot to knock. Dad said I have to knock now."

She gave him a smile, "Well, at least the door was open this time. When it's shut you have to knock, all right?" Seeing him nod, she turned to Jack, "Want to watch us play Battleship?"

Realizing there was something to the whole barging in thing, he decided to let things go for the moment. He was sure the lock had more to do with Tim, but to push her anymore would just bury her in her lie even deeper and he didn't know if either of them could handle that.

Chapter 11

A week or so later, Jack woke up to the sound of Sam bouncing on his own bed, "Why are you awake? It's like," looking at his clock, "6 o'clock. We don't have to be up for another half hour."

"It's snowing!"

Jack's eyes sprang back open, "It's snowing?"

"Yeah. You can't even see across the street and Dad said they're canceling schools already."

By now, he was sitting up, "You sure?"

"Dad just said the schools are closed." Resuming his bouncing, "Can we go sledding?"

"After some breakfast, we sure as heck can." Standing up, he reached for his sweatshirt then stopped when he saw Emily in the doorway, "Don't tell me school is back open."

Shaking her head, "No, but you gotta get up."

Still grinning, "What? You want to go sledding right now, too?"

"No, Will said he's taking Elizabeth to the hospital."

Sam stopped moving and Jack began digging up a pair of pants, "What's wrong? Is she having the twins?"

"I don't know. He just told me to come find you."

Pulling his jeans on over his flannel pants, he raced down the hall and Emily turned back to Sam, whose face had already crumpled. Opening her arms, he came in for a hug. "It'll be all right. She just wants to get a few things checked out, that's all." Holding him for another minute, she then asked, "You hungry?" She felt him nod into her stomach, "Well then, come on down and I'll make you some breakfast."

She met the other boys in the hall and after filling them in, all headed to the kitchen, Nate asking, "Where's Jack?"

"I think he's probably cleaning off the car or shoveling it out."

Dave spoke up then, more worried than he let on, "Why didn't they call an ambulance?"

Turning towards all four boys, "Not sure, but it's under control. So what do you guys want for breakfast?"

Three of the four called eggs, so eggs won, Tucker losing his beloved waffles. Emily was soon scrambling a huge pan full while Dave warmed the sausages and Tucker made toast. Just as she finished up, both Jack and Tim stumbled through the side door, yelling loudly at each other, "Go back to bed, Tim!"

"No. Tell me what the hell's going on?"

"I did already, dumbass. I yelled it through the door, but your hung-over ass couldn't comprehend 'Mom' and 'ambulance' and 'get the hell out here and help me shovel' so I gave up and dug out the entire driveway by myself! If you weren't so fu …" He trailed off when he saw the four boys and Emily staring at them, "Sorry."

Tim, however, didn't care about the level of his voice, "Next time, knock harder!"

As Tim slammed back out of the house, Jack glared after him, yelling at the now closed door, "Any harder, Moron, and I'd have broken the damn door." Taking in the scared look on Sam's face, his annoyance with Tim drained away, "Sorry guys. Mom and Dad are on their way. The ambulance said it would probably take them longer to get here than for Dad to drive her, but she's gonna be fine. She said she'd call later on."

Emily, almost positive there was more, doled out the eggs and sausage before catching Jack's eye. He shook his head, continuing to eat and talk lightly with the boys. The conversation turned to Sam and his sledding and Jack suggested they hit the big hill before the crowds. The food was inhaled at this point and soon the kitchen emptied, the boys going to change. Jack followed Emily to her room and sat on the bed, "Mom really did say she'd be fine, but Dad had this weird, panicked look in his eye and I wish they'd call already so I'd know they at least got there in one piece."

She nodded, "Dare I even ask about Tim?"

"I think you heard most of that one. He apparently didn't hear me knocking and yelling for him the first time, so when I went back up to find out if he was still alive, he got all pissy because I was yelling at him." Hanging his head down, "And it's not even 7am yet."

Stroking his hair, "Do you want me to stay here by the phone?"

"I figured we'd take them sledding, so I told Dad to call my cell."

After tilting his face up and kissing his forehead, "You're a good boy, you know that?"

"Thanks."

♦♦♦

Within 20 minutes, they were all bundled up, trudging the five blocks to the hill and, since it was so early, they did indeed have the place to themselves. Jack and Emily alternated between holding the phone so it wouldn't get lost in the snow, though they did put Dave on phone duty several times so they could ride down the hill together.

They spent almost two hours on the sleds before finally calling it quits. The struggle to get home through the new snow that had fallen seemed to take twice as long. Halfway back, Tucker nudged Nate and whispered something, then they elbowed Dave and filled him in. Once Dave had grinned and nodded, the three of them moved in closer, fully ready to tackle the trio ahead of them.

Only, somewhere, somehow, the gods of karma and playful fun caused Emily to have the same idea moments earlier and before she could talk herself out of it, she turned, suddenly flying through the air and taking Nate and Tucker down in the deep snow of some poor neighbor's front lawn. The boys weighed at least twice as much as she did, but the total surrealness of seeing her scarf-wrapped, snow-caked figure rocketing towards them had them going down without a sound.

Jack, fast-footed, even in heavy boots and with exhausted limbs, instinctively ducked low and took out Dave's legs, picking him up and carrying him a good five feet before landing in a drift, Dave's body disappearing completely.

Sam, for his part, dropped and began fashioning snowballs as fast as his half-frozen hands allowed. He wasn't stupid and knew that this could have only one logical outcome and he knew he needed as much ammunition as possible; that and to make sure he got Emily on his side before any of his brothers claimed her.

For a few moments, silence hung over the yard, everyone's brain assessing, processing, planning, understanding, and finally, "Snowball fight!!!!"

It was only once everyone could see that Emily and her arm, with Sam the mad ball maker at her side, were going to win that Jack called a truce just as Tucker took one last launch from Emily in the throat. Gasping and laughing, Tucker waved his arms, croaking, "We give up! We give up!"

Satisfied with their victory, Emily stood, Sam next to her, everyone finally getting their first good look at their surroundings, the snow having slowed for the moment. The yard was an unholy mess; the house and tree peppered with errant ammunition.

And one of their neighbors was standing there, shovel held in defense in front of his body, looking ready to deflect at a moment's notice. "Morning, Callaghans."

They had completely forgotten they weren't in their own yard. Giving the house a squint, Jack saw that more than one of their snowballs had hit the owner's front window, at least three or four were stuck to the bricks of the porch and one had knocked the mailbox beside the front door askew. Emily, embarrassed, raised her hand, pointing towards the mailbox, "That one was mine, I think. I'm sorry."

Mr. Coleman, their recently retired neighbor, laughed, "At least you didn't break any windows. It was kind of a shock, though, to come around the corner here expecting to see a quiet sidewalk and then find World War Three waging instead." Lifting his shovel for a moment, "Glad I came out with a shield."

They all now noticed one snowball mark in the center of the shovel, "Oh, crap. Mr. Coleman. We're sorry. We're stupid … a lot."

With another chuckle, "It's alright. Nothing's broken. Besides, if this yard can take my own kids' abuse, I'm pretty sure it'll last through the Callaghan clan."

In return for using his front yard as ground zero, Jack sent Dave and Nate running to get some shovels and they all pitched in, cleaning Mr. Coleman's drive and sidewalk, as well as three other houses before they reached their own. Tossing shovels against the side of their house, they trooped, all drenched, into the laundry room and stripped before the boys raced upstairs in their underwear and t-shirts.

Emily, having gone down to a modest pair of thermal underwear and shirt, laughed at the shivering Jack, who stood there in boxers and bare feet, jamming wet clothes into the dryer, "Would you go upstairs and find something warm before you catch pneumonia?"

"Why don't you?"

Herding him into the kitchen, "'Cause at least I'm wearing pants and my room is down here."

She had the hot chocolate going by the time everyone re-appeared and, leaving the cooking to Jack, went to bundle herself up. Soon, the drinks had been drank, the graham crackers eaten and the boys were settled in front of the TV, hashing out what movies they were going to watch. Catching Emily's attention, Jack nodded towards her room as he asked the boys, "You gonna be all right if me and Em disappear for a bit?"

Dave waved them away, "Would you quit babying us and go? Even Mom doesn't hover like you do, Jack. You could teach her a few things." Shooting his big brother a grin, "And thanks for the sledding. Kinda made things easier."

With a light shove to the back of Dave's head, "You're welcome."

Before Emily walked away, Dave stopped her, "I meant to ask before, but how come you attacked us?"

Blushing, she gave them a shrug, "C'mon, we made it through two hours of sledding without one incident of insanity. I couldn't handle it so I decided to start my own. Besides, I knew you guys would be launching your own attack sooner or later. I figured I'd beat you to it."

Nate, mouth full of the crackers he was still eating, nodded to her while talking to Jack, "Total keeper, that one."

♦ ♦ ♦

Jack flopped down on her bed, "Could this day get any longer?"

Looking at the clock to find it only a little after 10am, "Yeah, it could."

He just smiled and held his arms up, "Hug please."

"You sound like Sam."

"Whatever works."

♦ ♦ ♦

They slept for a few hours and woke to a silent house. Finding the four boys fast asleep all over the living room, Jack eyed them, then whispered to Emily, "Should we enjoy the silence?" Seeing her nod, they headed back

122

to the kitchen, Emily digging up lunch while Jack went to empty the dryer. Returning with a basket of still warm clothes, "When did we go domestic?"

"'Bout six this morning. Soup for lunch?"

"Perfect. What'dya need me to do?"

The boys woke up to the smell of food and while they were slurping down the vat of soup and noodles, it somehow came out that Emily had never seen 'Star Wars'. This was considered a major sacrilege in the Callaghan household and, not being able to fight the barrage of ribbing aimed at her, she quickly agreed when a marathon was suggested. "You really want to watch all six? In one sitting? That'll take us into tomorrow morning, won't it?"

Nate, with a twinkle in his eye, "We'll find ways to keep you awake, promise."

"Oh, God."

Luckily, Jack's phone rang before they started and after a few minutes, he hung up, a guarded smile on his face, "She didn't have the twins and everything seems to be okay, but they're going to keep her overnight anyway, so it's just us tonight, guys. Dad's gonna stay there with her."

The mood in the room lifted considerably and a few minutes after Jack called Tim with the news, Tim came in with a remorseful look on his face. Standing awkwardly next to the couch, "Sorry for being an ass this morning."

The boys grunted their acceptance of his apology and Jack slid closer to Emily, giving Tim room to sit, "Sorry for not breaking your door down."

Emily just held out the bowl of pretzels to him, "There's also soup in the fridge if you want some. It's probably still warm."

♦ ♦ ♦

Surprisingly, not only did she not fall asleep during the first two movies, but found herself yelling at the screen more than once, much to everyone's amusement. Dinner was the leftover soup and several pounds of spaghetti, courtesy of Tim, after which they returned to the living room for 'Star Wars 6', because, as Tim so artfully put it, 'you have to watch the awesome older three before you watch the crappier new three or else you'll never make it to the awesome older three because the crappier newer three make you never want to watch any Star Wars ever again'.

Finally, around 9 o'clock, everyone called it a day, having unanimously decided not to watch all six of the movies in a row. Tim said goodnight and after the rest of the boys headed upstairs, Emily and Jack were left alone on the couch. The quiet was a blessing and Emily sidled up to Jack, slipping her arm under his, "You did good today."

"I didn't have much of a choice."

"Doesn't matter. You still did good." Twisting to stand up, she stopped and groaned, "Oohh, found my sledding muscles."

Using the opportunity to put his hands on her butt, he pushed her up, then stood beside her, "You know, I can do a mean massage."

"I bet you can, but you should probably get to bed. We've got to get everyone moving in the morning."

"It's still snowing. Maybe school'll be shut again tomorrow."

"True, but you can't fight the fact that the minute you go in my room, your mom will know and she'll call screaming."

"She does have a habit of interrupting us, doesn't she?" Pulling her towards him, "But I don't think her radar covers living rooms."

"Well, I guess we can take a few more minutes."

♦ ♦ ♦

After finding out the schools were closed again, Jack snuck into the bedrooms at 5am, turned off the alarms, then crawled back under his covers. Snow days were wonderful, but he saw absolutely no need for any of them to be up at 6am two days in a row.

Later in the day, Will pulled up to the house to find five snowmen staring at him. With an exhausted smile, he made his way into the house to discover everyone back in the living room, watching another Star Wars and eating hot dogs. He was greeted with a chorus of 'hellos.'

Sam was the first one up, racing into his dad's arms before the rest had a chance to move, "Dad! Where's Mom?"

Giving his youngest a tight hug, "She's gonna be at the hospital until at least Saturday." After also telling them that once she did get home she would be on bed rest until the babies arrived, he looked specifically at Jack and Tim, "That means extra help."

As Emily warmed up some lunch for him, she heard Tim say, just a hint of annoyance in his voice, "How much help?"

Will seemed to be too tired to catch his son's irritation, "Anything she needs you for." As he wolfed down his food and tried to stay awake, "We'll need to work out a schedule and divvy up the chores later on, but right now, I'm exhausted." Pushing away from the table, "I'm gonna go take a nap."

Once Will had disappeared upstairs, Jack turned to everyone, "Should we hammer out the schedule now?" When everyone but Tim nodded, Jack ignored him and dug up some paper, "So, first, lunches? Who wants lunch making?"

They had the chores re-assigned within ten minutes, Emily reworking Jack's scrawl into something legible and organized. Hanging it on the fridge, they went back to the movie, happy that everything seemed semi-okay.

Will didn't come back downstairs until after 11 that night and by then, everyone but Jack and Emily was asleep. Emily was making the lunches for the next day and Jack was folding a load of laundry, "Hey, sorry I slept so long. I didn't mean to."

"S'okay Dad, we've got it under control."

"Where's Tim?"

Not really in the mood to mention Tim's off-handed comments about Jack taking over, he shot a quick glance at Emily before, "He's at his place. We're just doing a few things before bed."

Will looked at the list on the refrigerator, "You really do seem to have things fairly under control."

"Well, we figured we'd get it out of the way."

Giving each of them a hug, "I'm sorry things are gonna be a little harder around here."

"Mom'll be back in a few days anyway, then she can run the world from her bed or the couch."

With a yawn, "Still, it'll be interesting."

Chapter 12

Everybody followed the chore list fairly carefully and when Elizabeth came back home, she did indeed run the show from the couch, much to everyone's amusement. One thing she realized she should stay out of was the cooking. Jack had completely taken over the kitchen and, luckily, he cooked just as well as she did; most things even better, but not one of the boys dare say that out loud.

By now, it was early December and both Christmas and the Winter Formal were fast approaching. Claire had to shop with Emily this time and, regardless of how much fun Claire was, Emily found herself missing Elizabeth. Luckily, it didn't take long for them both to find dresses, even given their varying taste and the several slightly frightening stores Claire dragged them into. Once they arrived back home, Emily shooed Jack away so she could model the entire outfit for Elizabeth. Twirling in front of her, "Did I do okay? The zipper's not too long on this one, so I can reach it."

"Honey, you did wonderful. You look beautiful."

Stopping her spinning, she gave Elizabeth a smile, "I wish you could have come with us. It didn't feel right without you."

"I wish I could have too. I may even let you yell," pointing at her belly, "at these two when they're old enough."

Kneeling down, careful of her dress, she leaned over into Elizabeth's belly, "Roar."

Laughing, "That all you got?"

Putting her head on Elizabeth's stomach, Emily looked up, "I can't wait until they get here."

As she ran her fingers through Emily's long hair, "Neither can I."

She would have stayed longer, feeling the babies move under her cheek, but Jack yelled from the kitchen, "Can I come in yet or what?"

◆ ◆ ◆

Finally the 23rd arrived and with it, the Winter Formal. Dex and Jack wound up lounging in the living room while Claire finished Emily's hair and make-up. Dex had cleaned up remarkably well, the cheesy metallic dark red of his discount tux rental complemented Claire's silver dress perfectly and Jack, in his black suit, couldn't wait to see Emily, his foot bouncing on the floor in anticipation.

When he saw her emerge, it was all worth it. She floated out of the bedroom, a vision in deep green, her hair twisted up with tendrils trailing down her back; her neck sparkling in a delicate gold necklace Claire had lent her. And between her flushed cheeks and her dancing eyes, Jack didn't know how he kept his distance.

Emily, however, never one to miss his stares, came towards him, hands to his cheeks as she kissed him, "Hi."

"Hi."

"Ready to go?"

"Can't I just stay here and look at you?"

Elizabeth laughed, breaking the spell, "I don't think so. You need to go break that dress in."

Taking her hand, Jack spun her around the room, "You up for a little dancing?"

"As long as it's only with you."

Dex butted in here, "Hey, what about me? I get at least one dance, don't I?"

Claire swatted him in the chest, "Only if I get one, too."

Emily grinned at the crowd, "Wow, I've never had anyone fight over me before."

Claire gave her a most serious look, "Well, when Dex is dancing with you, the only person left to dance with will be Jack so I'll need to dance with you to offset settling for him."

Jack jumped in as they organized themselves for the camera, "Hey, Cousin, you don't need to act quite so repulsed by me."

Clapping him on the back, "You know I love you."

Giving her a big, smacking kiss on the cheek, "How could you not?"

♦ ♦ ♦

After Dave played photographer yet again, this time prepared with props and Sam manning the dimmer switch in the front room for 'mood lighting' as he called it, he told them he'd be Photoshopping in the fake snow and Christmas elves while they were gone. "It'll cost you though. Elves don't come cheap."

Dex tossed him a dollar bill and told him to splurge on the elves, then escorted Claire through the door, Jack and Emily following close behind. The dance was beyond perfect and, with only a minor amount of fake complaining, Jack did indeed dance with Claire while Emily danced with Dex, then with Matt, who in turn,danced with Claire, as well as every other female who looked his way. Eventually, Claire spun Emily out on the dance floor, swinging and dipping her, Emily returning the favor with her own whirls and twists.

The boys opted to hang out while the girls danced, deciding they could go without dancing with each other. Grinning from the sidelines, "Do you know we have the prettiest girls here?"

129

Jack smirked, "Just don't tell Claire I thought she was pretty. She'll never let me live it down."

"So, you don't mind that I demanded a dance with Em, do you?'

"Dude, she was your friend way before me. Who am I to argue with that?"

He'd witnessed the not-very-well hidden flames of annoyance in Jack's eyes when Matt had taken Emily out on the dance floor so he thought it best to ask, "Just didn't want you to be pissed."

"As long as you don't kiss her, we'll be all good."

Dex grinned, "Dancing'll do just fine, don't worry."

◆ ◆ ◆

By the time 11pm rolled around, nobody wanted to go home and there was a round of good-natured booing when the last dance was announced. Jack pulled Emily close, his arms tight around her, "Did you have fun tonight?"

"I couldn't imagine it being any better."

"Speaking of it being better, Mom told me curfew was lifted again. Have anything in mind?"

"Just being with you, maybe wrapped in a blanket on the couch in the dark, pajamas optional."

The mental images, oh, the mental images, "Please tell my you're not just teasing me to make me squirm."

She laughed into his chest, "You never know. You'll just have to wait and see."

"You are pure torture, woman."

Claire, skirting curfew as usual, couldn't stay and hang out at the house, so once again, the couples parted ways in Jack's driveway. He and Emily must have looked funny slogging through the snow, Emily in her dress and winter boots she'd stashed in the car while Jack hustled behind her, carefully placing his shoes in her footsteps so he wouldn't soak his pant legs.

Finally, they silently made their way into the house, praying that everyone was asleep. Wish granted, Emily immediately tiptoed to her room, working the pins out of her hair as she went. Jack followed and, standing behind her, he slid out the last of the clips, then finger-combed the long locks, "Just when I don't think you could get any prettier, you do."

Emily looked at him in the mirror, "I wasn't teasing before."

Moving her hair aside, he lowered his lips to her collarbone. Kissing her slowly, "I was hoping you weren't." As he dragged the zipper open at the back of her dress, the sleeves slid down, giving him even better access to her perfect shoulders. The dress was about to hit the floor when Will appeared in the doorway.

At the sound of his dad saying his name, Jack didn't turn around, knowing that if he moved, Emily would more than likely lose her dress or, at the very least, the gaping zipper would scream what had been going on, "Yeah, Dad?"

Will, looking away immediately after a glimpse of the pair's reflection in her dresser mirror, decided to live in ignorance for the moment, "Your mom's having contractions, so I'm taking her to the hospital. It'll probably be awhile, but I'd feel better with her there."

Jack nodded, still not turning around, "I'll be out in a second to help."

Already on his way back to Elizabeth, "Thanks."

Once Will had gone, Jack quickly zipped her back up, "Sorry."

Emily turned, a giant grin on her face, "I'm just glad you didn't turn around," and shoving him towards her bedroom door, "now go help Elizabeth."

Finally getting his parents to the car and receiving a laundry list of instructions from his mom, Jack came back in the house to find Emily still grinning, "You're awfully happy for 1am."

Flying into his arms, "Aren't you? There's gonna be two new people here soon."

His grin spread, "Kinda cool, huh?"

As she kissed his chin, "Very cool."

"Suppose I should go tell Tim."

"Already called and filled him in."

"Productive, I love it."

"I do what I can."

He let her go a minute later and, turning off the kitchen light, led her to her room. Moving behind her once again, "Now, where were we?"

Emily smiled, "I think you know exactly where we were."

◆ ◆ ◆

An hour or so later, they were curled comfortably around each other, Emily's back tucked into the curve of his chest, "Thank you."

Jack, whose face was buried in the back of her neck, "For what?"

"For not pressuring me to have sex. Most guys, I imagine, wouldn't be so easy-going about it, especially with their half-naked girlfriend in bed and his parents gone."

"It's called 'all the time in the world', Em. Besides, there're still four other people in the house. Like I'm gonna risk any of them catching us. It'd probably scar poor Sam for life. I mean, seeing the love of his life with me doing that would probably kill him."

132

Emily just shook her head, "Very true." As she snuggled closer, "And slightly off subject, but not really, do you realize that I could have been the one at the hospital right now? Having our kid instead of being here with you waiting for the twins?"

As his breath tickled her ear, he whispered, "Can I tell you something?"

"'Course."

Still in a whisper, "I pictured us having a boy, with your red hair, your eyes, your crooked ears and your bony knees. He'd be able to cook like me and draw like you and stand on his head for hours if we let him, like Sam. He'd have your smile … and the night after you said you weren't pregnant, I discovered I missed him."

Worried she might go all girly on him and start crying, she instead turned over, the sheets twisting around her, "Someday we'll have him, but not before we're ready … and we're sure your parents won't kill us both when we tell them." Blinking quickly anyways to hold back a stray tear, "Will you stay here with me tonight?"

Deciding his boxers were enough to sleep in, too comfortable to leave the warmth to find some sweatpants, "I will stay any night you ask."

"Good." She squeezed him tightly before a final kiss to his nose, "G'night."

♦ ♦ ♦

Emily woke up to a soft tapping on her bedroom door. Sitting up on her elbows in confusion, "Yeah?"

The door opened and Dave stuck his head in, "Um, Em, do you know where Mom and Dad are?"

Only when she felt Jack sit up next to her did she remember what was happening and, checking the blankets fast, saw that she was mostly dressed, but her thin tank top definitely was not enough to cover the fact that her bra was across the room. Dave also realized what was going on and shut his eyes quickly, "Sorry, um … I'm sorry."

133

Jack, nonchalantly pulled the covers up over her head while he grinned, "It's okay. Dad took Mom to the hospital last night. She should be having the twins any time now."

Dave's eyes popped back open in excitement, "Really? How cool will it be if they wait until tomorrow? We'd have Christmas babies."

Tim, who had just made it into the house, poked his head around Dave, "Hey, Mom or Dad call yet?"

"Nope. The babies are taking their time apparently."

Eyeing the lump beside Jack under the comforter, "Morning, Em. Thanks for calling last night."

Her voice came through muffled, "Um, you're welcome."

Jack, amused by the whole situation, just sat there, bare-chested, sheet only to his waist, "So, anybody hungry?"

Sam, who had just slid across the kitchen floor and was trying to see around Tim into the room, called his answer loud and clear, "Waffles!!"

At this point, Emily stuck her hand out from the burrow of blankets she was hiding under and pointed towards the door, "Out!"

All the boys laughed and Tim tossed Sam over his shoulder, "Come on kid, we'll go start your waffles." Calling back into the room, "Take your time."

Dave made sure to shut the door firmly behind him and Emily made Jack go lock it before she'd move the covers off of her. Catching her before she managed to start getting dressed, he hugged her, "That was entertaining."

"Sure it was. You didn't have to hide."

"I was wondering how long it would take you to kick them out."

Returning the hug quickly, she turned around, searching for her bra and straightening out her thoroughly twisted pajama pants, "And I wouldn't put it past them to come busting back in here, either."

"The door's locked."

"Do you really think that would stop them if they really wanted to get in here?"

Grinning, he pulled on his undershirt, scooping up his dropped suit coat and pants, "Good point."

◆ ◆ ◆

Jack went to the laundry room before he returned to the kitchen pulling on a pair of sweatpants. Yanking a sweatshirt over his head next, he leaned against the counter, a grin on his face, "You really didn't have to come in, Tim. You knew we were in there."

Tim, innocent expression abounding, "What? I thought you were having a party."

Dave laughed, "I really didn't mean to interrupt anything, I swear. I just couldn't find Mom or Dad."

Emily walked into the kitchen, "You didn't interrupt anything. We were just sleeping and at least you had the common courtesy to look embarrassed." Smacking Tim on the chest, "You looked like a fox in a henhouse."

He grabbed her wrist quickly, "It's not often you get to catch your brother in bed with his girlfriend."

A twinge of fear zinged through her belly and pulling her hand away, she repeated "We were just sleeping."

Jack, leaning over the counter to peer through the living room sliding door to see if they'd gotten any more snow, didn't see Tim's hold on her, "Yeah, remember sleeping, Tim? It's that thing you do at 2am after you ship your parents off to the hospital so they don't have your little brothers or sisters on the kitchen floor."

Not letting it go, "And to think, I figured I'd be getting more action than you by now, but I guess I was wrong."

135

Jack turned slowly towards his brother, "Excuse me?"

Tim's eyes rolled in annoyance, "I'm just kidding. Calm down."

Not sure what to do, Dave stood by quietly, realizing for the first time that something had changed with his oldest brother. He may have only been 14, but Dave was pretty sure Tim was not joking around anymore. Emily had backed up a few inches, now standing closer to him and, another first for him, without thinking, he reached over and pulled the back of her shirt, moving her even further away from Tim.

She didn't fight the gesture and now left a gap open to be filled with Jack's next words, hard-edged, "We were just sleeping, Tim. Regardless of what you think, that was it. Now, what you do and where you do it is your business, but when I tell you the truth, which, if I recall, is more than I ever have to tell you in the first place, don't get in my face about it and definitely do not get in hers, understand?"

"Glad to know where I rank these days, little brother." Deliberately giving him a smile, then looking towards Emily, "Sorry. Jumped to the wrong conclusion, it seems."

Emily didn't like that smile, "It's okay."

Turning to the cupboard, Tim pulled down a pile of plates, "Who's setting the table?"

Dave sidestepped Emily and took the stack, "I will."

Jack turned quietly and disappeared into the laundry room, the closest place he could get to before clenching up his fists. Emily followed once Tim began digging up the waffle irons, "Don't, Jack, please."

His face was the color of a tomato, his teeth grinding behind closed lips, his jaw muscles jumping with the effort of not screaming the obscenities Emily knew were lurking so close to the surface, "Why not?"

"Because he apologized and the kids are awake and Dave looks like he just realized one of his heroes is a big, giant asshole and I don't need him giving you that look as well because if you go out there and start something more, he will. And that'll kill me."

He desperately wished for Amelia at the moment, but remembering the things he'd learned from her at the beginning of his therapy, he began sucking in deep breathes through his teeth while whisper-counting down from 100. He reached 58 when Tim stuck his head around the corner, his face apologetic, "Hey man, I suck at waffles. Wanna come make 'em so I can burn the bacon and life can go back to normal?"

"Are you still gonna be a dick?"

"I'll do my best not to be, all right?" Nodding his head at Emily, "We okay?"

Wondering how much of an honest answer this was, she nodded, "Yeah. We're okay."

"Cool. Now get moving. I got starving boys out here and I can't hold them off for long."

After he disappeared once again, Jack looked over at her, "Are you lying?"

"Not sure yet." Taking hold of the hem of his shirt, "Come on. Hungry boys await."

♦♦♦

"Emily? Will Santa really wait until Mom's home to bring our gifts? He won't forget about us?"

Will had called them during lunch and talking things out with him, they'd all decided that Santa's gifts would wait until Elizabeth and the twins were home; that tomorrow morning, around the tree, the kids would just open their gifts to each other. Sam, though, still seemed to have his lingering doubts about the plan. Emily couldn't help but smile as she crouched in front of him, "I know he will definitely not forget us. He's probably very proud of the fact that we're waiting for everyone to be here."

137

Looking a bit more relaxed, "Can I leave him a note tonight telling him to wait? I mean, he may show up on accident or something and not know he's supposed to wait."

"I'll help you write the note, okay? Remind me before we go to bed."

With a huge sigh of relief, "Thanks."

Ruffling his hair, "Now, do you need any help wrapping your gifts?"

"A little."

Standing, she took his hand, "Lead the way, Sam my boy."

♦ ♦ ♦

Tim made mounds of grilled cheese and tomato soup for dinner and eventually, everyone was in the living room, first finishing their last 'Star Wars' then moving on to 'Raiders of the Lost Ark', yet another film franchise Emily was in complete ignorance about. After the movie, a good portion of the crowd was half-asleep and before anyone moved, Jack, olive branch extended, tapped Tim on the head to get his attention, "Hey, what'dya say to sleeping in the house tonight?"

Rolling his head along the floor to look up at his brother, "You willing to give up your bed 'cause I'm not spending Christmas Eve on the couch."

With a not so subtle wink at Emily, "Depends if I can find somewhere else to sleep."

She rolled her eyes and flung the pillow in their general direction, "You're both impossible, you know that?"

"Does that mean Tim's sleeping at his place?"

"I didn't say that."

About 40 minutes later, the house was quiet and Jack turned off the final light in the kitchen before heading to Emily's room. Stopping in the doorway, he watched her sitting on her covers, wrapping one final gift.

138

After the last piece of tape went on, she looked up, a shy smile spreading on her face, "This is new."

"What is?"

"You coming to bed with me."

"Kinda weird, isn't it?"

"I could get used to it though." Watching him come towards her, she suddenly remembered, "Did you make sure to eat the cookies Sam left?"

Jack nodded, "And I answered his letter." Wriggling his left hand, "He won't recognize it was me." Lying down next to her, "Tired?"

"Yeah. You?"

"Enough to want to lay down with you, but not enough to go to sleep just yet."

After switching off the table light, she snuggled her back against him, "Then do you mind just hugging on me for a bit?"

"Are you kidding?" His arm went immediately around her waist, his fingers just under the hem of her tank top, "I will never, ever, ever mind hugging on you."

"Very good."

Not wanting her to fall asleep yet, "You want to know something?"

"Sure."

"The twins are never going to not know you."

This re-woke her brain a little, "Huh?"

"Everybody here remembers what it was like before we met you. The twins, on the other hand, will never know what it's like to not have you around."

Her smile returned and he could feel her cheek pull up against his arm, "Another reason to add to the list of 'why I like it here'."

◆ ◆ ◆

Jack's cell phone rang at about 2:30am, scaring the hell out of Emily. Thinking only about shutting it up, she answered without thinking, not even sure if she was actually awake yet, "Hello?"

"Ja ... wait. Emily, is that you?"

Unsuccessfully trying to clear her throat, she rasped out, "Yeah. Will? Is anything wrong?"

"No, um, I just thought you might want to hear some news and Jack ordered me to call regardless of the time."

Jack, who was by now propped on his elbow, reached over her shoulder and hit the speakerphone option, "Hey Dad, good news?"

"Ah. Hi there. And it's always good news when you've got two new brothers."

Letting out a low holler that had Emily smiling, he began firing questions at his dad, "Really? When did they get here? What're their names? How small are they? I need statistics, man, geez."

They both heard Will laughing on his end, "Well, they got here a little after one and Ethan's older and about 5 ½ pounds while Xander's the youngest at just over 6."

"Ethan and Xander? I like 'em. Good choices."

"Glad you approve. And your mom said to make sure to tell you that Xander's spelled with an 'X'."

"Well, you can't fight a lucky letter."

Emily just shook her head in amusement, "How's Elizabeth?"

140

"Pretty good. She's exhausted, but happy. I'll tell you everything when I come home tomorrow and pick everybody up for visiting hours."

Jack spoke up again, "She's really okay though? No lying?"

"No lying, I swear." Jack watched as Emily let out a face-splitting yawn, which Will heard on his end, "But now I'll let you guys get back to sleep. She sounds kinda tired."

"Sorry," as she yawned again.

"Well, it is 2 in the morning."

Still with a smile plastered across his face, "All right. 'Night Dad."

"'Night, you two, and Merry Christmas."

"Oh my God, I forgot. Merry Christmas and tell Mom when she wakes up."

"I will. Love you."

Both Jack and Emily, in unison, "Love you, too."

Hanging up, he let out a happy wiggle reminiscent of Tucker whenever he beat someone's high score at anything, "They're here!"

"I know. Eight boys. Nearly enough for a baseball team."

"If you'll be catcher, we'll be all set." Pulling Emily back down to the pillow, "I did just realize that by us doing the whole speakerphone thing, he probably knows we're together."

"Maybe he'll just assume we fell asleep on the couch or something."

"Well, I guess we'll just have to worry about that later. Right now, I want to go back to sleep with my hand," nonchalantly sliding one under her shirt, "right about here."

She went all warm and not succeeding in keeping her voice steady, "G'night Jack."

"G'night."

♦♦♦

The next morning started much like the previous. She woke to a tapping and, opening her own eyes, saw five wide-open sets of them staring back at her from the already open door, all brown and all curious. As she sat up, Jack's hand slid down to her waist, the movement waking him up.

Missing her warmth immediately, "Where're you going?"

"I just thought maybe your brothers would like to hear the news."

Struggling to sit up next to her, he rested his sleepy head on her shoulder, "Go ahead."

With a grin, "Ethan and Xander got here about one this morning."

The explosion of hollering from the previously silent group made her jump and the sudden onslaught of bodies on the bed in a collective pile had everyone laughing. It was only after the bed board cracked and the whole mattress dropped to the ground that they calmed down slightly. "Holy shit, Em, we broke your bed!"

"Holy shit, Nate, watch your mouth, it's Christmas."

This set them all laughing once again and, finally standing, Sam shouted out what had just occurred to him, "It's Christmas!!!"

Tim grabbed him and tossed him in the air, "Yes it is. Now if everybody goes and gets ready, we can go to church, then come home and open gifts and eat breakfast and figure out who won and who lost bets because, after all, that's what normal people do on Christmas."

Sam was about to protest, then he saw his oldest brother's pointed look, "Okay, but can I at least go see if Santa ate his cookies?"

"Sure, just hurry up."

142

The rest of the boys, including Jack, ran to various bedrooms and bathrooms, leaving Emily on her own, to stare at her broken bed. About to shut the door to get dressed, Sam re-appeared, the biggest smile covering his face, "He's not mad that he couldn't leave the gifts under the tree but he had to leave them in Mom and Dad's room because he wasn't sure if the reindeer would be able to get back down here again this year." Holding the empty plate up, "He must've been hungry too, 'cause he ate all eight cookies."

As Sam scurried upstairs, it occurred to Emily why Jack hadn't been tired last night; he'd been riding a sugar-cookie high. Smiling, she attempted to close the door again when Tim appeared, "We'll fix your bed this afternoon, okay? Sorry for the pile-up, but when we Callaghans get excited, we jump on beds." Winking at her, "We leave in 20 minutes." After he disappeared, she continued her grin, relishing this brief glimpse of the Tim she loved and the sounds of the feet pounding on the ceiling above her, everyone singing Christmas carols at the top of their lungs.

◆ ◆ ◆

After they'd crammed themselves into the van and suffered through what seemed like an endless amount of brotherly poking and pinching, they arrived unscathed at church. Given they were regulars, everyone asked about the twins and Tim, slipping into adult mode, told the story before mass began.

Once everything was finished and the family was back home, the first thing they did was eat, the stomach growling occurring during church had been mortifying by any standards. Emily, Nate and Dave mass-produced pancakes, sausages and scrambled eggs and, after eating, finally … finally … finally, they all took pity on Sam as he sat bouncing in his chair, a small explosion waiting to happen. Tim pointed upstairs, "Everybody go get your gifts, the dishes can wait a little while."

The expected chaos ensued and soon, all were sitting around the tree. It took over an hour for them to open everything, each person doing a few gifts before letting the next person go. All the gifts were inexpensive and mostly homemade, making them all the more fun. Emily's gift from Tim was by far the biggest. She unwrapped the paper to find his old wood drawing board, sanded and varnished to perfection. Looking over at him, "Tim?"

"I figured it was time you got rid of that beat up thing you use."

"But don't you need this one?"

Shaking his head, "Nope. Sarah gave me a new one for my Christmas gift after I mentioned I was gonna give you this one."

Pulling him into a hug, "I love it. Thank you."

Jack mumbled, in amusement, "Geez, I get her 100 not blue Pixy Stix and nothing. You give her an old piece of wood and get a hug. What is the world coming to?" Emily let go of Tim and attacked Jack, slobbering kisses all over his face until he pushed her away, "Good lord woman, not here. There are children present."

"And one Tim who may need to throw up."

♦ ♦ ♦

After piling the gifts in their appropriate sections around the tree with Emily's nestled in the corner next to Jack's, Nate asked, "If Dad's coming to take us to the hospital, what're we gonna do about dinner?"

Emily stopped to look at the older two, "I don't know. We can't leave the turkey cooking while we're gone and won't we all get food poisoning if we partially cook a bird, then come back and finish it."

Will, who had snuck in the side door quietly, "Well, how 'bout we go to the hospital now, then we can cook when we get back?"

The younger boys rushed to their dad, nearly knocking him over, "Can we really go see the twins?"

"Sure. Just let me warn you of a few things."

The room went suddenly silent as Jack asked, in a quiet voice, "Warn us?"

Will, realizing how his statement sounded, "That came out wrong, sorry. I just meant that since there're so many of you, I don't think you'll be able to stay long. Also, the boys are really little, so I'm not sure who'll be allowed to hold them."

Tucker, still looking worried, spoke for everybody, "As long as we can see them and Mom, we'll be fine."

After Emily had made Will some breakfast, everybody showed him their gifts; then, while he was showering, they cleaned the kitchen and the living room from the morning's insanity.

Splitting up between Will's car and Elizabeth's van, which Tim drove, they were soon at the hospital. As usually happened when they all traveled together, they drew quite a few stares. Emily, never one to enjoy being ogled at, asked Jack in a low voice, "Do people ever not look?"

"Come on. If you saw the pack of us approaching, you'd have the same look." Scrunching his face for a second, "As a matter of fact, you do get that look every now and then."

"Really?"

Winding his fingers with hers as they got on the elevator, "Well, we do get a little overwhelming, especially on Christmas morning."

The boys laughed at the memory of the pile-up and Will looked at them, "What happened this morning?"

Before Jack could make a move to stop him, Sam answered, "We all jumped on Jack and Emily's bed and we broke it."

There was silence on the elevator ride and try as she might, Emily just couldn't sink into the floor in horror. Will turned to all of them once they were in the hall, "Well, there was a lot to be excited about this morning." Catching Jack's eye, "Later, all right?" Once Jack nodded, he continued, "Now, your mom might be asleep and the boys probably are, too, so be quiet when we go in."

Passing the desk, one of the nurses smiled at Will, "You weren't joking when you said they all look alike."

Tim called out before Will could answer, "Genetics can be a blessing or a curse."

With a laugh, "Merry Christmas."

♦♦♦

They had to leave way before they would have liked, but everybody got and gave Christmas hugs, including Tim, Jack and Emily, who also held the twins. Soon though, Tim waved the keys in their direction and led the whole group out to the parking lot. Will told them he'd be home later on that night and he'd call if he wasn't going to make it.

Dinner went smoothly, with everyone chipping in, then the older ones took turns calling relatives with the baby news while Emily kept Sam occupied. After Jack had finished his share of the calling, he went in search of the two, easily finding them right where he'd left them an hour earlier, Emily with her new board propped on her knees and Sam laying on the floor, the thick pad of paper Emily had given him open at his fingertips. Both were so intent on what they were doing that neither heard Jack slide into the room and settle on the carpet behind them.

Sam was slowly drawing and shading boxes, only looking up when Jack sneezed. Surprised to see his big brother only inches from him, "Jack! You scared me."

"I've been here for a while, buddy." Turning Sam's paper slightly towards him, "You're pretty good. Keep this up and you'll be giving Em here a run for her money."

Jack saw the edges of her lips curl as she drew on, letting him fill Sam with all kinds of praise. Eventually, he let his brother get back to his paper and scooted over towards Emily, "What're you working on?"

Sliding the board a little closer, "Nope. Not until it's done."

146

Grumbling, he fumbled around in his pockets until he produced his iPod, "I thought you gave that rule up?"

"I have re-instated it for the moment. Go away."

"Never." Emily's eyebrows shot up and, as he caught her eye, she saw twinkling there. Mouthing an 'I like you' in her direction, Jack slid his earphones in and, dumping the contents of a Pixy Stix on his tongue, shut his eyes.

♦ ♦ ♦

Will called later that evening, telling them he'd be staying at the hospital. This wasn't much of a shock to any of them. Luckily, no one had made any wagers. "Sucker bet," Tim had mentioned earlier, "who's he kidding, thinking he's gonna come back here. He's got us to do all the work."

There was something just on the edge of his voice that made Emily shoot a look towards Jack, who shrugged and watched his brother leave the kitchen, "God, even Mom isn't this moody and she's been pregnant for the last 17 years."

"Probably not the best time to ask him to help us with my bed, then?"

"Hell no." Calling out to the house in general, "Anyone within the sound of my voice, come on down and help fix Emily's bed. All y'all helped break it so get in here."

Tim was conspicuously absent, Nate telling them that he'd already went back to his apartment, mentioning something about Sarah coming over. Jack was fine with this since 'asshole Tim' seemed to be showing up more often than 'cool Tim' these days. After scouring the house and the garage for twenty minutes and coming up empty handed for substitute bed boards, the boys simply put the mattress on the floor, "We'll have to go to the hardware store tomorrow or something."

Emily shrugged, "I slept on the floor for years. It's fine, really."

"Well, it won't be years this time, promise."

Sam looked at her in confusion, "Why did you used to sleep on the floor?"

He had been just six when she moved in and hadn't asked many questions about it. It was kind of a joke between the rest of them, Nate putting it best with 'he doesn't care how she got here, just that she's here because he looooovvvveeeessss her'.

Even now, with him being older, he had never asked this type of question before, but instead of breaking the illusion, she answered simply, "Because I liked it. I didn't have to clean under the bed."

"I hate that. Mama says the dust bunnies are gonna rise up against us one day."

"She's probably right."

♦ ♦ ♦

After devouring some leftovers while watching "A Christmas Story", everyone was in bed by 10:30, Tim, presumably at his own place for the night, never reappearing after leaving the first time. Jack headed towards Emily's room after locking the doors and turning off the lights, finding her square in the middle of the mattress, now in the middle of the room, pencil moving diligently. Leaving the bedroom door half open behind him, he crawled next to her, "Do I get a preview yet?"

She shook her head, "Only the finished product, my friend."

Grinning, he curled his finger at her, "Can I at least get a good-night kiss?"

After shifting the board to one side, "I think it's a guarantee."

Chapter 13

He didn't remember falling asleep, but he must have because he was suddenly opening his eyes at about 3am, at least according to the blurry numbers on his watch. The room was dark save for the nightlight in the corner, by which Emily was hunkered down, still drawing.

"Em?"

Even in the soft blue light, he could see the mixture of excitement and exhaustion on her face when she looked up, "I'm sorry I woke you. I just had to get this done."

Propping himself on his elbows, "Same picture?"

"Uh-huh and I think I'm done."

"Do I finally get to see it?"

Standing, she groaned a little as her stiff knees creaked, "In the morning." After making her way towards the bed, she climbed in next to him, laying on her side and resting her free head and arm on his chest, "But right now, I just want to be here with you."

Already halfway back to sleep, "Do you think I could stay here every night?"

As her hand drifted up and down his bare chest, "I wish you could."

"Maybe it's time I had a little chat with Will and Elizabeth."

Emily smiled into him, "Do you have some sort of death wish?"

Tracing his finger down her spine and several of her scars, his eyes drifted closed, "Just looking for somebody to keep me warm."

Drifting off as well, "Warm is good."

♦ ♦ ♦

This time it was Emily who woke to an empty pillow beside her. Looking over her shoulder, she found Jack sitting on the floor staring at her drawing. Settling in next to him, "I said I'd show you in the morning."

"It's morning."

"It's 6am morning. I was thinking more along the lines of 10am morning or sometime after that."

"Exactly why I didn't wake you."

With a yawn, she rubbed her hands up and down her arms for warmth, having forgotten how drafty a floor can be in the wintertime, "Well, since we're here, do you like it?"

On the paper was a picture of his two youngest brothers, curled around each other, as they had been when everyone first laid eyes on them. For the last nine months, they'd been wedged together and as they slept, they'd sought out the same position, snuggled in the bassinet and sleeping soundly. Emily had made sure to take in every detail, knowing exactly what she would be doing when she got home.

"I love it, but where'd you get the picture?"

Tapping her head, "In here, which is why I couldn't stop until I was done. I didn't want to lose it."

He just shook his head in disbelief, "You realize you're amazing, right? I don't think even Tim could do this."

She just shrugged, "Imagine if I hadn't found my first pencil."

150

About to ask her about that first pencil, he was distracted by the footsteps coming across the kitchen. Before Jack could make a move to stand, Will appeared in the doorway, "Awake already?"

Scrambling up immediately, he walked a few steps towards Will, "Dad? What're you doing here?"

Will tried to look at the situation from any other standpoint than an exhausted parent, but he couldn't, his anger at finding them blatantly disregarding the house rules rushing up and out before he had time to bite his tongue, "Did you sleep in here again? I let yesterday go and this is how you respond?"

Jack hadn't woken up enough yet to keep himself under control either, "Yes, I slept in here again, Dad. Slept being the key word. I fell asleep in here watching her draw and woke up five seconds ago to you screaming at me from the doorway!"

Knowing he should be quiet, should take a deep breath and walk away from the anger of his son and the fear he saw blossoming in Emily's eyes, he instead listened to himself lose control, "God-dammit Jack! I give you one rule to follow. One! I ask you to do one simple thing and you can't even follow through on that. I ignore coming in here and finding her dress half off because your mother needed me. I ignore yesterday's comment about you and Emily in bed because I thought I'd be one of those really awesome parents and chock it up to stupid error, but you knew I knew and you did it again!" Looking towards Emily, "You, too. We talked about the rules of your room when I put the lock on your door." Lost in his rant, he took several steps closer into the room without thinking, steps towards Emily, "I trusted you, both of you, not to disobey me! Do I have to start watching everything you do because that, my lovely children, will thoroughly piss me off!"

The moment Will raised his voice, Emily began fighting her flight instinct, knowing somewhere deep down that this was her Will and he was tired and yelling because he was a parent and that was his job sometimes. She knew it, so she clenched her jaw tightly, teeth grinding loudly in her ear, determined to hold on as the waves of fear slammed through her. This was Will and Jack, two of the very few people in the world she trusted with her body and with her life. This was Will and Jack. It was Will and Jack. Will and Jack. Willandjack. Willandjackwillandjackwillandjack ...

Then he moved towards her, her feeble grasp on common sense that had been fighting to be heard vanished completely.

Will stopped his ranting abruptly when he saw her body drop to a crouch in the corner beside her dresser, heard Emily's low chant rising in pitch. Jack turned to follow his father's sight line and immediately flew over the mattress, feet catching on blankets, nearly sending him sprawling in his efforts to get to her, to stop her from hitting herself harder than she already was, her fists banging her ears in rhythm with her words, each landing blocking out his voice momentarily.

Jack caught her forearms, surprised at her strength as she pulled against him, still trying to hide herself from the painful beating that always followed the yelling. He finally had to let go, her muscles so taut her entire body rolled forward instead of just her arms. Sliding his hands over her head instead, he winced as her fists hit him rather than her skull. "Emily? Em? Please stop. It's me. It's Jack, okay? Please? Em, please? It's just me and Dad. He's just being Dad without sleep. Honest. He won't hurt you, I promise."

◆ ◆ ◆

Why wouldn't he go away? He'd been quiet for so long. He'd left her alone for so long she'd forgotten what it was like. Her stomach clenched. Somewhere in her foggy mind she remembered the last time he'd kicked her and it'd hurt so bad she had no choice but to curl around her abdomen, clutching and fighting the bile rising in her throat. This left her head exposed, as well as her back, for now she was hunched over on the floor instead of against the wall where she had started. Feeling the tip of something pierce her back, her body screamed silently, as did her throat, all sounds having deserted her in her agony. The foot connecting to her face, however, seemed a blessing, momentarily moving her attention from the screwdriver in her back to the blood pouring from her nose.

But only momentarily.

◆ ◆ ◆

152

Will was also by now crouched beside her, but when he reached out to help, Jack shook his head, "Don't touch her. You'll hate yourself even more because she doesn't know it's you." Jack was feeling remarkably calm given the circumstances and he only winced once when her hands whacked his particularly hard.

Just as Jack was about to send his father out of the room, Dave popped his head in, "Dad, what are you doing here?" He took a step back, however, when he saw Emily, "What's wrong?"

Jack looked at him, making a calculated decision that he prayed Emily wouldn't hate him for later, "Come here. Dad, go wait in the kitchen, would you?"

Both of them did as instructed, Dave on the verge of tears, but holding them back as he hovered over his brother, "Jack, what's going on?"

"Just … help me get her on the bed … watch her legs though. Get a good grip on her or else she'll probably kick you once we start to move her."

Wishing he'd stayed in bed, Dave shut his mouth and wrapped his arms around her legs, watching Jack let go of her head to lift her by the shoulders. Emily went back to assaulting her ears and in that moment of distraction, Dave forgot to pay attention to his job. His hand brushed her bare ankle below her pajama pants and her leg shot out, catching his knee and knocking him down. She curled back into a tighter ball, her shirt pulling up enough in the back to reveal the things Dave knew little about, but the scars told him what he needed to know and he stood again, arms ready, knee pain ignored, "Let's get her moving."

Her father never lifted her up before. He'd always left her where he'd finished with her: kitchen linoleum, bathroom tile, living room carpet, bedroom floor. The feeling of the soft mattress beneath her however, took her back to the last horror she'd experienced before she finally escaped from him and to the reality that she would soon be raped again. Even the boxing of her own ears couldn't keep his voice away, telling the stranger to do whatever he wanted with her. Finally she relented, realizing all her fighting couldn't keep the next few minutes at bay.

Although this time, it wasn't her father's voice or the scum of the Earth her father sold her to, but another one, one she struggled to recognize, repeating a phrase she couldn't hear until now.

"I killed him for you."

♦♦♦

Dave listened to Jack repeat those words over and over again until it became only a string of sounds that made no sense and held no meaning. He sat for what seemed like hours, his knee throbbing, his head aching, his heart screaming and his mind picturing the scars he'd seen. Putting two and two together hadn't been difficult, but to have been able to do such an equation made him want to cry, so he did, swiping several tears before finally giving up, letting them run down his cheeks, dripping from chin to shirt, his chest soaked before he managed to stop.

Something, however, eventually changed in the air that made Dave fall back to reality. Clearing his head with a shake, he saw Jack laying her arms down on the mattress in front of her, sitting up and wincing as his back and knees cracked. Nodding towards her feet, which were curled and clenched tight, he asked him, "Can you pull those straight for me? Don't force them, but she can't stay like she is."

Taking them slowly and gently by the ankles, Dave pulled her legs towards him, only getting them to move a few inches, but at least she didn't heel him in the face, which he was grateful for. Her toes, however, wouldn't uncurl and beginning to massage them, he felt the muscles start to relax as he waited quietly for Jack to tell him what to do next.

Jack, for his part, could feel his chest beginning to tighten, his brain kicking into high gear and the chant he had used to bring her from her waking nightmare plunging him into his own. Knowing he wasn't far from meltdown himself, he motioned Dave out of the way and, covering Emily with her quilt. He slipped from the room, finding Will sitting on the floor against the cabinets of the kitchen. Dave moved from the bedroom to sit beside Will without a word while Jack hesitated, torn in two by the girl behind and the man in front. He chose to sit as well, leaning his head against his father's arm, still able to see Emily through the open bedroom door, "She loves you, you know that, right?"

154

Will nodded, the tears still sliding down his cheeks, "But that doesn't help very much right now."

Dave turned to look at Jack, "Will she be all right?"

Jack's response was to begin rattling off the presidents in alphabetical order, the adrenaline and fear catching up to him at last, his fingernails cutting further into his palms with every second that passed.

♦♦♦

Will disappeared upstairs to his room, dealing with the turmoil of his morning in solitude, leaving his two sons in the kitchen. Somehow, someway, by some provincial twist of fate, everyone else was still asleep at this point and Jack needed to make a decision, "Do I work or no?"

"What?" Dave was still on the floor, eyes closed, head against the cabinet door.

"I'm supposed to be at work in a half-hour. Do I go in or stay here because right now, I think my brain can't handle the choice."

"Do you think she'll wake up soon?"

Jack shrugged, "I have absolutely no idea. I want to stay, but it's not fair to call off work this close to when I'm supposed to be there. A lot of people took time off for Christmas."

Wondering if this was totally stupid on his part, Dave offered, "Then how about I keep an eye on her? I wasn't doing anything else today anyways."

He wanted to hug his brother for making the choice for him, "If anybody asks, just tell them she's sick. Sam'll be the only one who'll keep trying to bug her, but just keep him busy and he'll be fine." Knocking his forehead with his fist several times, "God damn it. Why the hell did today have to happen like this? If I had just gone upstairs last night, everything would be fine. It would be a perfectly good day and that ..." growling again as he looked at his brother, eyes burning with self-loathing, "God, I am the biggest fuck-up in the history of the whole damn world."

155

"Jack ..."

Shaking his head to silence whatever comforting words his brother might offer in his direction, "Don't, okay? Thank you for watching her for me, but please don't try to make me feel better. I don't deserve it."

Dave had never wished more to escape from a day. He desperately wanted to rewind time until he was back upstairs and in bed, then, instead of coming down to Emily's room after going to the bathroom, he'd crawl back under his covers and hold onto his childhood a little while longer. But given that would be impossible, he chose to nod, "I won't leave her alone."

With a defeated sigh, "Just check on her, okay? She might not be the happiest camper when she wakes up. Ten to one, she'll be embarrassed as hell and want to be alone. Just ... you know ... don't be hanging around staring at her for the next eight hours or something, all right?"

In a deadly serious voice, "What happened to her, Jack, and don't tell me I'm too young or that I don't need to know? I can't un-see what I saw so I get to know everything ... something ... anything ... please?"

Crouching in front of Dave, "Her father abused her. That's all you need for now and nothing to the other kids, understand?"

Accepting that it was better than nothing, he only needed one last instruction from his big brother, "And what about Dad?"

Jack wished for some drugs for his headache and a miracle to erase his snowballing error, "He needs a nap and then some sleep and then just tell him that all this is my fault and that I'm sorry." Barking out a sudden, single chuckle as he scrubbed his face with his hands, "Also maybe mention how he should never, ever, ever yell at her again 'cause, holy shit, that is a really bad idea if ever there was one."

Knowing Jack didn't really mean the last part, Dave could only nod again, beginning to feel like a bobble head gone wild. Soon, Jack disappeared into Emily's room to say good-bye, he then sped out the door, leaving the rest of the house to still wake up, a normal day ahead of them and not a care in the world.

♦♦♦

Dave fielded a few questions from various waking up brothers, then happily settled into silence, choosing to stay at the kitchen table to hear Emily if she needed anything while playing a steady stream of what felt like every board game on the planet, Sam's choice every time.

Will appeared later that afternoon resembling a zombie, shuffling through the kitchen and hugging every son he could find before sitting down across from Dave and Sam, "How's she doing?"

"She's still sick, but I haven't heard anything from in there most of the day."

Catching on, he gave Sam a smile, "And how are you, little man?"

"Okay." He continued to put away the parts to 'Pay Day', "I'm goin' outside in a minute 'cause Nate and Tuck wanna build an igloo."

"Carry on then." Waiting until Sam had disappeared to look towards Dave, "She's been quiet?"

"Yeah. When I snuck in there about an hour ago, it looked like she hadn't moved at all."

Will immediately began to stand, but Dave stopped him, "She's breathing, Dad. I checked."

"What did you tell Tim?"

"Nothing. He hasn't been in here yet."

Finishing his getting up, Will stood staring at Emily's door, "I'm sorry about this morning."

"Jack said he is too. He had to go to work so I said I'd make sure Emily was okay until he got back."

"I wish he hadn't pulled you in like he did. You shouldn't have to deal with this kind of thing."

Dave looked at him like he had a third eye, "She's part of the family, Dad. Was I supposed to go watch cartoons or something?"

"I guess not." Ruffling Dave's hair, then patting him on the back of the shoulder, "I can keep an eye out if you want to go outside with your brothers for awhile."

It felt odd to tell his father no, "I promised Jack I'd stay, so I'm not moving until he gets back. Is that okay?"

Will gave him a smile that held more sadness than anything, "That's fine. I think I'll go stop the igloo making before they get too involved and see if they'd like to go to the hospital with me. I, uh, I probably shouldn't be around when she wakes up anyways."

Dave felt his father's heart breaking with that single statement.

◆ ◆ ◆

Will disappeared to the hospital for a few hours, taking Sam, Nate and Tucker with him. Jack turned up a little later looking defeated, having begged off the last few hours of his shift. Dave, who still sat glued to the kitchen table, gave him a pathetic look, "You … just … wow, you need a nap."

Dave was the only one at this point who could have gotten away with that statement and, moving past his brother to Emily's door, "She's been quiet?"

"Not a sound. She is alive though, I've been making sure she's breathing when I go in there, which," looking at the kitchen clock, "I need to do. It's been about an hour."

Jack looked at him with a mixture of admiration and pity, "Have you been sitting here all day?"

"Yeah. My butt is killing me."

Jack's first smile of the day came through, "I've got this one."

The one thought that kept running through Dave's mind all day finally fell out of his mouth, "How can you not be scared of her? Of what might happen? I've been freaking out all day that she'd wake up and just … do that again."

With his hand on her door, he gave his brother a small shrug, "I am scared of her, but I'm more scared for her. Kinda makes my choice to do this pretty simple." Jack came back out a few minutes later, finding Dave pulling his snow pants on, "You going outside?"

"Yeah. I gotta go do something. Too much thinking and not enough doing." Yanking his boots on, "Gonna go find something to shovel."

"Where's everybody else?"

"Dad took them to the hospital for a little while. I think Dad said Mom's coming home tomorrow afternoon."

"Tim?"

"No idea. He hasn't come over today."

Jack settled himself in Dave's chair, "Then I think I'll take a nap."

"On the table?"

Starting to put his head down on his arms, "I sure as hell ain't gonna fall asleep in there with Em and the couch is too far away." Waving his hand across the cluttered kitchen table, "Hence, my new bed."

"G'night Jack."

"Don't freeze … and thank you."

♦ ♦ ♦

He woke up, sitting straight in his chair, the straining in his ears telling him he had already heard something, he just didn't know what yet. Before he could think to turn and check on Emily, he heard her small voice, a whisper

159

seeming like shouting compared to the near-silent sound she made, "Jack?"

Whipping his head around, he saw her, standing small in her doorway, her face white, the skin around her eyes a pale blue, her lips chapped to a bright red color. Looking like she was made of fragile wax and ready to break, he approached slowly, hand out towards her, "Hi."

Jack watched her swallow once, her slender throat moving ever so slightly, then again before, "Was that a dream?"

Silently cursing himself for causing all this, he gripped the back of his chair as he answered simply, "No."

"Are you sure?"

"Pretty sure."

She sat down right there, halfway through the door, and with her head propped on her hand, she looked at him, "Do you hate me?" His tears were impossible to hold back and instead of replying, Jack crouched down and kissed her, figuring that would be a much better answer than anything he could say out loud. Even as he felt her crying with him, he didn't let go, keeping contact until finally she, half-laughing, half-choking, pushed him back a little, "I can't breathe."

"Use your nose like everybody else."

"It's all clogged up." She did indeed sound awfully stuffed, "I tried breathing through my ears but it didn't work."

Standing, Jack retrieved the box of Kleenex then sat back down in her doorway, "You should try harder next time, then I won't have to stop kissing you."

Squeezing the wad of now soggy tissues in her hand, she shut her eyes against the embarrassment of the day, "Trying to lighten the mood?"

"Just sayin'."

The front door opening had Emily scrambling into her room, not willing to face anyone else at the moment. Jack let her go, shutting her door just as Tim walked in the kitchen. Stopping by the counter, he wore a smirk that Jack wanted to hit him for, "Damn, you really are getting more than me."

"Shut up."

"Hey, we do what we can, or who, actually, with the time that we have."

"Shut ... up."

His face got hard, "Why? It's obvious that's what you're doing. Dad's gone. And from the sound of it, everybody else is gone, too. It's called an advantageous situation."

He bit down on his cheek so hard it bled, the metallic taste simply angering him more, "Go ... home ... now."

With a shake of his head, "Whatever. I need some food."

Jack could feel his heart banging in his ears, his neck, his fingers, any place with a vein throbbed with annoyance, but before he could semi-politely toss Tim out of the house on his ass, Will's voice caught them, "What's wrong?"

Jack bit down again, his lip this time, the only way he could keep from swearing, but still get out a strangled, "Nothing."

Tim's face went red, but he also replied with, "Nothing."

Will was not the utter idiot his sons apparently believed him to be and he told them as much, "You know what, I'm not stupid," looking from Tim to Jack, "you two let go of whatever just happened because nobody in this house needs that right now. Do you understand?" Both boys nodded, but even Sam, with his seven-year-old distracted wisdom, could tell this wouldn't be going away easily. Will knew it as well and let himself simply sigh, "Tim, are you staying for dinner?"

Responding with a snort and heading out the back door, Tucker spoke up, "I'm pretty sure that means no, Dad."

Will let out his second sigh, then turned to Jack, "Is she awake?"

"Yeah, but she, uh … she's still not feeling very good."

Emily, just on the other side of the door, hated herself for doing it, but reaching down, she ran her fingers over the smooth metal of the small twisting lock. She could open the door now and face them all, tell them she was sorry and move on. She could open the door, pretend to be feeling better, eat dinner and return to her bed. She could open the door, ask for Will and grovel at his feet for the stupidity she now felt from head to toe. She could open the door, explain what happened and talk it through.

She turned the lock.

Jack heard the sound, his eyes dropping shut for a moment in defeat, then opening again to find Will staring at the door.

They left her alone.

Just before Jack headed up to bed that night, he slipped a note under her door, "I love you. We all do, but I love you most." Forehead against the door for a few moments, he then went upstairs, relishing the knowledge that tomorrow had to be better.

◆ ◆ ◆

It had been a terrible day, but nothing compared to the night. Emily tried to fight the memories of her father crowding her brain, pushing and shoving to get to the head of the line, to be the next thought that broke her a little more. She lost every battle, moving from silent sobs into her pillow to restless sleep to panic-filled jerks awake after only a few minutes rest. Time got away from her, logic ran like hell away from her, reality didn't even attempt to enter the room; he was back, he was loud and she gave up trying to get away.

He won that night.

Over and over.

And she gave in.

162

Sam wanted his mother. Plain and simple. Something was wrong in the house, but he didn't know what it was. Emily was sick, but he noticed no one asking her if she was okay. Tim looked mad all the time and didn't even say hi to him when they got home from the hospital. Dad had been just plain grumpy all day, but that, he figured, was just because he missed Mom and the babies. Mama had given him extra hugs before he'd left her, but now it was dark and strange and different and he wanted more hugs.

Knowing how to navigate their bedroom in the dark, he expertly crept around Jack's bed, then to the stairs and down without a sound. After that, he tiptoed across the front room, which looked fairly creepy to him because of the orange streetlight glowing outside, causing all kinds of weird shadows that sent shivers up his spine. Emily's door was still shut, but he tried the handle anyway. Locked, which he had worried a little about, but the creepy shadows were still behind him which compelled him to tap lightly on the door, whispering through the wood, "Emily? Can I come in? It's Sam."

He had to say it again and tap a little louder before he heard the lock turning. It only took another moment before he saw her standing in front of him and, immediately, he felt so much better about the darkness around him. Emily would tell him why things felt strange and she'd give him the 3am hugs he required.

"Sam?! What's wrong? Are you okay? Are you sick?"

Sam let out his breath; these were the questions his mom would ask him if he'd shown up by her bed in the dark. The world felt right again, "Can I sleep in here? I miss Mama and I didn't get to say good night to you."

With those few words, her heart reassembled itself, not perfectly, but enough to give him a slight smile and crouch down, "How about we go back upstairs and I'll lay down with you for a few minutes, okay? Just until you fall asleep again."

Nodding, he took her hand, whispering up to her, "I won't let the shadows get you. They're really scary though, so don't let go of my hand, okay?"

She had the protection of a seven-year old boy. At that very moment, it was just what she needed, "I won't let go."

Both snuggled in his bed a minute later, Sam generously letting her have most of the pillow, "When is Mama coming home?"

Emily adored how he only called Elizabeth that when he was tired, "Tomorrow or the next day at the latest. Then we'll have Christmas again and then there's New Year's and tacos and pot banging and snowmen and sledding and visiting your grandparents. It's gonna be pretty cool."

He smiled, his eyes already getting heavy and closing for longer and longer periods of time, "Will you promise to always say good-night to me? I didn't like it tonight when you didn't."

Emily wiggled forward enough to kiss his forehead, "I promise I will always say goodnight to you, no matter where I am or what I'm doing."

"Even if you're far away, like in Cleveland or something?"

"Even if I'm in Cleveland."

Still holding her hand, he fell asleep moments later, leaving Emily sleepy as well. She had time to ask herself if she should go back downstairs, but was asleep before she could answer.

The following morning, entirely too 'the sun won't be up for a few hours' early, Jack woke to the sound of muffled giggles. Rolling over, he saw Sam with his flashlight aimed at the wall and Emily making shadow puppets with her fingers. It appeared that they hadn't heard him move so he contented himself to lay there watching the pair and their parade of animals, UFOs, family members and fairy tale characters march through the beam of light. Wondering how much longer his bladder would allow him to stay there quietly, he realized not as long as he'd like and, about to move, Sam and Emily suddenly said, in a louder voice than the whispers they'd been using, "Good morning, Jack."

"Curses. How long have you known I was up?"

"Since you rolled over. I told Emily 'cause she didn't hear you, but I knew it when you rolled over and didn't move again." Turning on the mattress to face his brother, "You never roll over just once. You flip and flip and flip until you end up in the same spot that you started in."

Jack sat up, staring at Sam in surprise, "Seriously?" Rubbing his head, his hair in fifteen different directions, "Sorry, kid, I had no idea."

Sam grinned, shrugging, "It's okay. I just figure you must be dreaming of flipping pancakes at work."

Now he laughed, "Probably." Disappearing quickly to the bathroom, he returned to find the pair lying back down, flashlight switched to black light and making the stars on the ceiling glow. Jack settled the other way on the bed, feet up near Sam's head, "How long have you guys been awake?"

"About a half-hour."

"Who woke who up?"

"I woke up first," holding the light steady on one particular star, Sam answered, "but last night after everybody was asleep, I missed Mama and Emily forgot to say good-night to me so I went and got her."

Wishing he was little enough to do such a thing and to talk about it with absolutely no embarrassment, Jack gave him a smile, "Cool."

Will found them an hour later, all fast asleep in Sam's bed, Jack's hand wrapped loosely around Emily's foot and Sam wedged in between the two, mouth open in a smile. His guilt still weighing him down, he felt just a little better seeing her with his boys instead of alone; she could still find a safe place in the chaos.

Back downstairs, just as he had finished cleaning things up a little before the rest of the family woke up and he went to retrieve Elizabeth and the twins, he heard a loud creak in the floor behind him and turned to find Emily in the entryway to the kitchen. Tentatively he offered, "Morning."

Jack and Sam hovered behind her while she hesitated, then with a deep breath, "Morning."

"I'm sorry."

Pretty sure he'd never looked more sorry in his life, she took a second deep breath before walking over to him, looking up, "Me, too."

"Still like me?"

After nodding, "Still like me?"

"The same amount as most of the boys and a lot more than I like Jack over there."

Jack grinned, glad they were one step closer to normal, "Whatever," picking up Sam by the waist and holding him sideways against his hip, the little boy's arms dangling and feet kicking, "I've got Sam and the girl 'cause you know she'll go wherever he does."

Will risked squeezing her shoulders while she stood beside him, "Your mother will just make tacos, though, and you'll all come running back."

"Damn it."

The issue seemed over for the moment and Will chose to save his next conversation for a better time, namely a few days from now, when things were back to normal, or at least as normal as their house knew how to get.

That made him smile.

♦♦♦

That night, Will was finally able to have a full conversation with Elizabeth, in the comfort of their room with only the twins hanging around to listen. After telling her more completely what had happened with Emily, Elizabeth could only shake her head, "Do we get her some help or do we let her work it out herself?"

Will, who'd been asking that same question to himself constantly for the last two days, "I think we need to offer it to her, but not be angry if and when she doesn't accept it."

166

"You think she'll say she's fine?"

"Yeah. I think she knows she's not fine, but that she's been dealing with it a lot longer than we have and it's gonna take more than yesterday to finally get her to realize she can't get by on willpower and stubbornness alone."

"Sometimes I'm pretty damn sure she actually is your child."

"I wish that more than once a day, believe me."

After so many years with him, she knew when to end a discussion with a hug, so she did, also kissing his cheek before she slowly stood up, still tired and sore, "Can you keep an eye on the boys for me for a few minutes?"

With a sudden grin in the direction of the small, rolling crib that was now on its 11th and 12th use, having worked its way through the Callaghan boys as well as Claire's family four weeks at a time, "I think I can manage that. Can you give her a hug for me, please?"

"How do you know I wasn't just going to use the bathroom?"

Giving his wife a half-smirk which included, at no extra charge, a wink that made her stomach jump, "The same way you knew to end our talk with a hug and a kiss. 21 years, eight months and some odd days, woman ... I know that look on your face better than you do."

Glad he could still make her blush, she returned the wink, "Four days."

He just smiled as she disappeared around the corner.

Once downstairs, she found Emily just turning out her bedroom light and, as was her habit now, she thumped her feet a little harder on the floor to make some noise, warn Emily she was coming, never wanting to scare her. Emily turned from her bed, sheets in hand and about to climb in, "Hi."

"Hi."

Dropping her covers, she walked towards Elizabeth, "Everything okay?"

Elizabeth pointed towards the bed, "Mind if I sit down? Standing isn't much fun at the moment."

Reaching to click the light back on, Elizabeth stopped her, "I don't mind the dark."

Emily suddenly knew what was coming and, bracing for it, guided Elizabeth over to the bed, which Jack and Will had fixed up that morning, replacing the popped screws and bed boards, "Does make some things easier, doesn't it?"

Not answering until she was settled back against the wall, "My sister, Jenny … Claire's mom … and I loved the dark. We told so many things … secret crushes, awkward kisses, what we thought were horrible confessions, bad grades … in the dark. Did you know that the day Will asked me to marry him, I had Jenny come over and stay the night at my apartment? I turned out all the lights before I told her because it was just such a big thing that I needed the dark to make it seem more real?"

She couldn't help but understand, "I needed the dark to tell Jack about myself."

Reaching over to find Emily's hand, "Would it be okay if I told you a secret?"

"Of course."

After a second or two of silence, "I'm glad your father's dead. I couldn't be happier to know that he can never, ever touch you again. Even with what it did to Jack, it was worth it, in my mind, to get him away from you for good." Squeezing her fingers, "But you have 13 years of nightmares, plus all the aftermath, that are going to follow you around for the rest of your life. So, I'd like you to promise me, right now, that when it gets to be too much, and I am pretty sure it will eventually, you will find me, take me into a room, shut the door, turn out the lights and ask me to help you."

"Eli …"

She cut Emily off, "I want you to promise me. Don't just say so for the sake of shutting me up. I want you to truly promise me that when you can't fight it anymore and are at your wit's end and think the world isn't worth living in, you", punctuating each word, "find," with a hard squeeze to Emily's hand, "me." Emily felt herself nodding, words escaping her for the moment, but Elizabeth wouldn't accept that, "Say it out loud for me, please."

Emily swallowed hard, then, her lower lip quivering, whispered, "I will find you."

Elizabeth gave her a smile, squeezing her hand a final time, "Very good."

Needing to return to some kind of normalcy, Emily shifted carefully, climbing off the bed and turning the light on before picking up the picture she'd drawn of the twins. Handing it to Elizabeth, she prayed her voice wouldn't break, "This is what Jack was looking at when Will came in the other morning."

All words escaped Elizabeth at this point and, gazing at her youngest sons frozen in time on the paper in her hand, she could only reach out, taking Emily's fingers in hers, hoping that the contact would convey her admiration and her thanks.

Emily understood completely.

♦ ♦ ♦

After some assistance Elizabeth made it back upstairs about 20 minutes later, Will looking up as she came in the room, "Everything okay?"

"About as good as it can be for the moment." Settling heavily on the mattress, "But I have a feeling this isn't anywhere near over."

Happy to finally have his wife beside him again, he chose to agree, "I think we need to wait this one out, though."

Will was nearly asleep when Elizabeth, who had been laying quietly stroking the closest baby's foot through the crib bars, asked in a whisper over her shoulder, "Did Emily show you the picture she did?"

It took a second to register the voice, "Uh ... um ... what?"

169

"The picture of the boys that Emily drew? Has she shown it to you yet?"

Too close to dreaming to be sad, "Not yet, but she will … when she's ready."

Removing her hand from the crib, she shifted towards Will and his furnace-like warmth, "I missed you."

Nose buried in her neck, he mumbled a contented 'missed you, too' as he drifted back to sleep.

♦ ♦ ♦

They had their second Christmas a day later, the whole family present and accounted for. The twins were pretty much the best gift any of them could have gotten, but, according to Sam, his shiny new bike came in a very close second.

Bouncing up and down, he waited impatiently as the chaos was cleared away before going over to Tim, "Can you go outside with me so I can try my bike? There's no snow on the sidewalk. Please?!!?"

Tim wrinkled his nose, "Dude, it's like ten degrees out."

"Just for a minute. Please? Mom won't let me outside unless somebody goes with me."

He just shrugged, going back to his small pile of gifts, "Sorry man, I'm not freezing my butt off."

Emily was about to offer to take him out when both Jack and Dave, who'd been listening, spoke at once, "I'll go out with you."

All three grinned and Dave pulled his new hat down over his ears, "Great minds freeze alike."

Jack, reaching for his gloves and making sure not to look at Tim, "And, really, what's a little cold when there's a new bike."

Sam, whose face had fallen rapidly at Tim's response, perked up immediately, "Yea!"

As he raced out of the room to find his boots, Emily glanced over at Tim, who looked kind of stormy, "You sure you don't want to come out with us? We may be forced to have a snowball fight ... make Dave into a real life snowman."

"Nope. You seem to have it pretty well covered."

Pulling himself up off the floor, he headed into the kitchen, nearly running into Elizabeth, who had poked her head in, "Sam just flew through here saying something about going outside to ride his bike. Are you guys taking him?

Dave nodded, "Yeah, we're just getting our stuff on. Is it okay?"

"Sure, just don't get too cold."

Tucker tumbled in then, "So, I hear we're having a snowball fight."

Jack stood with a grin, "Alright. Assembly, outside, five minutes. Choose your sides." Holding out his hand to Emily, "You coming?"

"'Course, but I'll keep an eye on Sam, so warn your troops not to attack us. Although we might join in later, if that's all right?" Eyes twinkling in his direction, "We can beat you regardless of when we start anyways."

Not able to argue such a valid point, he stuck his tongue out instead, "I'll make sure everyone's updated."

Sliding on her new sweater, "Just let me go get my other pants on and more socks and my second sweater and my scarf and gloves and boots and hat."

Dave shook his head, "Geez, it's not the Arctic."

Echoing Tim's earlier comment, but with a touch of sarcasm thrown in, "Dude, it's only ten degrees out."

As Dave pulled his own sweatshirt on for a second layer, "Good point."

Before heading outside, Emily tried Tim again, "You sure you won't come out? Freeze your butt off with the rest of us?"

"I think Jack's got the big brother thing covered, thanks."

"Come on, it'll be fun."

Pulling his boots on for the trip back to the garage, "Catch you later."

♦ ♦ ♦

The next day was New Year's Eve. Tim bowed out of the festivities, but Dex and Claire came to dinner that night, along with Dave's friend Brian; Matt declining the invite on account of being in Phoenix with his family for the holidays. After several hours of game playing and taco-eating, the two boys were introduced to the pot-banging festivities, much like Emily had been the year before. Claire, who had been doing it with the Callaghans since she was little, giggled with glee when Will called them all into the kitchen.

Brian wore that look of confusion Emily knew well. Pulling him aside, she handed him a spoon and a lid, "Just bang the hell out of it and run when we tell you."

Elizabeth had already moved the twins to her room upstairs and she called down to them quietly, "For the love of God and all that's Holy, please try to be quiet."

The eleven of them looked at her with a collective grin and Jack gave a wink, "Yeah, sure, Ma, no problem."

She just shook her head and shut the bedroom door, knowing full well the babies would be waking very soon.

Emily loved it. Packed together like sardines on the front porch, woefully trying to be quiet while giggling and waiting for the ball to drop on the TV so they could whack the hell out of all of Elizabeth's dented and dinged up metal cookware at just the proper moment. The anticipation of the cacophony of sound that would imminently echo through the neighborhood made her insides shiver and when she heard Will, who was on TV countdown duty, tell them to go, she made her contribution to ringing in the New Year in traditional Callaghan style.

Brian had the decency to stop a few seconds later with the rest of them, but Dex was in his glory, loving, with a little too much enthusiasm, the idea of being able to make legitimate, obnoxiously loud noise. Jack, herding everyone inside, had to grab his friend by the back of his shirt and drag him through the door, laughing and telling him to shut up at the same time. Claire snatched Dex's ladle from his hand before he could hit the pot one last time, and in an effort to keep him from yelling about the theft of his utensil, kissed him, wishing him 'Happy New Year'.

He kissed her back with gusto to rival his earlier pot-banging, then pulled back, looking over her head towards Will, "I could get behind you people doing this every week. Sanctioned noise making is totally freaking awesome. I should have skipped Texas last year and come here instead."

Laughing while shaking his head, "Happy New Year, Dex."

"Back at you, Mr. C."

The next few minutes were spent doing male-type bonding exchanges amongst all the boys, Emily patiently waiting for Jack to finally extract himself from the crowd and find her. That he did, kissing her before she had a chance to wish him anymore than 'Happy New ...'"

"Year," once he let go of her.

"Have fun?"

She gave him a wide smile, her face lighting up, "Best use of New Year's Eve ever."

In a loud voice, Jack called to the rest of the crowd, eyes still on Emily, "Same time, next year?"

Everybody joined in on the reply, "Same time, next year."

Dex kissed Elizabeth, who had come downstairs holding two now wide awake babies, on the cheek with a loud smacking sound, "I love you. Thanks for letting me partake in the insanity."

"I love you, too, Dex."

"I think I broke your ladle."

Elizabeth, as she handed one of the babies to Will, who was now beside her, "You can buy us a reinforced one for next time."

"Sweet."

♦ ♦ ♦

After a few more rounds of Uno, Will broke up the party by sending everyone upstairs to bed, leaving Jack, Emily, Dex and Claire in the living room, each of them getting a good night hug before he headed to bed himself, "Don't stay up too late."

"Of course not, Uncle Will. We'll be asleep before you can get your comfy flannel jammies on, promise."

"Smart aleck."

"It's smart Claire, Uncle Will, remember? Not Alec."

With a final smile, "Goodnight, smart Claire."

Once their sleeping bags, blankets and pillows were laid out, Dex flopped down, "So, what's on the agenda this evening folks?"

Claire, poking him in the chest with her toe, "Sleeping is usually good."

"Not on New Year's Eve, it's not. I don't care how slowly 'Uncle Will gets in his jammies', I will not be asleep anytime soon. We need to watch at least two movies, gorge ourselves on leftover tacos, have a pillow fight …"

Emily piped in on this one, "A pillow fight?"

174

With a patent-Dex grin, he leaned back, hands behind his head, "Well, you girls can have a pillow fight, me and Jack'll just watch."

Claire took a flying leap at this point and landed like a ton of bricks on him, thus the tickling began. Amidst the distraction, Jack led Emily into the kitchen, "While they're busy, I think I'd like another New Year's kiss."

Pulling herself up onto the countertop, she was now eye-level with him as she leaned in, "Just one?"

"Well, we'll start with one and move on from there."

Dex gave them about 10 minutes before poking his head around the corner, "Um, I hate to break this up, but my bladder's gonna explode and the only bathrooms are through the love den here."

Emily laughed as she slid to the floor, "I should probably go get my pajamas on anyway."

◆◆◆

Soon enough, they were all sprawled on the floor, watching *Mystery Science Theatre 3000* and munching on re-heated tacos. Claire was the first to fall asleep around 3, bundled beside Dex in her well-worn red sleeping bag. Dex went next, wrapped in a cast-off sleeping bag from his sister, bright pink and yellow checkered.

Noticing it was after 3:30am, Emily left Jack to his dozing and moved the plates to the kitchen, turned off the TV and finally crouched down next to him, discovering him watching her with half-closed eyes. Kissing the end of his nose, "You awake or asleep?"

"Both."

"Happy Anniversary."

His brain raced through what in the world she might be talking about then, remembering, he woke up and grinned, "Has it seriously been a year already?"

"Give or take an hour or so."

Reaching up, he pulled her down for a kiss, toppling her over accidentally, and when she landed square on top of him, she couldn't help the uncharacteristic giggle. Jack, in turn, laughed as well and before they could rearrange themselves, Dex called out from his corner, "Would y'all just get a room? Some of us are trying to sleep here."

"Shut it, Dex."

"Is it so much to ask for a little shut-eye? I mean, my God, it's 3:30 in the damn morning."

"Shut it, Dex."

"The appalling nature of this slumber party is just astounding. First, no pillow fight, then woken from a sound sleep by you two doing God knows what over there. I may have to file a complaint."

Emily was already up and sitting on Dex's chest, pillow ready to swing, "Shut it, Dex."

"No."

He did indeed get his pillow fight. Granted, it was rather one sided at first, but soon, Claire was awake and an all-out war began.

By 4:30, everything was back to quiet and, in the dark, Emily placed her forehead gently against Jack's sleeping face, "Happy New Year."

A half-hour later, Emily slithered out of her sleeping bag, retrieved the picture of the twins she'd done, then, quietly putting it in the frame she'd had Jack pick up for her earlier that day, she used her ninja skills and was back beside Jack in under a minute, the picture now safely leaning against the wall of Elizabeth and Will's bedroom.

By the time Emily stretched herself awake, the picture was perched on the mantle to one side of the shoe picture ... Emily's guardianship paperwork on the other side.

A sign in the middle of it all, written in thick black marker, stated simply, 'The Callaghan Kids'.

Chapter 14

Dex decided he truly hated February as they all huddled on Matt's porch, waiting for their doorbell ringing to be answered, "December's got Christmas so that's essential, January has New Year's so that needs to stay too, but February hasn't got any damn use at all except …"

Emily cut him off, "Valentine's Day is in February."

"… except for Valentine's Day which exists simply to make me feel guilty about not spending money on my woman. So, given that pleasant little horror, February hasn't got any use except to drag out winter to its bitter pain-in-the-ass end."

With a grin, Claire interjected this time, "Groundhog Day. You totally can't forget Groundhog Day."

Throwing up his gloved hands, "Shit. There goes my rant. Groundhogs are awesome."

Claire then lifted her foot and kicked him lightly on the butt, "You also said ass."

"Just thinking about the best one here."

Jack's face emerged from his striped scarf, his cheeks bright red and freezing, "Thank you."

"Do you really think your ass is high on my list of things to think about?" Jack made to answer when Dex just held up his finger as the front door opened, "Say it and you will regret it." Looking up smoothly at Matt, who now stood in the open doorway, "Hey! Happy Birthday! I think you need to move this whole party thing to July so I don't freeze my parts off."

Waving them inside, Matt shut the door quickly, shivering, "I would if I could. I hate the cold!"

Jack, still chuckling, "You ought to live in Chicago for awhile. That makes this weather look tame."

"No, thank you. I have no desire to be any more frozen than I am now. I have two layers of everything on right now and I'm still cold." After coats had been hung in the closet, Matt led them through the kitchen, introducing his mom before heading towards the basement door, "Come on down. Mom's forcing us all down there until dinner's ready. Cor has some of her friends over, but they're not as mean and bitchy as you might expect. Also, given Cor is boyfriendless at the moment, I have been the only male until now, so thank you very much for getting here on time."

Claire responded with something, but Emily didn't hear her. The only thing she could hear was her pounding heart and the long string of swearing in her head as she cursed whoever the hell invented the basement in the first place. She fought valiantly, though, and must have looked at least semi-normal because everyone else began disappearing through the door. Jack, however, hadn't made it past the first step before turning around for Emily's hand. Seeing her face morphing from rosy-cheeked happiness to chalky white terror, he knew immediately what that meant and hated having that knowledge. He whispered low while Mrs. Quatermass' back was turned, "Do we need to leave?"

She managed to shake her head at him which lead Jack to the conclusion that he needed to get her out of there anyway, regardless of what her answer had been. He didn't have time, though, to come up with any kind of exit strategy before Matt's mom turned around.

The expression she saw on Emily's face made her spine shiver and on instinct, she moved towards the girl, "Honey, are you all right? Do you need to sit down?"

The sound of her voice woke Emily and apologizing suddenly, "I'm sorry, um ... I just ... I'm sorry."

Jack, hands on her waist and brain moving fast, "She, uh, doesn't do well with basements."

From her view, this was putting it mildly, but Mrs. Quatermass threw them an unrealized excuse, "Are you claustrophobic?"

Jack latched on to this with gusto, lying through his teeth, "Yeah. Pretty bad, too. Um, do you mind if we stay up here instead? Is there anything we can help with?"

Wondering if Emily would turn back to her normal coloring any time soon, she nodded, "You can make the biscuits for me, if you don't mind."

"From scratch or tube?"

This led her and Jack to a discussion of cooking that gave Emily time to contain her scattered emotions into the tidy little box in her head marked 'do not open under any circumstance ever again'.

♦ ♦ ♦

By the time the biscuits were in the oven, Emily had loosened up and relaxed. Jack kissed the back of her head after washing his hands, "I'm gonna go down for a minute and say hi. Back in a flash."

Matt's mom chimed in, "Can you tell them to come up in about five minutes? Dinner'll be ready by then." With a 'yes ma'am,' he was gone, leaving the two of them to finish icing the cupcakes, "You sure you're okay?"

Finally answering in more than nods, "I'm fine. I just can't ..." trailing off, she waved in the general direction of the basement door.

"Well, I'm glad for the help, so thank you."

With her first genuine smile of the evening, "Thank you back."

♦ ♦ ♦

180

When Matt asked where Jack and Emily were, Dex simply shrugged, swimming in happy ignorance for once. When Jack showed up a few minutes later, he explained, "We were actually helping your mom with some things and we're all supposed to go up in about five minutes."

Satisfied with that explanation, he introduced everyone again.

◆ ◆ ◆

Once the party moved back upstairs, Emily joined in enthusiastically and, with 11 people jammed in the kitchen, Jack couldn't help but comment that it felt just like home, only with a few more elbows and girls' voices.

Emily poked him, "Well, with seven boys, it's not like you can hear me or your mom anyway. We'd need way more people than this to drown you guys out."

"Hey, we're not that loud!"

"Oh my God, the snoring alone could kill a person."

Corrine's friends and Corrine herself were fairly fun to hang out with for the evening. Claire knew them from school, but had never really had a conversation with any of them. Luckily, they all found common ground in music and movies, card games and general gossip about classes and other such trifle. After gifts, small, but amusing things like a light-up belt from Emily and a new winter hat with a yarn Mohawk from Dex, Jack taught the new people how to play Nertz, which they played with loud, swearing delight. By 11:30, they considered themselves friends enough for hugs when it was time to leave. Thanking Matt's mom as they trooped by, they all called good nights to each other before racing to their freezing cars.

After such a loud evening, Jack and Emily's ride home was quiet and even the amusement of him dropping her off at her bedroom door at the end of their 'date' didn't make her smile as widely as he'd hoped, but he tried one last time, "I'd ask to come in, but I've gotta work in the morning."

Still feeling stupid for her reaction to the basement earlier, "I hate work sometimes."

181

"Agreed." Kissing her good-night, he didn't pull back, instead asking quietly, "You okay?"

"I'm an idiot, but I'm okay."

"You're not an idiot."

"Okay. Just plain flipping dumb then."

Knowing his words would fall on deaf ears, he tried anyways, "You were fine and you have never been stupid, dumb or an idiot a day in your life."

With a deep breath, "I appreciate the effort to make me feel better, but it still boils down to the fact that I made an ass of myself tonight."

Trying another approach, "Are you gonna be okay down here tonight? I can stay here if you want to go up to my room."

Finally she let out a deep breath, the corner of her mouth turning up in a slight smirk, "You just want to dig through my sketch books."

"Can't blame me for trying." Kissing her again, he yawned against her forehead, "I just might fall asleep here anyways so you'll have to go upstairs."

Pushing him away gently and aiming him towards the stairs, "Go to bed before you fall down."

"Love you."

"Love you, too."

It wasn't long before Jack was well on his way to dreaming upstairs and Emily was lying in her bed, now extremely wide-awake and thinking.

Now, thinking can be a good thing or a bad thing, and this line of thinking was definitely not conducive to sleep. Alone, in the dark, all she could focus on was how stupid she'd been and how completely messed up her life was. After a good hour of this, her blood was boiling and by 2am, she decided she was going to finish it.

Sliding out of bed, her stocking feet carried her silently across the kitchen linoleum and she stopped in front of the door to the basement. Before she could lose her nerve, she pulled the door open and flipped on the light, illuminating the wooden stairs.

♦♦♦

And that's where Will found her at 6:10 the next morning, slumped against the wall facing the still open door, eyes staring ahead, rimmed with exhaustion. "Em?"

Swinging her head around and up to face him, "Hi."

As he sat down next to her, "You all right?"

"Sure."

"Then, um, what're you doing?"

Matter-of-factly, "Just looking."

Beginning to think she may be sick, he touched her forehead, "Emily? Why are you on the floor?"

"Did you know my father's down there waiting for me?"

He certainly hoped she was speaking metaphorically, but from the look in her eye and the far off way she spoke, he needed to be sure she didn't really believe he was physically down there, waiting in the shadows, "He can't be down there, Em, you know that."

"No, he's down there. He's been down there since the beginning."

"Emily, you saw him in the morgue at the hospital."

"But in my head, he's still down there."

Reality began to shape itself, "Have you been trying to go down there all night?"

183

"Yup. Got the door open about 2:30 this morning. Been sitting here ever since."

Before he could say more, Jack walked in the room rubbing his head tiredly, stopping short when he saw them, "You don't see this every day." Looking between their two faces, then at the open door, "Are we waiting for something to come up or go down?"

Will nodded his head towards the other side of Emily and Jack, still confused, took a seat beside her, "I'm still trying to find out."

Jack, waking up more, realized he already knew, "Em, you don't have to worry about last night. No one cared."

"I did and I hate it."

"So you were trying to go down by yourself last night?"

After nodding, they all sat in silence for a minute, Will trying to sort things out and Jack playing with the soft skin of Emily's knuckles. Suddenly, Emily swung her hair over her shoulder and put Jack's fingers on the scar running across her neck at her hairline, "I got this down there."

Will, thinking this might be a good moment to give them space, went to stand, but Emily's other hand clamped down on his thigh, keeping him there as Jack asked, "Will you tell us?"

◆ ◆ ◆

It took her a good five minutes before she spoke again, "Can you go downstairs with me first?"

Jack gave her a startled look, "You want to go now?"

"I've been sitting here for three hours and if I don't go now, I'll never do it."

He stood, holding his hand out, "Then let's go."

Sliding her fingers in his, she haltingly took each step, heart pounding, blood rushing, head spinning, until she was finally at the bottom of the fifteen steps. Pulling Jack to a stop once they hit the cement floor, she sat, head on her knees, "Give me a second, would you?"

Flipping the switch on the wall, the rest of the basement lit up behind him, "Take as long as you need." Will, following silently down, settled a few steps behind them, sitting with elbows on knees. Leaving Emily to her own timetable, Jack explained to Will what happened at the party the night before.

After they had quieted again, she raised her head up to meet Jack's patient stare, "I was never good at math, even when I was little. I was one of those who counted on my fingers until the fifth grade. Teachers tried, but I just could never quite get it."

Continuing on after she took a deep breath, squeezing her hands together tightly until the fingers turned white, "Usually, I could squeak by with a C, but once, in fourth grade, I ended up with a D on my report card and where I went to school, any D required a parent/teacher conference. I had to take it home and show him and tell him about the meeting."

At this point, Jack motioned for her to scoot over and, sitting down, "You still okay?"

Nodding, "He acted like he didn't really care at first and stupidly, I thought it might be okay. I turned around to leave the kitchen and he suddenly grabbed me by the hair." Pulling the ends of her tangled mass over her arm, "It wasn't anywhere near this long, but it was enough for a good length braid." Letting go of it again, "Anyway, he dragged me down, then across the kitchen and over to the stairs. I couldn't get my feet under me to stand and whenever I tried to move, he just pulled me harder."

Jack could see the glassy look in her eye and knowing she was once again miles away and years ago, he slipped his hand over her knee and waited.

"All the hair here," running her hand over her neck, "was already pulling, but once he shoved me down the stairs, my hair caught. They were these old, horrible wood steps with cracks and nails sticking out." Her body tensed as her hand continued to trace the raised scar, "My braid caught on one of the nails and I could actually feel the skin tearing as all the hair down here ripped out."

Jack felt his insides curl as he listened, "It just seemed to make him even more angry that I didn't make it all the way down to the bottom. He pounded down the stairs, yanked the braid free the shoved me down the rest of the steps with his foot. I thought he'd leave me alone after that, but he seemed to be on a roll. Maybe it was me crying that fired him back up, but either way, he pulled me up and pushed me over to this old laundry tub that was down there …"

Trailing off, she put both hands on her neck and, hanging her head to rest, her forehead on her knees once again, Jack heard a muffled sob. Reaching around to rub her back through her pajamas, he pulled her closer, "It's okay. Remember, I told you I won't let anything else hurt you."

She rolled towards him, craving the warmth as she was suddenly chilled to the bone, "He had this old Swiss Army knife he used for everything. He ate with it, opened old boxes, fixed things. I mean, it was disgusting and after he leaned me over the wash tub, I felt him reach in his pocket and pull it out." Stopping suddenly, she stood up, "You know what, I'm hungry. You hungry?"

Floored by her sudden shift, "What?"

"I'm starving. I've been up all night and I really want some waffles."

Will stood at this point, coming down to stand beside her. Taking her face in his hands and tilting her head up, "Don't stop, Emily. You're so close."

With chin quivering, she held his gaze for another minute before, "He kept saying that he could make me really cry if he wanted to, then he slid the knife where the skin had already broken and just … he finished the job."

Will rubbed his thumb over the tears falling, desperately wishing he could beat the hell out of her father as his son had, but holding his anger in check, he kept his eyes steady and focused, knowing if he cracked, it would all go to hell, "Go on."

Not even blinking at this point, "I could feel the blood running down my cheeks and I watched it puddle at the bottom of the tub. I wasn't even crying anymore. I just remember the pain and the red rivers running down the drain. He was screaming at me the entire time, but all I could focus on was the color." Cocking her head slightly, "It was such a bright red. It looked almost beautiful against the dirty sink in that dark basement in my little corner of hell."

At this point, Jack slid his hand over the back of her neck and Emily turned away from Will, focusing in on Jack, his other hand following the first, fingers twining together as she continued, "Then he was gone. I don't even remember him leaving, just the lights going out and the basement door shutting, then my whole body screaming."

Will spoke, his anger barely veiled, "He left you down there?"

Not really hearing his question, "I woke up on the floor later and cleaned up as best I could, but I didn't have any soap or warm water or any real light to see by so, needless to say, I didn't do a real good job." Resting her forehead on Jack's chest, "By the time he let me back up, I knew I had an infection."

Talking into the top of her head, "How long were you down there?"

The safety of Jack's arms did nothing to keep the violent shudder that coursed through her at bay, "Three days. Long enough for him to go to the conference and pretend he gave a shit about me and long enough for him to get pissed all over again."

"He kept you down there for three days?"

"Yeah … and it was January and I swear, colder than it is now. The floors were cement and made your feet freeze, even in shoes."

Jack went cold as well, asking a second time, "Three days?"

Nodding, head still on his chest, "Luckily, I could drink the water, but let me tell you, it's not real fun to sleep on top of an old washer and dryer. I debated whether I could fix the dryer, then get inside so I could turn it on and keep warm." For some reason, she found this funny and as her shoulder began shaking, "Oh my god, I actually had an hour long debate with myself about which would keep me warmer, fluff or permanent press." As the tears flooded her eyes, she lifted her head, "The only thing he said when he opened the door was, 'I guess I'll have to try harder next time'."

The three sat in silence.

Hugging her close, Jack held her for quite a while before whispering in her ear, "Still feel like getting those waffles?"

"I think I need to see the rest of the basement."

"Drenched in syrup, covered in butter, with a generous side of chocolate milk?"

"Jack."

"I'll even tell you my secret ingredient."

"Jack."

He stopped rambling and pulled away far enough to look at her, "Yeah?"

"Will was right, I can't stop now." After a slight pause, "I need to do this."

♦ ♦ ♦

Will crept up the stairs while Jack and Emily ventured on. Two hours later, he came back down to find them curled on the sofa in his study in the basement, asleep in a comfortable pile under several of the old blankets he kept stacked in the corner. Jack's shirt was still damp from her tears, but her face was dry now, half buried in Jack's neck, the tension he'd seen hours before gone away, hopefully for good.

Lifting up the bottom of the blanket, Will found four stocking feet tangled together and choosing the largest of the bunch, began tickling the bottom of it. Instantly the foot jerked away from him and he heard a grunt at the other end of the couch. Will couldn't help his smile, which grew

188

exponentially when he heard Jack's graveled voice, "So help me God, I'll put your hand in a vat of warm water tonight."

The rest of the feet began to wiggle now as well and Emily, her voice faint, muffled under Jack somewhere, "Just kick it. Maybe it'll go away."

For that, Will grabbed Emily's toes, "Please, I've been kicked by bigger feet than this."

Suddenly, her head emerged over the top of the blankets, "'Morning again, Will."

"'Morning Miss Emily. Can you tell my son he's got to be at work in a half-hour?"

Chapter 15

She never meant to feel it. It came out of left field and stopped her in her tracks, her hand hovering two inches from the doorknob, two seconds from stepping into the kitchen. She heard his humming through the hollow core door and she froze.

Listening, her ear pressed against the wood before she knew what she was doing, she heard Will's nameless tune.

She knew he was out there, following his usual morning routine, awake, breakfast in silence, dressed, brushed and out the door by 6:45. She knew that. He did it almost every day.

She knew that.

And it didn't make sense that, for the first time, she didn't want to open her door and say 'good morning'.

She had to be the stupidest person in the world.

The most paranoid, dumb, idiotic and moronically stupid person in the entire world.

But she waited anyway, still as stone and just as quiet, waiting.

Suddenly, her brain registered the quiet and, shaking her head, she caught a glimpse of her watch ... she'd been standing there for almost 15 minutes and she had absolutely no recollection of it at all.

What the hell was happening?

◆◆◆

Everything was fine again until one evening a week later.

Emily had just finished quizzing Nate through the Middle Ages and after she waved away his undying devotion, she remained on the floor of her room, realizing ten seconds too late that Nate's textbook was still at her feet. Struggling to stand and take it to him, she came face to face with Tim, who was poised to knock on her doorframe. His fist hovering in midair, eye-level with her, had her ducking on instinct, the looming hand blocking out the familiar face.

Tim's face screwed up in confusion, "What the hell? I'm not gonna hit you!"

Recovering fairly quickly, she lifted her head back up, "Don't do that!"

"What? Should I have just busted in here?"

"Make some noise first, would you? Scare the hell out of me sneaking up like that." Tim cocked his head, trying to choose between annoyance or apology and, about to apologize, Emily cut him off, head suddenly pounding and hand moving up to massage her forehead, "What did you need?"

Taking her hand movement as annoyance instead, he fired back, "Nothing now. Maybe when the queen calms down, I'll let her know."

"Tim …"

He passed Nate, who had come back to retrieve his book, "Watch it or she'll bite your head off."

Nate looked from his brother to Emily, who looked about as far from angry as he'd ever seen her. Walking slowly towards her, "You okay?"

Emily pushed down her urge to cry, instead holding out his history text in her hand, "Just a misunderstanding, I think."

191

Shrugging, "Tim misunderstands a lot. We like to call it 'him being an idiot'."

"No, it was my fault. He just surprised me and I wasn't very nice about it."

"Well, he wasn't exactly nice about it either." Moving on, like any 12 year old would, "Thanks for the help. If I fail, I'm blaming you."

She nodded, wishing she felt the happiness that ought to be behind the smile she gave him, "Because it will, of course, be totally my fault."

"Totally."

It took until about 11:30 for her to finally give in and, slipping out of bed, she locked her door.

◆ ◆ ◆

Things were okay again … for a few days.

Until the following Monday, when she suddenly and inexplicably woke at 2:30 in the morning drenched in a cold sweat and shivering, her blankets pulled from the bed and tossed halfway across the room. Checking the door instinctively, she saw the lock still in place and, sitting up, she waited for her heart to stop pounding before re-making her bed.

Laying back down, however, was not the most appealing option at the moment. Instead, she dragged out her art board and set to work on her next assignment, diligently ignoring the fact that her nightmare had been filled with a sickeningly familiar voice.

She opted not to tell anyone and slept soundly the next night, exhaustion pushing all things but peaceful sleep out of the picture. Thinking maybe it had been just a fluke, it scared her even more the next night. She was beginning to hear fractions of the words he yelled and when she woke this time, her own scream was already rising full force in her chest. Having just enough comprehension in her frozen mind, she held her breath until the urge dissipated.

The fear, however, remained and before she could talk herself out of it, she was halfway up the stairs, zeroed in only on the safe warmth of Jack's arms. She didn't make it that far though; when she passed the twins room, she heard one of them whimpering. Detouring, she picked Ethan up carefully, "What's up, little man?"

He quieted instantly in her arms and enjoying both the warm bundle and the company, she settled in the rocking chair, whisper-singing one of the songs Claire had been practicing recently, as she moved. It didn't take long for Ethan to fall back to sleep and for Emily's thoughts to calm. She was about to drift off herself when she felt a hand on her shoulder, "Em? I'm gonna put Ethan back in bed, okay?"

Eyes popping open, she saw Jack and nodded, surrendering the baby to him. Once finished, he held out his hand to her, "Come downstairs?" Following him down, she stayed silent as he dug through the fridge, coming up with a pile of ham and some cheese. Sandwich made, he motioned with his head towards the living room, "Want to hang out for awhile?"

Not quite willing to go back to her room just yet, "Sure."

As he smiled with bits of ham in his teeth, "Thought maybe I'd check in on the Weather Channel. The 3am tropical updates are totally awesome." Holding out his sandwich to her, "want some?" After she shook her head no, he did indeed switch the TV right to the Weather Channel and after a few minutes of updates on the floods somewhere in South America, he took his last bite, then muted Bob Stokes, who was being a bit too enthusiastic with his meteorological terms. Not turning to face her, "So, you trying to de-throne me as resident insomniac?"

Facing forward as well and far enough from her terror to answer in a steady voice, "Bad dream."

"'I'm naked in the school hallway covered in pudding' bad dream or 'Holy hell, I'm never sleeping again' bad dream?"

"Pudding?"

"Don't change the subject."

Leaning her head back on the couch, she rolled it towards him, "Chocolate pudding or butterscotch?"

Knowing exactly which dream she had, he played along, "Depends on which you like better."

"Why?"

"Future reference." Placing his arm over her thigh and tucking his hand under her knee, he slid his head next to hers, "Was he in it?" The involuntary spasm of every muscle in her body answered for her and, not pushing it, he ran his thumb over her knee, "You know, I think there's some pudding in the cupboard."

He felt her begin to relax as her face pulled into a slight smile, "I think I'd just like to stay right here with you, if that's all right?"

With an exaggerated sigh, he clicked off the TV, "Denying me pudding is just plain vicious, you realize."

Wiggling closer, she slid her hand over his leg as well, "I've always been a chocolate girl."

"That is very good to know."

◆ ◆ ◆

Jack was just coming into the kitchen, still mostly asleep, when he ran smack into Will, "Jack? What're you doing up so early?"

Pointing over his dad's shoulder, "Bathroom."

After poking his head in the living room and finding Emily asleep, still sitting up on the couch, Will made his tea while waiting for his son to return. Once he did, "She all right?"

With a yawn, "She had a nightmare."

Will looked surprised, "I thought those had stopped?"

194

Emily, stumbling into the kitchen then, afghan wrapped tightly around her shoulders, answered quietly, "So did I, but it seems that my trip to the basement woke up the beast. It'll quiet back down, but until then, here I am." Stopping in front of Will and ignoring the apprehension suddenly filling her, she looked up at him, "'Morning."

Studying her red eyes, "Why don't you go back to bed for awhile? You can still get at least an hour or so."

Heading towards the fridge, "If I go to bed now, I'll never wake up." After pulling out the gallon of milk, she hit the cupboard for the cereal, "Anyone want any breakfast?"

Seeing his dad nod, Jack went to get bowls and spoons, plus the orange juice. Once they were settled at the table, Will asked her quietly, "Want to talk about it?"

She felt Jack's hand slide onto her knee to stop the leg-jiggling she hadn't realized she'd started, "Um, not particularly, but I could really go for a game of Scrabble."

Smiling at her gently over the cereal box, "Can't deny a request like that, can I?'

After he'd soundly beaten her by a good 200 points, Will stopped her as she was cleaning up the board, "It doesn't matter what time it is. You come and find me and we'll play again, alright? I don't want you sitting down here scared."

Knowing she'd never wake him up, she nodded anyway, "Thanks."

"Well, I've gotta go." Dropping a kiss on Emily's head as well as Jack's, "Have a good day."

Once he had disappeared out the front door, Jack looked over at her tired eyes, "Gonna stay awake today?"

Plastering on a cheesy smile, "Of course. Can't promise I'll learn anything though."

With a giant yawn, "Fair enough."

♦♦♦

She made it through the day, with Jack keeping a surreptitious eye on her, at least in his mind. To the rest of the world, he stared at her every chance he could get.

But she didn't mind. She was too busy trying to stay awake to mind.

Either way, she made it through school, then work, finally stumbling in the front door after 10, stumbling being defined as tripping on the door frame and flying, arms flailing, into the hall. Luckily, Tim was digging in the front hall closet for something and she ran into him instead of the floor.

"Hey!"

Trying to regain her balance, she used his shoulder as leverage to stand back up, "Sorry. Tripped on the door."

"You okay?" She started to nod when he continued, "'Cause you look like shit."

Fires lit, "Why are you such an ass lately? You never would have said that before."

Waving her off, "You look like someone went over you with a steamroller, but hey, who am I to comment. Go let Jack tell you you're perfect and the world'll be happy again."

This stopped her, "I'm far from perfect, but you don't have to make me feel worse than I already do."

As she walked away, he called after her, "Stop spazzing out then."

She kept going, save for the rather unexpected middle finger that popped up in his direction.

Telling Jack about it a little later, he chuckled, "Really? Oh, I wish I could have seen that."

196

"It's just, he never used to make me feel bad. I didn't do anything, did I?"

With a small kiss to her shoulder through her t-shirt, "No. I'm beginning to think that getting his own place, even if it is just in the backyard, made him crazy."

"But it's just an apartment."

"Yeah, but he always used to make little comments about how he would love to be on his own, away from us, especially right before we fell asleep and the toilet would flush and doors would slam and we'd all be yelling goodnights down the hall, he'd look at me and go, 'did she really have to have this many of us?'"

"So he's having his mid-life crisis and his teenage rebellion all rolled into one?"

"More like graduating from the 'Idiots School of Jackass Training and Moronic Dillholeness'."

Already feeling better and getting sleepy against the headboard where they were sitting, "How do they fit that on the diploma?"

Getting up to let her settle under her covers, Jack then headed towards her door, "Very tiny letters."

"Hey."

"Hey what?"

Emily propped herself up on her elbows, "Do you think that's why he never brings Sarah around anymore? I mean, she was never here much anyways, but we don't see her at all now."

Jack shrugged, rolling that through his brain, then answering in a voice low enough so Elizabeth, on the couch, wouldn't hear, "I think he doesn't really like any of us very much right now." Taking a deep breath and stuffing his hands in his pocket, "Tim has morphed into someone I don't recognize, I don't like and am beginning to not really care about. I've told him as much, so now I see it as his own damn problem." Giving her a crooked smile, "I just hope he knocks it off before he goes too far with us."

"Us?"

"I'd choose us over him." With that, he left, not realizing his unexplained words would provide her another sleepless night.

PART 2

Chapter 16

Her nightmares, an unseemly mixture of her father, Will and Tim, became regular again over the next few weeks. Soon, she didn't even try sleeping in bed. Sometimes, she'd come out after everyone had gone to their own rooms, dozing on the couch, only to be woken up as the fear set in. Many nights, she stayed in her room, lights blazing and door locked.

But she never went back upstairs to visit the twins, knowing that if Jack, or anyone, found her there again, there'd be too many questions with answers she didn't want to give.

But try as she might to keep to herself, Jack still found her late one Thursday night. Rubbing his eyes, he came around the corner and into the living room, half expecting to see his mom sitting there with one of the babies, but instead he saw Emily, glowing in the light of the TV, eyes half shut and shoulders curved. Before he had time to warn her he was there, she noticed him and sprang from the couch, hand over her mouth instinctively, to keep from yelping too loudly. Once she managed to realize it was only Jack, her temper flared, her whisper slicing through the air, "Would you fucking people learn how to make some noise? I swear to God, one of you is gonna kill me soon." Not knowing how to respond, but at least realizing it was exhaustion talking and not actually his Emily, Jack crossed his arms, squinting in her direction, waiting for the silence between them to become uncomfortable enough to crack her, which it did after a few moments, her sitting down first before looking up at him, "I'm sorry. I didn't mean that."

"It happens when you forget to sleep for a few weeks."

"I haven't forgotten."

Giving a yawn, he crawled across the couch, resting his head on her thigh as he settled in, "I'm here. You can go to sleep now."

Emily figured he would be dreaming before he could ask anything else and sitting quietly, she felt him fall asleep, his head getting heavier and his back relaxing.

She couldn't remember what it was like to sleep that peacefully.

♦ ♦ ♦

The following morning, Will's muffled sneeze warned her he was on his way downstairs, but too tired to move, she remained at the kitchen table, her sketch pad in front of her and Jack snoring on the couch in the living room. She'd retreated to the table when she couldn't stand staring at the wall anymore and she worried the TV would wake Jack up.

Will was about as surprised as Jack had been in finding her, but he covered fairly well, pausing only for a second before, "Up for some Scrabble?" Seeing her shake her head, he tried again, "How about some breakfast? I've got time for pancakes."

After a second no, she kept her eyes on the pad of paper she was drawing on. Settling in across from her in silence, he continued to look at her until finally she spoke, her head still hanging, "Why are you staring at me?"

"Because this should have stopped by now."

"It's just a few bad dreams."

"Emily. Look at me."

Still, she ignored him, her face aimed at the paper below, "I'll be fine."

"Look at me, please."

Her latest nightmare had had Tim in the forefront so she managed to look at Will without too much fear leaking through, "What?"

202

She'd been avoiding him for the last few weeks, but he'd been able to explain it away because of the normal swirling chaos of the house around them, everyone always being pulled in a thousand different directions, but now, she had his undivided attention and he had hers, "Why won't you tell me?"

"Tell you what?"

"Exactly what's going on." Biting his lower lip, "We've been running into each other in this kitchen more than we should be."

"Will, I'm fine."

"If you were fine, you'd be sound asleep in your bed instead of hunched over, drawing," glancing quickly at the pad of paper, "some fairly scary things and looking," trying to choose the right words, "like you haven't shut your eyes in weeks."

Anger and annoyance reared their ugly heads, "Everybody has nightmares, Will. If you would just stop asking me about the damn things, they'd go away!" She stood up and ran right into Jack, who'd come in to inspect the commotion.

Catching her by the arms, "Hey, what's your hurry?"

As she pushed past him, "Go back to sleep."

Standing in continued confusion as she slammed her way into her bedroom, he then turned to his dad, "What the hell happened?"

Pulling the sketchbook towards him, he thumbed through the pages, "I think things are catching up with her again."

"No kidding."

Will looked at him intently, "What do you mean?"

Twisting, he cracked his back, then straightened up, rubbing his head, "She got detention a few days back for falling asleep in class."

"Emily? Really?"

"Yeah. Dex told me. He was in class with her and texted me about it last night."

Emily stormed back to the kitchen just then, "He did what?"

Jack's eyes widened at the rage on her face, "He was gonna keep quiet about it, like you asked, but then he realized he'd better rat you out and I'm glad he did because judging from your reaction right now, you sure weren't gonna tell me."

"How do you know that?"

"Would you have?"

Backing off, she balled up her fists, barely remembering to keep her voice down, "I'm fine. Why the hell won't anyone believe me? So I can't sleep. You didn't sleep for months and I never had anyone spy on you."

By now, his eyes were beginning to blaze, "Really? I'm pretty sure you had conversations with Mom and Dad and with Tim and probably Dex. Was that not spying on me? You may not have had them following me, but you sure as hell were talking to everybody."

"You needed help. I don't."

"Do you think you still live that solitary life you used to? None of us are as blind or stupid as we were back then. You've got an endless amount of people who, if you can believe it, which I'm beginning to doubt you ever will, want to help you. Who see you spiraling down this bottomless pit and have no idea how to pull you back out. Two Decembers ago, I cut class and lied to Mom and had Dex lie for me and got a black eye and a bloody nose thanks to your flying fists and I didn't tell a soul anything." By now talking in a low hiss, his words slurring slightly as they passed through his clenched teeth, "I love you way more now than I even thought possible then and this time, regardless of how much you bitch, moan, scream, complain, whine, object, swear and punch, I'll go behind your back if necessary to keep you from hitting bottom."

By now, Emily was white, her hands shaking and her jaw clenched, "I didn't tell anyone because I trusted that when you were ready, you'd ask for help."

The fight drained off his face as he moved closer and in a quiet voice, "But I don't think I can trust you to do the same. And I didn't ask, remember, you made me ask."

Going from white to gray, she turned and walked calmly into her bedroom, shutting the door firmly behind her.

Will, shocked by the exchange, put his hand on his son's arm, "Jack ..."

"Not now, Dad." Pulling back, he sat on one of the kitchen chairs, his head resting on his hand while he watched her closed door, "Please."

Emily came out of her room five minutes later and even though school was still more than two hours off, she left without a word.

Jack still hadn't moved by that time and only Will's voice jolted him back to reality, "She's gone. You can stop staring at her door."

"How bad did I screw up?"

"I don't think you screwed up at all. I maybe wouldn't have yelled it all in her face, but ..."

With a groan, he laid his head on the table, his cheek and ear pressed tightly to the smooth wood, "I promised myself I'd never yell at her."

"Sometimes yelling is the only thing that gets through."

His voice seemed to echo in his head as he spoke, the lone tear dropping to the tabletop, "I broke my promise."

◆ ◆ ◆

He tried to talk to her at school, but she walked passed him. He filled Dex in and, being Dex, he attempted the peace-making process with a Reese's Peanut Butter Cup and a serenade. Looking over at Jack as she ignored them completely and continued down the hall, "We're well and totally screwed, you know that?"

Keeping a steady eye on her, he ran his tongue absently over the gap in his teeth, "Yeah," then headed to class.

Matt came up a moment later, "Why were you singing to Emily?"

"Attempting to apologize. Both Jack and I are in the doghouse at the moment." Giving Matt the briefest of explanations, he shut his locker and shoved the Peanut Butter Cup into his friend's mouth, "But that does not make me less late for class. Gotta bolt."

Matt watched him disappear into the crowd, wondering in the back of his mind if he should go find Emily or just wait to see what happened. The bell ringing decided for him and he headed to class himself, chewing along the way.

Friday night she stayed at work later than normal and slipped into the house quietly, straight to her room, avoiding any and all who still might be awake at the late hour. Saturday she couldn't take refuge with Claire for obvious Dex and Jack related reasons, so after work, she found herself knocking on Matt's door, feeling strange and out of place, even though she had been there plenty of times by now.

He was rightfully shocked to see her standing on his porch, "Emily? What are you doing here?"

"Hoping you'll let me in so the neighbor over there will stop staring at me."

Gesturing her inside, he shut the door, "Mrs. Rourke keeps an eye on everyone. Don't feel too special."

"Thanks."

Matt shook his head, "That's not what I meant."

Emily couldn't help it. She gave him a small smile, "I know. Just messing with you."

Smiling back, "Did you walk here?"

"Yeah. It's nice enough weather out. It's even supposed to be kinda hot by next week. Last year we had a giant snowstorm right around now so anything is better than that."

Feeling weird talking about the weather like they were seventy years old or something, Matt gestured for her to follow him, "Come on. I'm tired of standing in the hall."

Emily noticed how quiet the house was, "Where is everybody?"

"Cor's with her latest victim, Blight or Bling or whoever and Mom's got Bailey at the movies with some of her friends, so it's just us." He suddenly felt awkward having her in the house, "Are you okay with being alone with me?"

Giving him a curious head tilt, "Who told you?"

With honest confusion flooding his face, "Told me what?"

"Um, nothing. And yeah, I'm fine with it being just us. Not used to it being so quiet, though."

"I'm using the quiet to my advantage." Reaching the kitchen, he gestured at the open textbooks, "May you be the first to witness that I'm doing homework at the beginning of Spring Break, not the ass-end of the week like a normal person, but the damn beginning of it." After scrunching his forehead in thought, "Actually, not even the beginning of it, but the weekend before it starts. Pre-Spring Break studying … how sad is that?" Matt shook his head, then settled onto one of the barstools, "Pull up a seat, join me in my hatred of anatomy."

Emily shook herself from her daze, "Um, sorry, can't hate what I've never taken, although I probably shouldn't keep you from doing your work, should I?"

"Distraction is a good thing, necessary at times." Seeing her slipping back into clouded-over mode, he leaned forward, his head bent to catch her eye, "I like the distraction, Emily."

Deciding to just be honest with him, for the most part, "Would you mind if I hide here for awhile?"

"Still fighting with Jack I take it?"

"Not so much fighting as … can we just not …," fiddling with the spiraled edge of his notebook, she trailed off, leaving the sentence hanging in mid-air.

Matt nodded, "I think I can refrain from talking about Jack tonight. It'll be tough, but I can manage." Finger-walking his hand up her arm, then to the top of her head, doing a little jig once there, "Feel like dancing?"

An impulsive smile lightened her face for a moment, "Dancing? I thought you had anatomy homework to do."

"That's what later is for." Matt stood, his fingers leaving her, "Come on. We won't dance, but we're definitely due for something fun. I've got seven seasons of *Doctor Who* upstairs we can watch and a fairly comfortable bed to sit on."

"First, what's 'Doctor Who'?"

Matt feigned horror, "Seriously? Oh, Emily, you're killing me. You watch 'The X-Files'. I totally assumed you'd have heard of the Doctor."

With a shrug, "Nope. Sorry to disappoint you."

"You need to be educated." As they made their way up the stairs, "The Doctor is a Time Lord who travels through space and time saving the universe from the bad guys. His time machine is a blue box called the TARDIS that's bigger on the inside and by bigger I mean infinitely large; it could hold the universe itself and still have room for the pool." Leading her into his room, stacks of DVDs piled on the floor, TV on the dresser, "He goes everywhere, does everything and will never die because he can regenerate into a totally different person and he gets to keep all his previous regeneration's memories."

Amused by his enthusiasm, she could hardly say no and didn't want to anyway. Instead she settled on the bed, stocking feet tucked under her, "Why is it called a tardis?"

"First off, you have to say it like it's capitalized. TARDIS, not tardis. Hear the difference?"

She couldn't fight the smile anymore, deciding to forget her issues for a little while and enjoy her friend's enthusiasm, "I can hear the difference. Thank you for clarifying."

"Second, it stands for Time and Relative Dimension in Space."

"Is that something I should remember?"

Finding the correct disc and putting it in the player, "Definitely. There may be a test later." Settling in beside her, an acceptable distance between them, "Do you have a fear of mannequins?"

"Um, not that I recall."

Hitting play on the remote in his hand, "Good."

During the menu and BBC logos, Emily texted Elizabeth about where she was and once she got an answer back, she stashed her phone in her pocket, planning to ignore it for the evening. Once the second episode had finished, Matt nudged her, "Still awake?"

Opening her eyes wide, she nodded, "Yup. Start the next one."

"Yes, ma'am."

It was nearly nine when her eyes slipped shut, something about the darkened room and the fact that she hadn't slept a full night since February working against her fight to stay awake. Matt didn't notice at first, but when she slid sideways down the wall and landed lightly on a pile of clean clothes, he had to laugh, shaking his head and telling her quietly, "Jack would have a fit if he saw you right now." Standing, he tossed his quilt back and over her, deciding he'd let her sleep for a while before he sent her home.

About an hour later he was having the debate about how to wake her up when Emily decided for him. She sat up suddenly, her hand over her mouth, a choking sound squeezing out through her clamped fingers and her eyes rolling rapidly in what seemed to Matt to be every direction imaginable. He jumped when she moved and, standing up quickly, he kept quiet, not sure what the hell happened, but not able to take his eyes off of her. He'd never seen someone that scared before, with eyes that tore around the room, looking for who knows what, but searching all the same. Finally they stopped their terrified scanning and focused in on him, Matt saying the only thing on his mind, "Who were you looking for?" Hearing her sucking breath through her fingers, he shook his head to get the rest of himself moving. Taking her hand from her mouth and nose and echoing the advice she'd given him the very first day they'd met, "Breathe."

Emily's shoulders loosened and she looked less likely to scream with each passing second. After a few large gulps of air, "Do I have to?"

"Helps with the whole staying alive thing."

She looked down at where he still held her hand then back up at him, feeling both shame and stupidity, "I'm sorry."

"For what? So you had a bad dream. Unless it was about weird plastic-controlling aliens, then it's my fault and I ought to be apologizing to you." Knowing it wasn't *Doctor Who* that set her off, he rambled anyways, "Or was it the skin-stretched face that got you? Still creeps me out."

"Matt."

"Although I figured after *X-Files*, you'd be fine with these. Maybe I should have warned you about the Face of Bo, I mean, a huge disembodied head isn't something you normally see."

By now, she had scooted towards the end of the bed, tugging on the end of his shirt with her free hand, "Hey, it wasn't the show, I promise."

Desperate to keep his mouth shut, but still hold onto her hand, he failed at both, "Then what was it? You looked ready to jump out the window to get away from it."

Pulling her hand back, she stood up, slipping around him so she wasn't cornered on his bed against the wall anymore, "Just, uh, just a stupid dream. It's fine. I'm fine." Pressing her lips together for a moment to shut herself up, she took a deep breath, then spoke, her voice back to its normal pitch, "I have them sometimes. It's nothing."

"Didn't look like nothing."

"It was."

Pretty sure he shouldn't believe her, he let it go, "So, um, I probably ought to get you home, but you think you'll need a place to hide tomorrow? 'Cause, you know, aside from the nightmare, I had fun tonight."

Having no idea what tomorrow would bring, Emily nodded tentatively, "You wouldn't mind?"

"Are you kidding?"

"No."

"Well, let's just say that there is nothing on Earth that would keep me from spending the night with you." She didn't know how to respond and Matt went scarlet, "I just totally made it awkward, didn't I?"

"Little bit."

He chuckled in her direction, not minding that she didn't return the laugh, "Then go get in the car and I can get you away from me before I say something really embarrassing."

He got her home, watching until she slipped into the house before he drove away. Once back in his room, he sent Jack a text, "Emily was with me tonight. We just hung out, but I thought you'd like to know she was safe and sound."

Jack replied a minute later, "Thanks. Is she still super pissed at me?"

Matt debated his answer, finally deciding on, "She didn't say much one way or the other. We talked some, we watched TV, I tried to get her to rip up my anatomy book, but she gave me some line about knowledge is power and books are our friends."

"Sounds like something she'd say. Thanks for keeping an eye on her."

He wanted to send back, 'it's not that hard', but not wanting to start anything with Jack, who he now considered a fairly close friend, instead just replied with a, "Good night."

◆◆◆

Getting out from his glamorous job of pet store restocking a little earlier than usual the next day, Matt drove to the Golden Dragon. He waited in his car until he saw her come out of the main door, still wrapped in a coat, but hat and scarf gone, her hair whipping around freely in the wind. Stopping in confusion for a moment when she spotted him, she then came over to his now rolled down window, "Coincidence?"

"I think not. It's Sunday and I got out early. Figured I wouldn't make you walk to the house this time."

"I don't mind the walk."

"Would you like me to leave? I can head home and wait for you if you'd like."

Emily gave him a smile, "I don't think you'd actually do that."

Shrugging, "Probably not." Aiming his finger at the door, "Just get in, would you."

Once she had her buckle on, he drove off. Not wanting to lie to her, "Um, I let Jack know you'd be with me tonight. I also told him after I dropped you off last night that we'd just watched TV."

Her stomach twisted at the thought of someone else telling Jack where she was instead of herself. It twisted even more when she realized that this couldn't go on for much longer and one way or another, she'd need to act sooner than later. But of course, Matt didn't hear those thoughts, just the, "It's okay and thank you."

212

"Thought you might be pissed at me."

"It'd take a lot more than that for you to piss me off."

"That's good to know."

Soon they were back in his room, after having said hello to his mom and sisters, dinner declined for popcorn and *Doctor Who*. It took until after ten for Matt to turn off the TV and nudge her with his elbow, "We've still got at least six seasons to go. Any prognosis on the rest of the week?"

"I don't know." Hesitating, she settled her head on his shoulder, "But if I decide to come knocking, you'll answer?"

"Of course." Together, they sat there quietly, a good couple of minutes passing in silence before, "Think you want to tell me what happened? Jack's not talking and neither is Dex ... and Claire just says to ask you." More silence until, "He didn't hurt you or something, did he? I mean, I can't see Jack doing anything like that and I certainly can't imagine Dex letting him get away with anything like that, but, I mean ... did he?"

Lifting her head up, she shook it, "I would tell someone if he did do anything. No one's ever gonna do anything to me again."

Surprised by that statement, he chose to steer clear for the moment, "Can I hassle you with another question then?"

"I think you deserve at least one more given I've invaded your life and all."

"Are you gonna be okay?"

Her answer was quick, taking him by surprise, "I don't think so."

It was his hand brushing hers that sent her standing, her speed and momentum nearly toppling her right back to the carpet. Watching her regain her balance quickly, he stood up as well, hand going back to her arm, "Hey, what'd I do?"

Eyeing his hand, then arm, "Nothing. It's not you."

"Then why don't you think you'll be okay?"

Now her eyes traveled to his face as she backed away slowly, "I need a TARDIS. Somewhere that I can store all my baggage and shut the door when necessary and still have plenty of room for a pool."

"The TARDIS would do it, but even the TARDIS sometimes can't contain the shit inside. Things stored in there like to fight back at times. I wonder if maybe your issues are more like a Pandora's Box kind of thing."

Amazement took control for a moment or two as she looked at him wide-eyed, "That's an even better description. Pandora's Box, looks all nice and neat and normal, but open that shit up and it'll crush you to dust, the world ending in the blink of an eye before you can possibly figure out a way to protect those who accepted you in the first place, pretty box and all."

Anyone with any kind of observational skills could see this as simply the tip of the iceberg and plowing ahead, "Did Jack get in the way of the onslaught of crap?"

"More like he chose to step in front of it."

"But that makes him a good guy, right?"

"That makes him the best guy," pausing for what seemed like a horrendously long time to Matt, she finally continued, "but even the best guys can only take so much of someone else's crap, especially 17 year old ones who could easily have a much better life without me."

Telling her the truth, "I think you're wrong about that. Jack's life definitely wouldn't be as good without you in it."

Her lips turned up at the corners ever so slightly, "Are you one of those good guys, too?"

"Sure as hell am."

Suddenly in need of a hug, she stepped forward against him. Momentarily stunned by her move, he wrapped himself around her loosely and stood silent, enjoying her warmth. A minute later, her muffled voice drifted to his ear, "Thank you."

"Anytime." And given she made no move to pull back, he decided to go with some blatant honesty, "And just to let you know, I'd really like to kiss you right now."

Emily, not surprised by the statement, "I know."

"I've wanted to kiss you since that first day you found me not breathing at my locker."

"I know."

"I don't have a chance, do I?"

Finally pulling away from him, she kissed him lightly on the cheek, "Sorry, I'm all Jack's, but if he hadn't found me, I'd have definitely found you."

"Promise?"

Running her hand down his cheek, she kissed him on the corner of the mouth before stepping back all the way, "Promise."

He gave her one long stare, then shook his head, rattling it back and forth, forcing himself to stop the stare, "Ppbbththh, moving on. Were you ready to head home?"

"Matt …"

"I'm fine, honest." He gave her what he hoped was a nonchalant smile, "Or we could just stay here, have a campout with Bailey in the living room."

"Hey!" She waited until he stopped his fidgeting and met her gaze again, "Are we alright?"

"Yes, we're fine, I swear. It'll take a few minutes to get over you, but I think I'll manage eventually." Picking up the hated anatomy book he'd tossed forgotten on the floor, he pitched it into the trashcan, "But this has got to go." Then, taking her by the fingers, "Come on, let's get you home so I can come back here and start cold-calling actual available girls to go on a date with." After a fairly quiet ride back to Emily's, Matt stopped against the curb, but kept the car on, leaning across her slightly to look out the side window towards the house, "You worry me."

Leaning over to study the house as well, "I'm sorry."

"Ever gonna tell me what's on your mind?"

Turning towards him, "Might be awhile."

"I'll wait."

"You're a good boy, Charlie Brown." As she got out of the car, she looked over her shoulder at him, "Thanks."

He watched her make her way up the walk. As he drove away slowly he couldn't help thinking about how he had his own little red-haired girl.

◆ ◆ ◆

After slipping into the house and telling the few who were still awake 'good-night', Emily knocked quietly on Jack's bedroom door and, careful not to wake Sam, "Can I borrow your laptop?"

Immediately, he stood, pulling on his sweatpants over his boxers, "Sure, let me unhook a few things and it's all yours." She waited silently until he handed it to her, "Here you go."

Without looking him in the eye, "I was over at Matt's. We watched *Doctor Who* and gorged on popcorn."

Nodding, "I'm glad you had somewhere to go."

"Can I keep this until tomorrow morning?"

"Sure." He watched her turn and walk down the hall, her retreating figure resembling none of the girl he used to know.

He waited a minute before following and finding her door closed, he knocked, "Can I come in?"

Opening it, "I'll talk to you in the morning, okay?"

"Really?"

She nodded, "Mm-hmm," and backing away before he could touch her, "Good night."

Not sure if he should knock again on the closed door, he thought better of it and returned upstairs.

Chapter 17

Spring Break officially started the next morning and Jack, having finally succumbed to a restless sleep around 1am, stumbled into the kitchen at 7:30. Dave stopped dead in his tracks between the fridge and the counter, "What're you doing here?"

Jack, not ready for much just yet, "I live here."

"Okay. Then if you're here, who has Tim's car?"

Still mostly asleep, "What?"

"Tim's car is gone. He blew through here, like, 20 minutes ago, totally ticked off that you took his car without asking and told me to tell you when I see you tonight that there'd be hell to pay on your part." Finishing his trek to the fridge and grabbing the jar of jelly for his cooling toast, "He thinks you took it to work."

Still confused, "But I'm here."

Dave shrugged, "Just the messenger, man. Call Tim and tell him you don't have his car. Maybe he just forgot what he did with it." When Jack continued to stand and stare at him, Dave raised an eyebrow and pointed over his shoulder towards the living room, "Do you want me to go get the big board so we can draw up suspects and make pie charts of alibis?"

Any other time, he'd have thrown something at his brother, either a dirty sock or a smelly t-shirt, but at the moment, his brain was shifting into gear as his stomach tightened, "Where's Emily?"

Pointing towards her room, "Still asleep, I guess. I haven't seen her." Dave moved towards Emily's closed door, but Jack beat him to it. Catching on to what Jack was thinking, "Do you think she took it?"

Pulling open her door, Jack found the room empty, "Shit."

"Maybe she took it to work or something?"

"Go find Mom!"

Sensing the urgency and distress in his brother's voice Dave quickly went searching while Jack picked up a note left on the bed beside his closed laptop. Elizabeth, holding Ethan and still attempting to get him into his shirt, found Jack standing in the middle of Emily's room a minute later, holding the paper, "Jack?"

"She's gone."

"Gone? What do you mean?"

Giving her the note, "Emily. She went to look for her mother."

◆◆◆

Emily ignored her phone ringing on the passenger seat. Without a glance, she knew it was him, or at least Will or Elizabeth and she didn't have the energy to deal with anyone at the moment. She still had a good four hours to go and her tired mind could only focus on the road ahead.

◆◆◆

"So she's headed to this Parkton, Indiana to find her mother based solely on what she dreamt her crazy father told her seven years ago while he was in the midst of attacking her?"

Jack, who was back in the kitchen, head once again on the table, nodded, "Pretty much."

"And she took Tim's car sometime late last night or early this morning to go chasing after a woman who happened to be named Annaliese Wesley Ward?"

At this point, he knew as much as Elizabeth and wished his mom would just shut up for a minute. Sliding the laptop towards her, where Emily had saved the picture she had found online, "You can't deny it's her. She looks exactly like Emily and the picture we found at her old house. Hell, when I first saw it, I thought it was Em."

Elizabeth paced through the room, the phone to her one ear and the other aimed towards him, "Why won't she answer?"

Finally lifting his head up, "Ma, she's not going to. Her note said she'd call when she got there."

Hanging up, she looked at her son, "Did you know what she was going to do?"

"Ma, if I had, I'd be the one driving right now."

"Jack ..."

"I'm the one who left her alone last night. I'm the one who broke my promise and I'm the one who should be next to her now." Standing, "She's pissed at me, she's pissed at her father, she's pissed at the world and I'm willing to bet she's pissed at herself." Not knowing what to do next, he figured he might as well let Emily take the reins for awhile and, moving, he headed towards the stairs, "I'm going to work, but when she calls, could you tell her I'll be here when she gets back."

With that, he disappeared upstairs and Elizabeth picked up the phone, dialing Will while strapping Ethan into his seat. Explaining to Will while sending Dave, who had been standing quietly by, upstairs to get Xander, she put the big question out there, "Do we go after her?"

Will shook his head slowly, glad to be in his office behind closed doors so no one would see his sadness, "I think she does this one on her own."

♦♦♦

220

Emily called as promised, but instead of the lecture she'd been expecting, Elizabeth told her to be careful as well as passing on Jack's message, but before hanging up, "Em?"

"Yeah?"

"You could have trusted us. You know that, right?"

"Yes, ma'am."

"Please, please be careful."

"I'll call when I leave." Suddenly remembering, "Wait! Elizabeth, can I talk to Sam a minute?"

With her eyebrows knit in confusion, Elizabeth told her to hang on and once Sam got to the phone, she handed it to him, "Emily wants to talk to you."

"Emily?! Why aren't you home?"

His voice sounded so close, she fought the tears welling up, "I'm gonna be gone for a few days, okay, but I didn't want you to go to sleep tonight without my saying goodnight."

Sam grinned into the phone, "G'night back. Can you call me tomorrow again?"

"I don't know, little man but how about we do a couple more and those'll cover if I can't call, okay?"

After exchanging several 'goodnights', Sam handed the phone to his mother, "She says she'll call if she can."

Taking the phone, Elizabeth heard a dial tone and hung up, then pulled her son into a hug, "I hope so."

◆◆◆

After hanging up, Emily curled up on the cheap polyester bedspread of the equally cheap hotel she'd found just outside the city. She'd napped periodically at various rest stops and McDonald's parking lots throughout the day and now, sheer exhaustion overtook her. As she drifted off, her last thought was of Jack, hoping against hope he wouldn't be angry with her for too long for leaving him behind.

By the time she woke up the next morning, she was beginning to wonder why the hell she had ever thought this was a good idea. She had the address she'd found online written on a wrinkled piece of paper, her phone's GPS fired up and ready to go and a raging suspicion that this could be by far the stupidest thing she'd ever done. Since it was essentially now or never, she swallowed the lump lodged in her throat and headed to the car, aiming for the only address she had leading to what might be her mother.

Chapter 18

It was very early Thursday morning and she had only one destination in mind, a singular thought fueling her, keeping her upright, for, without it, she'd be on the ground, crushed by exhaustion and what felt like massive depression. The room was dark, but that was the way she needed it to do what she had to do next.

Gently shaking Elizabeth by the shoulder, she only had to say her name once before her eyes opened up, "Hmm."

Afraid to speak any more, she stood there, not sure where to go next.

Elizabeth knew, however, and she slid back, thankful once again for the gigantic bed she had insisted on buying so many years ago. Emily, for her part, realized she had absolutely no other place she'd rather be. Carefully lying down, the moment Elizabeth touched her, she gave up.

She tried to keep her sobbing quiet, but given Will was only about two feet away, he woke and, taking in the situation, got up, whispered to his wife that he'd leave them alone, then disappeared from the room, pulling the bedroom door shut behind him. Stopping at the top of the stairs, he could hear Emily faintly and it was a sound he knew he'd never forget.

Heading downstairs, he'd just settled on the couch when he heard the kitchen floor creak. Turning, he watched Jack coming into the living room, "Did I wake you up?"

Jack had been sleeping in Emily's room since the day she left, so after he heard the front door and waited for her to come to her room, he finally ventured out to find out why she hadn't shown up, "No. I heard the front door. Did Emily come home?"

"Yeah. She's up with your mom now. I figured I'd leave them alone." Seeing him preparing to turn and head up the stairs, "Sit down for a minute, would you, please?"

He sat, remaining quiet.

Will, elbows propped on knees, scrubbed his head with his hands, "The way she was crying when I left, I just … I think you should leave them alone."

"She was crying?"

Nodding, "I don't know what happened while she was gone, but whatever it was, I think it broke her again."

Jack's hand began flexing quickly, "She can't handle any more, Dad. No one could."

"We all have a finite capacity for stress, Jack, then it shuts us down and makes us crawl, sobbing, into the safest arms we can find. She did that. She came home and she did that."

He could feel his chest tightening, "But they weren't mine, Dad. Why aren't they mine?"

Moving to sit across from Jack on the coffee table, he leaned forward, taking a good grip on his son's arms, "Because they aren't. There are a lot of people in this house that love and support her. You can't question it. You can't worry about it. You can't get mad over it. She needed a mom … your mom … plain and simple. I have absolutely no idea what happened while she was gone, but from the sound of it, please, just be glad she came home."

His heart pounding out of rhythm, making him dizzy, "I want to take her away. I want to get in the car right now and just drive with her until we're someplace no one can find us again. Someplace she has no past to worry about and no future to fear." As his vision tunneled, "Someplace where I can keep her safe and she never has to cry again."

"I know. Just remember, Emily has 17 years of shit, if you'll pardon my language, to deal with and it's gonna take more than just one night with your mom to fix things. It could and probably will be years, actually, but for right now, you need to remember she's as safe as she's going to get. This is all we can do tonight, okay? We just need to wait it out. That being said, since we have nothing else to do," Will, leaning over to kiss his son on the top of the head, "how about we focus on you for a minute and try to calm you down, okay? What are the ingredients for your grandma's crock-pot beans? Exact measurements."

♦ ♦ ♦

Emily didn't say a word, she just sobbed into Elizabeth's shoulder, wrenching, body shaking, racking sobs that made Elizabeth cry right along with her. Having no idea how long she held the girl, she was surprised when Emily began quieting down. Managing to steal a glance at the clock on her bedside table, she was even more surprised to see that nearly two hours had passed. It hadn't seemed long at all, but once she began to pay attention, she realized her arms were asleep, her neck muscles screamed in agony and she had a pounding headache the likes of which she had nothing to compare.

She didn't even want to imagine how Emily was feeling at the moment. Waiting another minute or two, she whispered towards Emily's ear, "I can't feel my arm. Can I get it back for a second?"

Not receiving an answer, she tried again to move and this time managed to get free, wincing with every movement until she was able to stand. Stretching for a minute, she then leaned back over finding Emily asleep, whiter than the sheet beneath. Gently feeling the pillow, she turned to dig in the clean laundry baskets behind her, coming up with a bath towel then wrapping it around Will's pillow and coaxing it under Emily's head. Pulling the covers up as well, she left to go find Will.

First, however, she hunted down some Tylenol and, after swallowing three, checked to make sure the twins were still asleep and the rest of the rooms were quiet before venturing downstairs. Not too surprised, she

225

found both husband and son on the couch, Jack asleep, but Will wide-eyed and shell-shocked.

"You look awful."

Will gave her a smile, "You look horrible."

"I feel worse." Sitting down on the coffee table across from Will, she nodded towards Jack, "How's he doing?"

"Okay now. I made him tell me all his favorite recipes and when he still hadn't relaxed, I forced him to do triple digit multiplication in his head."

"Did he just pass out?"

"Yeah, a little while ago. How's Emily?"

"No idea. She never said a word to me."

Jack, who'd woken as soon as his mother had come in the room, opened his eyes, surprising them both with a groggy voice, "Can I go see her?"

Elizabeth tilted her head in his direction, sympathy clear, "She's had a really rough time."

"I just want to make sure she's okay."

Relenting, Elizabeth nodded slowly, "Be careful."

Upstairs in a silent instant, Jack stopped cold when he saw her lying there and, kneeling down, he nearly jumped back in surprise when she opened her eyes to look at him. Now knowing what his parents must have felt when he did the same thing a few minutes earlier, he vowed never to do that again. Taking a deep breath, he whispered, "I thought you were asleep." Remaining silent, she simply stared at him, not blinking until he spoke again, "Do you want some company?"

This time he watched her nod twice, words being too much effort.

Settling in on the floor, he rested his head on the mattress, "I missed you."

Another nod.

"Do you want to talk about it?" Receiving a head shake of no, he let his eyes wander over her face, neck, any parts he could take in without moving a muscle. As his eyes adjusted to the dimly lit bedroom it was then that he registered what was different. "Where the hell is your hair?"

Whispering, "Cleveland," she shut her eyes, her last thoughts being of the wonderfully dark, quiet place her mind was retreating to.

◆ ◆ ◆

Jack woke with a start when he felt people around him. Opening his eyes and seeing Emily still in front of him, he slowly turned his head, feeling every movement deep in his stiff neck. That's when his crowd of brothers caught his eye and, shifting slightly, he whispered in their direction, "Can I help you?"

Dave spoke up first, "Is she okay?"

The rest started throwing out their own questions all at once, "Why are you in here with her? Why is she in here? When did she get back? Where'd she go? What's with the towel under her head? Is she puking? Should we go away? Where are Mom and Dad?"

The barrage made his eyes open wide in awe, "Dudes, hold the interrogation a minute. I still haven't processed the first question you fired point blank at me, thank you very much." Determination seemed to be the goal of the four boys crowded in the doorway, with more questions spewing forth, which Jack silenced with his hand, "Holy shit, would y'all calm down and shut up for a second. I will answer as soon as I can, but if you don't be quiet, I won't say a damn word, okay?"

The boys finally understood the request of 'shut up for a second' and stood quietly. Jack blinked a few times, rubbed his face and massaged his neck for a moment before he began looking between a still asleep Emily and his brothers, debating whether it was time.

She hadn't hated him after he'd enlisted Dave's help with her at Christmas and he prayed she wouldn't hate him now, "Sit down, would you, please? There's something you need to know."

Dave knew what was coming and as he settled on the floor, "Sam, too?"

"Yeah."

Sam looked at Jack, "Emily isn't leaving, is she?"

"I'm pretty darn sure she's not, little buddy, but there are some things I think you guys need to know to help explain what happened." Starting out simply, he gave the boys an overview without gritty details and examples. He also kept a steady eye on Sam, who digested the information fairly well, asking only a few questions and nodding whenever asked if he understood. It didn't take too long and soon, Jack was taking a deep breath, "Now, hopefully, she doesn't kill me when she finds out I held this little pow-wow without permission."

Tucker scrunched up his face in thought, then straightened it back out, "We won't say anything to her or to anybody, right guys?"

Nate nodded his agreement, then Dave, but Sam just stared at Emily, then gave her a smile, "Can I still give you hugs?"

Emily, who had woken up at the beginning of the discussion, had remained quiet, eyes shut until that moment, when she knew Sam must be looking at her. With the slightest of head nods, Sam knee-walked over to her, nudging Jack out of the way in the process. Leaning in as far as he could, he rubbed his nose on hers, whispering, "I won't tell anybody, Emily. I promise." Her eyes filled again and lifting up an arm, she beckoned him closer, squeezing him as tight as she could without injury. While nice and comfortable with his Emily, he asked her, as only he would have been able to do at that point, "Did you find your mom?"

Before Emily could even begin to fashion an answer that didn't include swearing, rage and torrents of tears, Sam floated away from her, Jack having picked him up, one arm under his legs, the other under his chest, "That, Mr. Samuel, is enough questions for now. Remember, you promised not to talk about this and not to treat her or me any different, okay? She'll tell you what she wants when she wants to. I probably shouldn't have told you anything, but I'm gonna plead the fifth or the third or one of them and tell you all to be quiet and get out like the heavenly angel brothers you are."

And they did, filing out solemnly, the weight of their newly acquired knowledge bearing down.

They were soon over it, however, when there was a thud and a giggle in the hall, followed by Nate bellowing he was hungry and Ethan screeching in glee at four brothers coming in to play.

◆◆◆

Emily sat up once the room had cleared out, Jack crouching down by her knees, tweaking the ends of her now wildly sticking-out hair, "Cleveland, huh?"

Her face still a chalky-white, the shadows under her eyes even more noticeable than before, her bottom lip quivered for a moment, "I'm sorry."

"I would have gone with you, you have to know that."

"I know. That's why I didn't tell you." Standing, she nearly cried, thinking just how far away her own bed was, "How pissed off is everybody?"

Deciding to leave Tim's little ranting fit about her stealing his car and the comment or two under his breath about her also having absconded with his easel and tackle box of art supplies in the trunk, "More worried than pissed ... for the most part."

She sat back down on the mattress, "Why don't you people hate me yet?"

Indicating the ruckus still taking place in the hallway and the twins' room, "Do you really think they could ever even come close to not liking you, let alone hating you?"

Nate's voice came into the room clearly, "Jack? I'm pretty sure Xan just peed on the ceiling."

229

"I'll be back." Emily nearly cracked a smile as Jack disappeared down the hall, "For God's sake, would you cover him with a diaper when you change him? Oh, wow, you weren't kidding."

By the time the group had calmed down, Jack returned to his parent's bedroom to find it empty. With all the boys following as quietly as they could, he headed downstairs, finding Emily's bedroom door shut and his parents still asleep on the couches. Stopping, the boys pulled to a halt as well and Jack, reaching for the closest cell phone, which turned out to be his mom's, dialed Dex, "Hey, you busy today?"

"Nope. Just hangin' and chillin' with Caleb… it's what all the cool kids are doing."

"Feel like doing me a favor?"

Mock debating in his head, he held the pause for a few moments, "Sure, why the hell not."

In an amazing feat of organization, soon the boys, Caleb, Dex and Matt were headed to Dutch Wonderland, a smaller amusement park not too far away. Claire was strapping the twins, their paraphernalia and herself into her mom's car, planning to take them back to her house for awhile, threatening to give them blue baby mohawks and feed them pureed pizza.

Jack was mostly sure he'd made a good choice in the twins' babysitter.

Somehow, his parents remained asleep. Granted, the minors of the house had been much quieter than usual, but Jack was still thoroughly impressed and he told them so before they drove off down the street, "You guys are awesome, you know that?"

Nate looked at him like he was stupid, "Um, yeah. Where have you been?"

Smacking his brother lightly on the back of the head, he turned to Dex and Matt, "Thanks. I owe you two … a lot."

Dex wiggled an inuendo-filled eyebrow at him, "I know."

"Go away."

"I expect a full story in here somewhere, you know that?"

"I know."

"Cool. Catch you on the flip side."

Soon, they were gone and Claire was gone and Jack decided he might just want to lay down on the front lawn and take a nap. Instead, he trudged back to the house, knowing full well that his day was just beginning.

♦♦♦

He walked in to find Tim banging on Emily's door, "Stealing my car! Don't even think about trying to explain. You stole my God-damned car!"

Jack hauled him, by the arm, away from her door, "What the hell are you doing?"

Tim was in no mood to be calm or rational, "She took my fucking car. I'd like to tell her that I'm," aiming his next words directly at her door, "THOROUGHLY PISSED OFF!"

Spinning around, Jack spied Tim's keys on a pile of newspapers where Emily must have left them when she came home. Throwing them at Tim, "She gets it, all right. The whole damn neighborhood gets it now. Would you just get the hell out of here?"

"I'm not done!"

"Yeah, you are! God, I really wish I knew the day you turned into an asshole so I could go back in time and beat the living shit out of you."

Moving towards him, Tim shoved him against the counter, intent on screaming at him instead of Emily when Will shouted loud enough to carry over both of them, "Stop!" Pulling Tim back, he pushed him to the other side of the kitchen, "I don't know what the hell is going on with you two, but this is not happening right now, I guarantee it." Looking from Tim to Jack and back again, "Do you work today?"

231

Tim glared, "Yeah and I'm gonna make it on time because," his voice raising substantially, "the little thief finally returned my car!"

"Go! Now!"

Grumbling and red-faced, Tim left, door slamming behind him. Will went after him and, Elizabeth, tears swimming in her eyes, sat down at the table, "What happened?"

Jack looked at her, deep breaths doing their best to keep his blood-pressure from popping every vein in his body, "You didn't hear that?"

"I meant … I don't know." Resting her forehead against an open palm, "Something happened with the three of you and I just …" She ran out of steam and words so she just shifted her neck until she could see her son.

He was so close to telling her about everything, but a small part of him still wondered if maybe he couldn't get Tim on a really good day and talk to him, make him see what was happening, make him realize he was hurting an awful lot of people, make him wake up to reality. He wanted to fix this himself; save his parents the worry.

"He's just really angry and he was yelling at her and I … I'm sorry."

Elizabeth looked at him with disbelieving eyes, but let it drop, her overtaxed brain still attempting to wake up.

◆◆◆

Emily, at the first bang on her door, shut her eyes and stuffed her fingers in her ears, scooting into the corner of her bed back against where the walls met, her humming not blocking out as much as she'd hoped. This time, thankfully, she stayed in the present, still scared, but fully aware of who Tim was and not flashing back to other screams and terror.

◆◆◆

"Damn it!" Jack turned from his conversation with Elizabeth and headed towards Emily's bedroom door. Knocking lightly while trying the doorknob, he found it locked, "Em? It's Jack. Can you open the door please? Tim left

232

already. It's just Mom and me. Dad's outside. Emily?" It took a minute, but he heard the lock click and then saw the door open inch by inch, Emily's face appearing slowly. "You alright?"

She nodded, knowing full well that everyone in the room knew she was lying.

"Will you come out? Have some breakfast?"

With another nod, she moved slowly into the kitchen, looking to Elizabeth as she sat down at one of the stools at the table, head down, "I'm not hungry, but thanks."

"Don't listen to Tim, all right? He's just … I don't know … he's being …"

Emily stopped her, "He has every right to be mad at me."

"No one has the right to scream at you through your bedroom door, though, or call you names." Elizabeth took a hold of her hand and Emily finally raised her head, "I'm sorry he did that."

"Should I go out and make sure they're okay?" Elizabeth gave Jack what could possibly have been the funniest look anyone could muster at that moment in time and Jack couldn't help but crack a smile, "Although that might just drive him more nuts, you think?"

"Why don't you just go get some cereal and hope they don't wake up the neighbors."

The next few minutes passed in silence, the only sounds being Jack's crunching of cereal and gulping of milk. Just as he slurped up the dregs from the bowl, Will came back inside, leaning quietly against the counter until Emily broke the silence, "Everything okay?"

"He'll be apologizing to you when he comes home from work tonight."

"He doesn't need …"

"Yes he does."

Emily wanted nothing to do with that, but, not able to argue, she simply nodded instead, choosing to plow ahead before she lost the last nerve she had, "And I need to apologize for everything I did ... I'm sorry ... for the car ... for scaring you ... and for just being horrible these last few weeks."

Elizabeth, shifting chairs so she was catty corner from Emily, tears already smarting in her eyes, "We love you, you know that, right?"

As Jack settled next to her and Will continued to hold up the counter, "I love you, too."

"And we know you're sorry and appreciate the apology, but right now, you need to tell us what happened." Elizabeth reached over and ran her fingers through Emily's wild mess of shorn off hair, "Can you do that?"

Eliminating preliminaries, she began, "I stopped sleeping about a month ago and at first, the dreams were about my father, but I couldn't make out what he was yelling at me. Eventually, I started to hear words and finally," looking at Will apologetically, "the morning I yelled at you and Jack was the morning after I remembered what he said."

Without thought, he prompted her, "Which was what, exactly?"

"That I'd be better off dead than with her. I didn't know what to do with the idea that she might actually still be alive somewhere and I drove myself crazy until I couldn't take it anymore. I borrowed Jack's laptop and started looking for her. I found her address around midnight and before I knew it, I was in the car."

She stopped here and Jack told her quietly again, "I would have gone with you."

Lifting his hand to her lips, she kissed his knuckles, "I know you would have."

Turning back to Elizabeth and Will, "I got there Monday afternoon and slept through until Tuesday, then went to her house. After sitting in the car for a good half-hour, I finally knocked, but nobody was there. The neighbor saw me and after I lied a little bit, she told me where my mother worked." Shifting in her chair, Emily pulled her legs up under her. As she felt Jack's hand move to her knee, she continued, "I found her work and waited outside …"

Chapter 19

Tuesday:

Sitting in the car, Emily slid low and watched as the employees came out after 5. She wondered if her mother would be hard to spot in the crowd, but suddenly, she saw a sweep of hair and when the crowd thinned, it felt as if she were looking in a mirror.

She knew she should probably get out, but dumb-struck as she was, her mother was long gone before she could even think about moving. Cursing herself, she headed back to the house and after some discreet drive-by stalking until well after dark, she returned to the hotel, both angry and disappointed that her mother had never shown.

Eating her chicken sandwich, she stared absently at the TV, willing herself not to stare at the phone. She could picture Elizabeth giving the twins their bath, Nate and Tuck would have been playing one of their video games while Dave would be over at Brian's house and Will would have Sam in his pajamas, coloring or playing Battleship.

Clearest in her mind, however, as she fell asleep once again, was Jack. He would be stretched out on his bed, wearing an old gray t-shirt with some forgotten logo washed off beyond recognition and his green and blue plaid flannels, iPod in his ears and stocking feet keeping the beat only he could hear. It was a comforting thought and the only one she hoped would fill her dreams.

Wednesday:

She was awake by 5:30, eating the granola bar she found smashed inside her backpack, thinking if she ate any more than that, she'd be throwing it back up anyways, probably on her mother's shoes, which most likely wouldn't be the best introduction. Sitting in front of the house by 7, the nice looking car in the driveway gave her hope and at 7:45, the front door opened. Sucking up the remaining air in the car in a final, terrified deep breath, she pushed down the panic and pulled the door handle.

The woman stopped short on the sidewalk, keys dangling forgotten in her hand. Emily saw the look of recognition clearly pass over her face, followed by what was, unmistakably, annoyance. Praying she'd misread the second look, Emily headed across the street.

"Yeah?"

Hoping her voice wouldn't quiver too much, "Are you Annaliese Ward?"

The woman's face hardened, "Haven't been called that in awhile; still hate how it sounds."

"I'm not … I'm not sure what else to call you."

"Did he send you here? I'll be damned if I'm going to give him money just because he sends you to do his dirty work."

By now, Emily felt as if she'd taken a kick to the stomach. Trying to keep steady, "He … nobody sent me. I found you myself."

"Then what do you want?"

This honestly had to be a disturbingly realistic nightmare she couldn't wake up from, "He told me you were dead and up until about a week ago, I believed him."

Scoffing, "He's still an asshole then?"

As her world crumbled around her, "He's dead. He died a year ago."

Her face twisted into an insidious grin, "Finally drink himself to death?"

At that very moment, the anger boiled, "You knew he drank?"

"Why the hell do you think I finally left? I stayed as long as I could, but what 20 year old stays with a guy like that?"

Her fists clenched, "One with a four-year old daughter. You left me there."

"Four years was enough. Believe me."

Rage festered, "It's your fault."

"What is?"

Right there, in the middle of a nice neighborhood with cars passing by and people walking dogs, Emily stripped down to only her bra. Walking within a foot of her mother, once again, "It's your fault," as she turned, revealing the products of the years after the woman had left.

Morbid curiosity drove her hand out to touch the closest mark. Emily jerked away at her touch and, turning around, "No! You don't get to touch me. You God-damned bitch! You ran away and left me with him, with a drugged up alcoholic!" Her voice already crackling in anger, "You left me with a fucking monster!"

Pulling her shirt back on, she held her head high as she started towards the car. She was almost there when her mother, hand on Emily's elbow, spun her around, the anger flashing in her eyes, "Do you have any idea what he did to me?"

"I don't care what the hell he did to you! You left your four year old daughter behind!" She couldn't contain her anger, feeling it in every part of her body, quaking, tingling, blood-pulsing, heart-thudding, blinding rage, "Why?!"

A touch of guilt crept onto her mother's face, but was quickly replaced by defiance, "He never touched you. I thought you would be fine."

With a shove that had the older woman stumbling backwards slightly, Emily left her mother without a word. Opening the back door to the car, she spotted Tim's tire iron innocently lying on the floor. Without thought, she took it, moved past her mother and walking up the driveway, swung with all her might through her mother's car's back window, punctuating each word with a swing, "I … was … four … years … old!"

As her mother screamed obscenities at her, Emily deposited the tire iron back in Tim's car, got in and drove off, not caring about the destination, just as long as it was away from that street and the woman who had abandoned her.

She wasn't sure how she actually got back to the hotel, but without comprehension, she found herself sitting on the bed, staring at the small crack in the wall. Her head ached, her stomach ached, her heart ached and she feared her meager breakfast would be all over the floor if she moved even an inch.

Logic, however, won out about an hour later and, knowing she couldn't sit there forever, Emily moved slowly to pack up what little she had with her. Heading first to check out, then to the car, she suddenly couldn't wait to get back home.

♦♦♦

It was after 1am when she found herself finally pulling to a stop in front of Matt's house. For some odd reason, she felt the need to go there first, even though her soft pillow was merely minutes away. Also realizing there was hardly a remote possibility he'd even be awake, she jumped when she saw the front curtains move, then the door itself open up. Heading to the porch instinctively, he pulled open the storm door, beckoning her inside with a look close to panic on his face. With a whisper while leaning into her, "What are you doing here? I thought you were gone … what are you … are you okay?"

Will power alone was keeping her on her feet at this point, "Why are you up so late?"

Matt looked at her as if she had a second head, "What? Who cares why I'm up? Are you okay?"

239

Taking a deep breath, "I hate Pandora and her damned box." When he gave her a blank stare, she shut her eyes, keeping the tears at bay, "I never should have opened it. I just never knew that what I'd find would be what I found."

"Will you tell me?"

"Not yet." Feeling his hand on her arm and his proximity, she leaned her head forward, forehead against his chest, "I'm just glad I made it back home."

"So am I. You also shouldn't have gone alone, regardless of who you were fighting with or whatever."

"Pandora's Box doesn't have a minimum requirement label for the amount of participants needed."

Instead of arguing, he pulled back, then, leaning down, brushed his lips over hers.

To his surprise, she didn't cold-cock him, but rather, leaned into the kiss for a few moments, her lips parting and his tongue grazing hers, before she turned her head, "Matt ..."

"Urrghh, I know, I'm sorry." Resting his forehead against her hair, "I'm stupid and it's late and ... I'm sorry." When she didn't pull away from him, he ventured quietly, "You know you're my little red-haired girl, right?"

Barely above a whisper, "I don't mean to be."

"Most little red-haired girls don't." Lifting his head from hers, "It's us blockhead Charlie Browns that have to move along. And this idiot here thinks that you just might fall asleep on his stairs, so you should forget about Pandora and all her crap for awhile, go home and get some sleep. Do you need me to follow you or are you gonna be all right?"

Wrapping her arms around his neck, she hugged him tightly, knowing she could dig up just enough energy to navigate her way home, "I'll be okay and just for the record, that blockhead was always my favorite."

"I'm glad you made it back."

"Me too."

◆◆◆

Back to Thursday morning in the kitchen, Emily told them everything, including her stop at Matt's, leaving out only the kiss. Jack removed his hand from her bouncing knee at the mention of Matt, but had it back by the time she arrived home in her story.

Elizabeth couldn't get past the encounter with the mother, "She honestly said that to you?"

Emily looked at her, nodding slightly, "That is one conversation I don't think I'll ever forget. Believe me." Eyes filling with tears, she shut them, scrunching up her face in an effort not to break down again, "What I can't even begin to understand is what did I expect to find when I actually met her? I mean, I had weeks to realize that she had to have left for a reason and that since she wasn't dead, then she fucking abandoned me." Not apologizing for her swearing, which she deemed appropriate at this moment, "Why didn't I think of that at all? I could have saved everybody so much damn trouble it's not even funny. I could have gotten really depressed and angry and yelled and screamed and when you asked me what was wrong, I would have told you and you could have been angry with me and given tons of advice which would have been way less apocalyptic than me stealing a car and finding out, live and in person, that my mother, which I never want to call her ever again, was an even worse individual than my father and that," shaking her head, her eyes now open wide and devastated, "is truly enough to make me ... God, I don't even know how to finish that sentence ... to make me ..." She couldn't finish and instead of waiting for her to come to him, Jack slipped one arm under her knees and the other behind her back, picked her up and settled her on his lap, his arms around her tightly while she sobbed into his shoulder.

Will and Elizabeth waited patiently and only a few minutes later, Emily quieted, peering over her shoulder to take in the adults who got to witness her complete and total breakdown yet again. Kissing the side of Jack's neck where her face had been buried, she slid off him and walked over to Will, who gave her a hug, not saying a word about her now being covered in

241

various wet substances ranging from snot to tears. After a good long squeeze, she moved onto Elizabeth, "At least I know I have the best mom and dad waiting for me when I come home."

Like his son, Will said the only thing left swimming in his mind, "But where's your hair?"

Emily managed a laugh, "Callaghan boys have an obsession with my hair."

"I take it I'm not the first to ask?"

"Nope. First Jack, then," looking around suddenly, "where is everybody? I know they were up and if they're being this quiet, they must have done something really, really bad."

Jack informed them all about the boys' whereabouts, with Elizabeth striking a horrified look, "You let Dex and Claire supervise my children? We may never get them back."

Will shook his head, "We'll get them back, but they'll more than likely be all hopped up on sugar and dyed various colors."

Jack shrugged, "Matt's there. He's a semi-rational voice in the chaos of Dexville."

That straightened out, all three turned in sync to look at Emily once again and with a shrug, "My hair is in some trash can at a gas station somewhere just this side of Cleveland." Playing with an end for a moment, "Her hair was longer than mine and the same color and I just couldn't stand it anymore." Feeling fairly stupid now about her spur-of-the-moment decision, "I bought some scissors and while I was filling up, I stood at the outdoor trashcan they usually have by the pumps and I chopped it all off. There was some woman who just stood staring at me, credit card halfway to the machine, the whole time I was doing it. Mouth hanging open and everything." Cheeks reddening, "I probably should have waited and let somebody talk me out of it, but I'll say, it felt a million pounds lighter when I was done." This time, she began biting her lip, "How bad is it?"

Will beat them all to the truth, "You look even prettier than before. I mean, you will once someone cleans up the edges and makes it look less like Tucker attacked you with the lawnmower."

Emily, who still hadn't looked in a mirror smiled at his honesty as she ran her hands through her hair, making it stand up even more than Sam's did, "I've seen Tucker's idea of straightly mowed lines so I have an idea of just how bad it is." Moving on because she felt like she was about to collapse to the ground in exhaustion, "I know I just came back from a major rule breaking spree, but I can't even focus my eyes anymore so would you mind, maybe, giving me my punishment now or kicking me out or whatever you think I deserve so I can go find a place to sleep for the next decade?"

Once she'd received a two week grounding of no leaving the house except for work and school, she stood, giving both Elizabeth and Will more hugs and kisses before stopping in front of Jack, "I need to talk to you later, okay?"

Hands settled on her waist, he gave her a half-grin, "I can't even begin to imagine."

Simply kissing first his cheek then his mouth, she disappeared back to her room, the door closing behind her. Jack looked at his parents, the half-grin disappearing, "She didn't ask for help."

"No. She didn't."

Elizabeth put her head down on the table, "I might need a nap more than she does."

Cajoling her away from the table and towards the stairs, Will tiredly climbed the steps behind her, "Come on. We can pass out together. I sent an email to Toby last night about not coming in today so I'm good for at least an eight hour coma."

Jack, for his turn, called one of his fellow waiters and swapped his evening shift for the early shift the next morning. That done, he began slowly gathering ingredients for dinner that night, cooking keeping his thoughts from racing about what Emily still might need to talk to him about.

♦ ♦ ♦

Emily's sleep didn't last long, however, her guilt getting the better of her. Coming out just as he was starting to layer the pans of lasagna, "Jack?"

"So much for napping, huh? Smell my food and wake up or just the thought of me covered in tomato sauce turns you on?"

Knowing she couldn't wait, she skipped any pretense of a light conversation, "Neither, actually." Taking the container of Ricotta from his hand and setting it on the counter, she also dispensed with all courtesy, saying it before she could stop herself, "Matt kissed me when I stopped over there last night."

Jack, still holding his calm demeanor, stuffed his sauce-stained hands in his pockets so she wouldn't see the twitching that signaled the beginning of an attack, "He finally tried, huh? Took him six months longer than I figured."

"Excuse me?"

"He's been watching you since you first met him. You had to have known that."

She shrugged absently, knowing he had her, "I guess I just hoped it would go away if he saw that I was most definitely not available."

Contemplating for a minute, he asked her quietly, ignoring what felt like an elephant sitting on his lungs, "Look at me." After moving to stand in front of him, "Did you like it? Honest truth."

"Honest truth, I have no idea. I was so messed up last night I'm not sure what the hell was going on. All I do know is I wanted to come home to you … to this house and to you."

He was having trouble keeping her in focus, "Can you at least tell me if you are still most definitely not available?"

"I am still most, most, most definitely not available to anyone but you."

By now, he could barely stand, having the singular thought that if he could just move away from her, hide in the bathroom or something, she wouldn't have to see him breakdown, "Then Dex and I will hold off on killing Matt for the moment."

Suddenly she noticed the tightness of his mouth, the rigidness of his arms. Pulling his hands from his pockets, she saw his nails cutting into his palms, knuckles bright white, "Are you okay?"

He remained still as a statue, sweat beginning to roll down the sides of his face, "Give me a minute and ask again."

"Jack!?"

"Shhh. It's okay." Teeth clenched tight, he breathed as deep as his spasming throat would allow, "Just talk to me."

Out of nowhere, placing her hands on the sides of his face and angling downward so he could look her in the eye, "Remember I was going to tell you about my first real pencil. I was a little over five years old when I found it. My mother was already dea-, gone and my father was passed out from something, who knows what and I was hungry. I went into the kitchen, very quietly I might add, because even then, I knew that if I was quiet, I didn't get punished as much. I opened the fridge and didn't find anything, so I climbed up on one of the counters and found a can of beef stew." Seeing him focused on her, she continued, "I knew I could get it open somehow and I remembered something about a can opener so I started looking in drawers. I found it, but I also found a fat construction pencil. You know, the square kind?" Jack nodded slightly. "I'd used a pencil before, but this one, the lead was oblong and flat and just to try it, I made a line on the back of an old envelope. I could make the line skinny or fat by just turning it. I swear, at that moment, a whole other world opened up for me. I realized I could make thick lines without having to try to trace my first line over and over again, and I could make shadows and smudge it with my finger. I totally forgot about the can of stew and I just drew all over that envelope until there wasn't any room left. Then I turned it over and saw more blank space so I opened the stew up and ate it cold while I sat at the kitchen table and drew the can." She stopped here, realizing Jack's muscles had relaxed some and his hands weren't fisted shut anymore, "Feeling better?"

Shaking his head to help clear his foggy brain, "You, um … you've never seen me do that."

"No, I haven't."

Suddenly exhausted, he mopped the sweat off his forehead and dropped to a kitchen chair, "I'm sorry. I didn't mean to freak out like that."

"You're apologizing for something that is completely involuntary? That's like apologizing for breathing."

Flexing his hands and jittering his legs up and down, trying to eliminate the feeling of ants crawling under his skin, "I'm still sorry you had to see it."

Moving to him, she kissed his forehead, "I set you off. I should be the one apologizing, not you." Asking before she lost her nerve, "Do you forgive me for Matt?"

"I forgive you for Matt. I promise." Wishing he could sit still, he resigned himself to simple foot tapping, "Whatever happened to the drawing of the can?"

"My father stumbled in an hour later, found me still sitting there. He picked up the envelope, looked back and forth from the can to the paper and," Emily actually smiled at this, "told me I wasn't half bad at the drawing thing. He then asked if I was still hungry and when I told him yes, he made me another can of something, I don't remember what."

Standing up slowly, he pulled her in close, "That's it?"

"Apparently he was having a good day." Not wanting to set him off again, she decided not to share that this had been one of the last good days she'd had for the next eight years.

Jack hugged her tightly, then backed up enough to find her lips, "I love you."

"I love you, too." Giving him a genuine Emily smile, "Gonna let me help with dinner?"

His hands were still tingling, the muscles sore from the tight fists he'd been making, fingers twitchy, "Just let me get some feeling back in my fingers so I don't drop everything."

"Whenever you're ready."

Pulling a stool over, he sat, then picked the cheese back up, sprinkling a layer of it before sighing and giving her a look, "That was exhausting."

"The cheese or the," waving her hand around helplessly, not quite sure what to call his panic attack, "the thing?"

A smile flashed across his face as he mimicked her gesture, "The thing, as you call it, but the cheese was pretty taxing as well."

She returned the smile, "Shut up," then pointed into the living room, "Want to go lay down? I can put this together if you'd like me to."

"Uh-uh. I started this and I'm gonna finish it. Just make sure not to let me drown in the sauce if I pass out or something."

"Will do."

Halfway through the pan, Jack decided he had enough of his sanity about him to finally ask Emily, in the middle of a conversation about Doctor Who, "Did I scare you when I yelled at you? Is that why you went over to Matt's for those few days? You were scared to be with me?"

"Seriously?"

"Yeah."

Dabbing a dot of sauce on the end of Jack's nose with the spoon, "You don't scare me. I was angry at you and I left because I was angry, nothing more. I was exhausted and a jumbled up wreck and I was angry." Carefully placing a single shred of cheese on top of the sauce, "And I dealt with it in a fairly juvenile way and I'm sorry for that." Next came the smallest corner of a noodle to join the sauce and cheese, "My brain's a mess, Jack, but I'm doing the best I can." Finally topping it with a tiny chunk of green pepper,

"So believe me when I say that I don't think I could ever be scared of lasagna boy."

Jack's laugh burst out, jostling everything off his nose, "Promise?"

"Very promise."

♦ ♦ ♦

Dex, Matt and the boys showed up only a minute before Claire and the twins and given how much Jack had cooked, Elizabeth met them at the door, demanding everyone stay for dinner. Matt, having no idea if he should follow the crowd inside, hung back by Dex's car, debating with himself about what to do. The invitation had been from Elizabeth, but he was positive that Emily had told Jack what he'd done and that he was the last person either Jack or Emily would want to see. About to slip away and walk home, Jack surprised him by coming around the car and punching him lightly in the arm, "Dude, why the hell are you still out here?"

"Not sure where I should go."

"Well, I think you ought to drag your ass in there and eat some of the best damn lasagna I've ever made."

Staying still, he regarded Jack with squinted eyes, "Did you poison the sauce for me?"

Jack, crossing his arms, but keeping a light smile, "I'm not gonna kill you, I swear. I won't say it didn't make me mad, but I get it … and I think you've learned what not to do with my girlfriend's lips, right?"

Turning scarlet on top of the sunburn he'd gotten from his day at the amusement park, "Yeah. I am now very aware of the parameters and proximity of your girlfriend and I will not forget them in the future."

"Don't make promises you can't keep."

"I try not to."

248

Taking Matt by the collar, much like he would any of his brothers, he dragged him towards the house, "Hurry up before it's all gone and we're stuck licking the plates."

Matt laughed and by the time they returned to the kitchen, both were in fairly good moods, Matt elbowing his way in between Nate and Dave, "Pass me a plate, would you?"

A paper plate flew at him from across the table. Looking up to see who the flinger was, he saw Jack grinning, "Enjoy."

Emily, for her part, made the rounds of the table, in turn hugging each and every person tightly from behind. The chaos slowed and their voices quieted as she did this, until she finished circling the table. Before she could say anything, Sam looked at her, "Are you gonna leave me again, Em?"

"No, Sam. I'm not gonna leave you again. I might go places, but I promise, you'll always know."

Nate looked at her solemnly over his forkful of lasagna, "Did you find your mom?"

"Yes."

Tucker took over, "Do we get to meet her?"

"No way in hell."

Matt, having been filled in by the boys and Dex during the day, "Are you gonna see her again?"

"No way in hell." Giving Elizabeth a shy look, "Besides, there's a pretty good mom here already," then looking around the table, "and I ought to thank you guys for sharing her with me."

After all the boys gave her the same happy grin, Dex, always Dex, swallowed his mouthful, then, "Good 'cause that other one probably ain't worth shit anyway. Would someone give me a roll, please?" Five of them flew at him, one fully buttered, which bounced off his forehead and landed on his plate. Swiping the butter from his skin, he licked his fingers, then looked at the bunch, "Totally glad I didn't ask for a knife."

During the chaotic burst of laughter, Dave's voice carried over everything, "Emily ... when are you gonna tell us what happened to your hair?"

♦ ♦ ♦

Emily excused herself shortly after dinner and, falling asleep immediately, slept until about two that morning, when she woke up suddenly, her familiar room comforting for the first time in several months. Smiling in contentment, she debated for a moment or two, then crawled out of her bed, pulling her bedroom door open quietly. She realized the sound that had woken her up had come from the living room and if she wasn't mistaken, it was the sound of one of her best friend's snoring.

And it was. She found Dex, Claire, Jack and Matt sleeping scattered around the living room, Dex's allergy-stuffed nose making all the racket. Staring at each of them for several moments, she realized she wanted to see the rest of the family ... her family.

Passing back through the kitchen, she ran her fingers lightly over the kitchen table and what everyone now considered her chair and her spot, smiling at the thought that it would always be hers. Turning to go upstairs, remembering to skip the creaky eighth step, she reached Will and Elizabeth's room first, standing in the doorway, catching them asleep in the moonlight. As a calm feeling spread through her, she continued down the hall.

Dave had an arm flung over the side of his bed while Nate, in the bottom bunk, lightly snored. Tucker, in the top bunk, had kicked off his covers, his bare toes just peeking over the edge of the mattress. Resisting the urge to tickle those tempting toes, she made her way across the hall into Sam and Jack's room.

Jack's bed, of course, was empty, his iPod waiting expectantly on the pillow for its nightly ritual while Sam, in his bed, had curled into a ball, knees to chest, arms gripping his beat-up teddy bear. Picking up the iPod after dropping a light kiss on Sam's forehead, she made her final stop of the evening.

250

Ethan was all bunched up in the corner of his crib and after pulling him out straight again, the small boy opened his eyes for a second, focused in on Emily and let out a gurgle, going back to sleep almost instantly. Xander, too, had worked himself into the corner, but when Emily moved him, he waved his arms and finding her finger, latched on, squeezing with his tiny fist. She stood silently for a few minutes until his grip lessened and he slept as well. Running her finger gently over his cheeks and nose, she slipped back downstairs, more than ready to have one of Jack's Emily-specific playlists lull her to sleep beside him on the couch.

Jack, however, had other plans. Once she'd carefully settled opposite him, one foot on the floor to keep herself from rolling to the ground and one stocking foot temptingly close to Jack's ticklish ear, he opened his eyes in her direction, "Hi."

To her credit, she didn't heel him in the nose but simply returned the 'hi.'

"Did you know that I'm having dreams about Dex's snoring?"

With a small chuckle, "It's not a dream. Him and the rest of the posse are asleep five feet from you."

"Really?"

"You don't remember them all staying here?"

Looking over her foot, then back at her, "I have a vague recollection of asking if they wanted to stay, but I don't recall what they told me."

"Apparently they told you yes." Smiling down at him, "Going back to sleep?"

"I'm not tired right now."

Raising an eyebrow at him, "You're not tired?"

"Nope."

After studying his twinkling eyes for a second, "Oh my God, you want to wake everybody up, don't you?"

Pretending to shrug non-committedly, "I mean, might be kind of fun. I haven't played glow-in-the-dark Frisbee in years."

"But I'm grounded to the house, remember?"

Already poised to get up, "If you stay on the deck, you should be fine. It's still technically the house."

Staring at him for a minute as he plastered on his ear-to-ear grin, she gave in, "You win."

Bouncing up off the couch, he whispered a "Yea!" then dropped to his knees beside Dex, "Dude! Dude, wake up!"

Dex answered with a, "Hhmmrrphh."

Not to be deterred, "Wanna go outside and play Frisbee? It's 3am, it'll be a blast."

Somehow this penetrated Dex's brain, "Frisbee?"

"Glow-in-the-dark."

His eyes opened at the same time he grinned, "Awesome."

Matt was an easy wake as well, only replying that Bailey should shut up because it was vacation before realizing he wasn't at home and Emily's voice was the one that woke him up. Lastly, they woke up Claire slower, given she had a tendency to come up swinging, but soon, they were all outside, Emily and Claire curled on the deck chairs under afghans while the boys chased each other around the yard.

◆ ◆ ◆

"So, Miss Emily, what's new?"

Claire asked this with a hint of humor, a little curiosity and just a smidge of caution. Emily answered with the same, "Hopefully nothing for a very, very long time."

252

Smiling, "Do you want to talk about it or hear about just how insane my sisters truly are?"

"Insanity works for me."

"Good, because have I got some gossip for you …"

For the next half-hour, Emily was regaled with the latest on Claire's sisters and their various boyfriends, fights, break-ups and make-ups, "My God, I've only been out of the loop for a few weeks!"

"This is what happens with four girls in one house."

"How do your dad and Ben stand it?"

"They spend a lot of time in the garage."

"The garage?"

"Yeah, I found them out there once sitting on a couple of old buckets playing cards."

Emily laughed, "What'd you say?"

"Hell, I joined them. You can only handle so much of Andi and her whining."

"Very nice."

"Yesterday was a God-send actually. My mom and Evie were going at it, so when Jack called about the twins, I practically flew over here. I figured that all arguing would stop once I presented them with babies. I was totally right."

"Why were they …" She didn't get any further because they all heard the jangling of the chain-link gate, telling them that someone was coming in the backyard. Jack, on instinct, clicked the Frisbee LED off and Emily held her finger to her lips. Claire saw this and swallowed the inevitable question she was about to ask.

From their dark corners in the yard, the four of them watched Tim stumble up the drive, giggling to himself and mumbling nonsense. Right before he reached the outside stairs to his apartment, he stopped suddenly, threw up all over the evergreen bushes and passed out in a heap on the concrete.

Everyone just stared in silence for a minute until Jack, his shoulders slumping slightly, turned to Dex and Matt, "You mind helping me with chuckles dumbass here?"

Nose wrinkled, Matt started moving, "As long as you know that if he hurls on me, I'm gonna kill him."

Starting towards his brother, "Not if I do it first."

The girls watched them struggle up the stairs, Matt bringing up the rear, hand on Dex's back, making sure he didn't tip over as Tim swayed back and forth. Once the group was inside, Claire said innocently, "Neither of you seem too shocked that Tim just passed out on the driveway."

Emily, pulling the afghan tighter around her shoulders, "We saw him like this after homecoming and a couple of times since."

"Homecoming? Seriously? That was months ago. News like that would have hit my family within the hour and we haven't heard a thing."

"We didn't say anything." Biting her lip and looking up towards the garage, "Ever since he started school, he's not the same. He hasn't shown me any of his art and he doesn't ask about mine. He's been horrible to Jack and he only really comes around when Elizabeth or Will tell him to. I don't know, maybe the whole freedom thing of being alone out there went to his head." Feeling Claire's finger poke her arm, she looked her way, "Yeah?"

"That's not right, Em."

Staring at the other girl, fighting her urge to spill her soul to her friend, "I know, but he's Tim."

♦ ♦ ♦

Meanwhile, once the boys got upstairs, they stripped Tim down and dumped him on the bed. He woke up briefly as Jack put the empty trashcan by the bed, "What the hell are you doing here?"

"Helping you, jackass. When you puke, aim for the basket."

He turned to walk away, but Tim grabbed his arm, "Don't call me names!"

Fire blazed in him, "Don't come home drunk off your ass and I won't."

"I'll come home any way I want."

"Then next time, I'll leave you lying in the middle of the driveway for Mom to find in the morning."

"Don't tell me what to do!"

"Fuck off."

He never even saw Tim's fist. All he felt was the sharp pain in his cheek and the momentary feeling that his eye was about to explode. Tim overbalanced as he swung and after falling off the bed, seemed to pass out again.

Dex, shocked, first checked on Jack, who waved him away. He and Matt then moved Tim back on the bed. Jack just grunted, "Leave him," and headed towards the door. Dex made his way down first, but Matt stopped Jack just inside the doorway, "Does Emily already know he drinks like this?"

"Yeah. Well, sort of. She's seen him once or twice, but not for a while. I've been trying to keep it quiet."

Matt didn't like the sound of that one bit, "I know you didn't kill me yesterday for stepping way the hell over my bounds, but I'm gonna say this and you're welcome to shove my ass down the stairs, but, Jack ... I only found out about Em yesterday and I am already damn certain you can't keep him around her or her around him. It's not good ... at all."

"Do you think I don't know that already?"

"Then what are you gonna do?"

Throbbing cheek taking a front seat at the moment, Jack just shrugged, "I'm still working on it."

"Dude, you better work fast."

Knowing Matt was right, Jack nodded, as he pointed out the door, "I know." After returning to the deck, Jack sat on the ground in front of Emily's chair, looking up at her, "Hi."

"What happened?" When he didn't answer, she turned his face gently towards her, taking in his already swelling eye, "I thought he'd passed out already?"

His lips curled in a mirthless smile, "He woke up."

Lightly kissing his also-swelling nose, "I'm sorry."

"At least he didn't hit the other side. I don't need that half broken again."

Claire slid out of her chair, "I'll go find you some ice."

Nodding slightly, "Thanks."

Dex, watching Claire until she was gone, turned to Jack, "You know you just sent the noisiest person in the free world to rummage through your freezer at 3am, right?"

Jack shrugged, "The parentals are only tuned to certain sounds, babies and kids crying, smoke alarms, carbon monoxide alarms and genuine shouts of fire, famine, plague and certain death ... otherwise, you could circle their bed with fifteen toilets and flush them in surround sound and they wouldn't flinch." When Dex looked at him curiously, he continued, "If they weren't used to the sound of kids going to the bathroom at all hours of the night and people going downstairs to use other bathrooms and dig in the fridge, they wouldn't have slept in the last sixteen years."

"My dad could hear a pin drop at fifty yards during a damn hurricane."

Emily gave Dex a smirk while still cradling Jack's face, "Luckily you never break the rules."

Claire returned in a moment, holding a bag of frozen peas towards him, "How're you gonna explain that in the morning?"

"Maybe they won't notice." Turning his head towards the garage, "Or maybe I should have just left him on the driveway."

"Jack …"

Wincing as he shifted the bag of vegetables more towards his nose, "I'll just tell Mom and Dad that Claire hit me when I woke her up. They've seen her in action. They'll believe it."

Matt leaned forward on his knees, "This isn't good, Jack."

Ignoring his friend, "Anybody wanna go back inside?"

Most of them nodding, they trooped inside and all returned to their original spots, Emily laying opposite Jack on the couch, both feet by his chin this time. Once settled, Jack curled his hand around her ankle, "This okay?"

"Trying to make sure I can't leave again?"

"Sam would be sad."

Matt, from his dark corner, "So would I."

"Me, too," came the simultaneous responses from Dex and Claire, who then proceeded to jinx each other until Matt shoved Dex with his foot and threw off their rhythm.

Emily, temporarily moving Tim to the back of her mind, gave them a sleepy smile, "I would never do that to Sam again."

Before letting her fall asleep, however, Jack wiggled her foot back and forth until she opened her eyes again, "I'll talk to Tim. See if I can make him understand how bad this is. If that doesn't work, then I'll tell Mom and Dad, okay?"

Nodding slowly, she went to close her eyes again when Matt's voice drifted over, "If necessary, I will lend my right hook to help him with his understanding."

Jack looked like he wanted to smile, but didn't succeed, instead calling quietly over to his friend, "I may need to take you up on that."

The next morning, Jack's black eye wasn't much of a ripple in the grand scheme of things, the only reactions he received were head shakes and mutterings of 'she should come with a warning label' and Sam's, "Maybe she should sleep in boxing gloves or something."

Claire liked that one and gave him a dollar for uniqueness.

He pocketed it happily.

♦ ♦ ♦

Tim apologized to Emily later that morning just as Will had said he would. Sounding fairly sincere, his face embarrassed and his eyes humbled, "I didn't mean to yell at you like that. I wish you'd have asked if you could take the car, but at least it came back in one piece. Anyways, I'm sorry. Will you forgive me?"

Not thinking she had much choice in the matter, she nodded, her heart aching for the Tim she'd met the year before, the Tim who would have at least asked why she'd taken the car in the first place. The Tim who didn't immediately turn away from her and look at Jack to say, "What happened to you?"

With Will, Nate and Dave in the room as well, Emily covered for Jack's stunned silence, "Claire. Um, Claire hit him when he went to wake her up."

Shaking his head, he moved towards the back door, Pop-tart in hand, "You gotta learn to move faster, little brother."

258

Chapter 20

And for a glorious few weeks, life seemed under control.

Emily slept through the night, mostly ... well, not much more than she used to, but at least enough to where she felt awake during the day, which is saying quite a lot.

Tim didn't stay out doing who knows what until morning.

And Jack put off confronting him.

♦ ♦ ♦

Near the end of April all of the kids, with the exception of Tim, gathered in the living room. Switching off the TV, Jack turned to the crowd, "So, Mom and Dad's anniversary's coming up? Any ideas?"

When the living room stayed silent, Emily chose to speak up quietly, trying not to disturb Xander, who was sleeping against her, "You know, they haven't had a whole night to themselves since the boys were born."

"But they went out tonight."

She looked at Sam with a smile, "I don't really think shopping for a refrigerator counts as a night off."

Jack, with Ethan asleep on his shoulder, "That's actually a good idea. I heard Mom mention something about gypsies and cheap asking prices the other day, again. That's usually a pretty good sign she needs a breather."

"Maybe we could ship 'em off to a hotel or something for the night, throw in a decent dinner, send them to a movie?"

Looking at Dave, "Now, if Dex were here, he'd make some comment about already having too many kids in this family and we don't need to send them off to conjure up some more, but," taking the crowd in, all staring expectantly at him, waiting for him to tell them what to do, Jack finished his thought, "I say we pool our money and see how much we have."

Tucker, silent until now, piped up from his corner of the room, "We totally forgot last year, so it's either find the money or find new places to live."

As Emily switched the baby to her other arm, "What about Tim?"

Pulling out his phone, Jack began typing, "I'll text him and let him know what we're doing. After that, he's on his own."

After pooling everything they had, including Sam's 11 cents, they found they had enough for a nice dinner and an honest-to-God, $9 per ticket new release movie including popcorn and M&Ms. The other option was a cheap dinner, cheap hotel, $1 movie and no snacks. Dave clinched it for them by adding, "If Mom doesn't get her popcorn, she's gonna be pissed the rest of the night."

Everyone except Emily nodded in agreement, having seen their mother in popcorn withdrawal. Figuring they knew best, she spoke up, "Popcorn it is then."

♦ ♦ ♦

The following Saturday night, Jack had just fired up the grill when Elizabeth and Will headed out for their kid funded date, dropping the twins off for their overnight at Claire's parents house on the way. Since it was nearly May and suddenly unseasonably warm, they'd all decided to BBQ for dinner. They'd also invited Claire, Dex, Matt and Dave's friend Brian over for the night.

Nudging Dave with his elbow, "Can you go see if Tim's at his place? Tell him we're eating soon."

Dave nodded and jogged across the lawn, only to come back a minute later, "He's not up there."

Shrugging, he began opening the hot dog packages, "Can't say we didn't try."

Just as they were finishing dinner, Tim and his friends strolled up the driveway and, after a half-hearted grunt 'hello', they headed to his apartment. Sarah, who'd been trailing after them, veered towards Jack, "Sorry. Tim just finished finals and they want to relax a little."

He'd heard the glass bottles clinking together in the paper bags they'd been carrying, "Why do you stay with him?"

"What do you mean?"

"You're apologizing for him, but you don't exactly seem in much of a hurry to go upstairs."

Emily took a different tack when she saw Sarah cringe slightly, "You're welcome to stay down here with us. We're gonna play some games, eat like pigs, hang out, nothing much."

Her face softened, but she turned towards the garage, "Thanks, but Tim's waiting for me."

"Well, we'll be here all night if you change your mind."

With one last foot shuffle and internal debate, she went upstairs, Jack audibly grinding his teeth. Emily heard his jaw popping, so she slid closer to him, "She's a big girl, Jack."

Giving her another of those unreadable shrugs, "Whatever. Tonight, it's not my problem." After standing up, "Ready to kick my ass at flashlight tag?"

The rest of the boys and Claire scrambled from the table at the mention of flashlight tag and soon, the flashlights were dancing across the yard, with Emily having the foresight to remind Sam to stay off the roof.

By 10 that night, Sam gave up, heading to bed, with Nate and Tucker giving in soon after. Will and Elizabeth returned around 11:30, happily thanking everyone still awake for the wonderful night off, then headed to bed themselves. By midnight, the rest of them had finished cleaning up and were about to go inside when Tim's door opened up, "Any food left?"

Jack, with the magic of the evening evaporating instantly, "Nope. We put everything away a couple hours ago."

As he came down the stairs, or nearly fell down the stairs actually, followed by several guys about as drunk as he was and Sarah, quietly bringing up the rear, "Dude, there's always food. Just turn the grill on and make us something."

"When the hell did I become your personal chef?"

As he staggered again, his words slurring badly, "God, I'll do it myself, then."

Visions of the grill, deck, house and family engulfed in flames filled his head. Turning to Dave, "Can you take the tank off the grill and put it in the house, please?"

Dave, who'd pretty much pictured the same scenario in his head, started to move when Tim called out, "What the hell? Don't touch that!"

In an eerily calm voice, Jack nodded towards the house "Now, please."

"Shit … I'm not gonna burn the damn house down. I just want a hamburger."

"Then walk down to Fred's and eat until you explode, but you're not cooking here."

"When the hell did you become my mother?"

"I'm not your mother. I'm not even sure I want to be your brother anymore, but just for shits and giggles, let's keep you from frying yourself to a crisp tonight, shall we."

It was the 'shall we' followed by Jack's tightening fists that brought Dex up beside his friend, "Tim, just go upstairs, would you? Order a pizza or something."

"I don't fucking recall telling you to speak."

This got a laugh from Tim's friends, but it drove Claire to the edge of the deck, "I don't recall telling you to be a dick, but there you are, doing it anyway."

"I wasn't talking to you, either."

Jack moved a few feet closer to Tim, "No, you were talking to me."

Swinging his head back towards his brother, "You're so fucking self-righteous, aren't you? What is it with your goddamned absolute need to come to everyone's defense? Stay out of everyone else's shit."

"I will definitely be staying out of yours from now on. Drink yourself into oblivion for all I care. Just keep the hell away from me and Emily and the rest of the kids and we'll be just fine."

Glancing over at Emily, then back at Sarah, "At least I don't let my girlfriend keep me from having a good time."

"At least my girlfriend doesn't wish she didn't have to spend time with me."

Sarah turned and walked out of the backyard without a word. Instead of going after her, Tim returned his now fired-up gaze to his brother, "What the fuck? She's on your side, too? I get away from seven whining kids, learn to live a little and you all hate me for it. There's some thanks for you."

"Why the hell would I thank you? I've done nothing but stress about your ass since September."

Getting on a drunken roll, "You should be thanking me because you're now about 50 feet away from your girlfriend. You can bang her in the privacy of her first floor room as opposed to some cheap hotel. What I find amazing is that Mom and Dad know you fucked her and they still give you free reign." Glancing once again at Emily, leering openly, "Then again, with her ass and that sob story, I'd be nailing her every chance too … if you don't mind sloppy seconds or thirds, actually, from what I recall. Hell, I'd probably pay more for her than the first guy."

Taking the final swig of vodka from his bottle as he said this, he pitched the empty container over Jack's head, not paying any attention to what or who was in its path.

Emily, frozen in place, never saw the bottle coming, only feeling it strike the side of her face, the pain making her stumble sideways and lean over, clutching her left temple. As she went forward, she hit the right side of her face on a sharp corner of the deck railing, the edge narrowly missing her eye, but taking a deep, long and large swath of skin from above her eyebrow.

Jack turned quick enough to see the bottle bounce off Emily and for her to drop to the ground, the smear of blood left behind on the wood enraging him further. Claire reached her before he could move and realizing she would be in good hands, he turned back to deal with the second person to hurt her on his watch.

◆◆◆

The backyard exploded in flying fists and tackling bodies. Jack went straight for Tim and Tim, vaguely aware he must have said or done something wrong, defended himself.

Both Matt and Dex moved towards Tim as well, pissed as hell that their Emily was a bloody mess on the ground.

Tim's friends saw this and fueled by Tequila shots, decided to join the fray.

Brian, as small as he was, had enough muscle on him to wrestle varsity as a freshman and, deciding where he was best needed, landed like a ton of bricks on the two who'd zeroed in on Matt.

Dave, for his part, scooped up Emily from the ground, moving her past Claire and getting her onto one of the lawn chairs before he turned to Claire, "Get Dad." Seeing her nod, he darted off the deck, stupidly thinking that if he could get Jack and Tim to stop, the rest of them would as well.

Dave realized a moment too late that that was definitely the stupidest thought in the history of the world. Pulling at Jack's arm, all he received was Tim's elbow to his face, his bloody nose staining a shirt already ruined by Emily. Backing up, he leaned over and barreled into the pair, knocking all three of them to the ground. Tim's fist hit him this time and without thought, Dave swung as hard as he could, connecting with Tim's cheekbone just as he felt something crack in his wrist. Backing away in agony, he huddled against the deck stairs, cradling his hand and wondering when the hell it would end.

Claire took enough time to press a discarded and hamburger grease stained kitchen towel to Emily's head, trying to stop the blood pouring out of her cut, before she took off towards her uncle. Will was out of bed only a few seconds after Claire had woken him up, shoving past her, taking the stairs down four or five at a time before sliding through the kitchen and out the sliding doors.

His mind couldn't comprehend, couldn't put together that Claire's terrified shaking of him awake only moments earlier, her trembling voice crying to him over and over again, 'wake up, Uncle Will, wake up! Tim's drunk and they're fighting! Wake up!' would lead to him seeing his backyard in chaos. People Will didn't recognize were beating the hell out of boys he did know … Dex, Matt and Brian, boys he treated as his own getting hurt while under his care.

Assuming Jack was in the center of the brawl somewhere, he was about to yell 'STOP' to see if that would bring any order to the insanity. Then he heard Jack's voice, coming not from the group, but from his left, along with the low grunting thud of unmistakable fist to flesh and bone. Turning, his heart stopped for a moment.

His two oldest boys, friends from birth it seemed, were now swinging at each other with such force every landed blow seemed to shake the Earth under his feet. He couldn't tell them apart while they struggled on the ground, dirt and grass being ripped up around them, a score to settle that would never have any kind of redeemable compromise. He knew deep down that this was the end of something no one could ever fully repair. There would be no winners in this fight and nothing would ever be the same again.

And if he didn't stop it now, one of his boys would end up broken beyond repair.

Yet he couldn't make his feet move, paralyzed by images of the final fight between his brother Larry and their father. It was happening again. The thing from his past, the one thing he had hoped his children would never have to experience.

One sober against one drunk.

Dave's voice and the smallest tug to the bottom of his shirt thrust him back to the present nightmare, "Dad?!"

"STOP!"

The sound of Will's loud, resonating order distracted Dex and in that moment, he took an unexpected and full-force fist to the nose. Both feeling and hearing the crunch of cartilage, he dropped to his knees, forehead smacking the dirt hard as he pitched forward, wondering if his nose had somehow been pushed up into his brain. Emily saw this and waved Claire over to him, "Go."

Everyone else had stopped fighting by now. Everyone except Jack and Tim.

Elizabeth had been only moments behind Will and she bee-lined first for Dave, who had worked his way up onto the steps, completely missing Emily on the chair. Watching her sons while she held Dave's head, she swallowed hard, praying this was just an ugly dream. Hadn't her family been through enough already?

Tim's friends stared at Will for a moment or two, then took off, running or limping from the backyard, nursing their wounds and not wishing to stick around to deal with the consequences.

Will let them leave, instead moving towards his still brawling boys. Brian, who'd dealt much more pain than he'd received, ran with Matt towards the pair, Matt clutching his side, but ignoring it for the moment. It took the two of them, plus Will, to get the fighting boys apart, Matt and Brian struggling to get Tim to the driveway and against the fence, soon dropping him there in a crumpled heap.

Jack, once he came out of his angry fog, stopped resisting and crawled to sit on the deck stairs, head down, covered in dirt, blood, spit, grass and sweat.

And it was quiet once again.

◆◆◆

Will, stationed halfway between Tim and Jack, drew in several deep breaths, counted up to nearly 400 before he felt himself calm enough to not scream at the top of his lungs. Seeing Tim's eyes rolling back and forth, he correctly figured that he wouldn't be getting much information from that direction, so he turned to the rest of them, somewhat lined up on the deck, all looking both pissed as hell and scared shitless.

"Will someone please tell me what the hell happened?"

No one said a word, mouths sealed shut, all of them thinking Jack needed to be the one to start the explaining. The quiet held a little longer before Jack, lifting his head up, bruises already showing at the corner of his jaw and around his eyes, "I went after Tim." Spitting off to the side of the deck, "I didn't know anyone else was fighting until you pulled me away and I saw them," waving his hand in Dave and Matt's direction, "looking like that." He couldn't look at anyone, however, the guilt beginning to weigh heavily on him as he realized what each and every one of them had done for him.

"You started this?"

Dave, eyes watering in torrents from the pain in his nose and his wrist, jumped in at this point, "Tim started it, Dad. He came down here drunk and he just," not willing to say anything about Emily, "he wouldn't shut up."

Confused by now, "What the hell did he say that would start this?"

Before answering, Jack, his head still down, asked, "Em … can you go inside for a minute?"

By now her dishtowel was saturated through and leaving it on the ground beside her, she pressed her discarded sweatshirt over the cut, "I was here, Jack. I heard it all."

His voice cracked as he whispered over his shoulder, "But I don't want you to hear me say it."

Heart breaking, she whispered back, "I promise not to listen."

Jack repeated verbatim what Tim had said, "Then everything disappeared. I've been so pissed at him for so long and when he said that, and I saw what he did to Emily, I just … " Leaving the sentence hanging, he stood up, moving next to Emily, taking the sweatshirt from her hand, "Let me see."

Before he could say anything about the injury, Elizabeth caught sight of it and gasping, stood quickly, "Emily! Oh my God!" Rushing over, she pressed the cloth against the still free-flowing blood, "We need to get you to the hospital, now."

Trying not to look at the ribbon of skin still stuck to the wood she had hit, she kept her eyes steady on Jack's, "I know, but not yet."

Knowing no one would be able to make her go until she was ready, Jack simply crouched down beside her, watching Emily, but addressing his parents, "He's been doing this since the end of September, at least. Em and I saw him after homecoming and when I asked him about it the next day, he got all snarly with me."

Will's stomach was twisting in an ever-tightening knot, "How many other times have you seen him like this?"

After swallowing a mouthful of blood and spit he grimaced before continuing, "I don't know. We found him in the kitchen once, he couldn't even stand up then. I've stayed with him a few times to make sure he was okay. Other times, I've just seen him through the sliding door when I couldn't sleep and was down on the couch."

Elizabeth reached forward and tilted Jack's chin up with her finger, some instinct telling her that she would be right, "When you told me Claire hit you last month, was that really Tim?"

Jack nodded, "He came in and passed out on the driveway. Matt and Dex helped me get him upstairs, then he woke up, said a few things, I said a few things back and he nailed me." Will nearly asked what else was said, but Jack leaned forward, head cradled on Emily's forearm, "I'm sorry I didn't tell you. I just ... he's Tim. I didn't know what else to do."

Elizabeth looked over everyone slowly, wondering how she and Will had missed all the signs, then knelt beside Jack, "I wish it hadn't come to this, but you don't have to worry anymore, all right? We'll take it from here."

"It should have only been me, Ma. I never wanted anyone else to have to deal with it. I didn't mean for anybody to get hurt."

Kissing the top of his head, "I know." She stood up, addressing Emily in a stern voice, "You are going to the hospital right now, young lady, no more arguing." Looking around to the first kid she could find, "Dex, what hurts?"

◆◆◆

Fifteen minutes later Dex, Claire, Emily and Dave crowded in the van with Elizabeth for a trip to the emergency room, Jack flatly refusing to go and Brian and Matt claiming they'd make it to live. After dragging Tim upstairs, Brian took up Will's offer of still staying the night and headed up to Dave's room where a sleeping bag lay waiting, having already been thrown on the floor earlier in the afternoon. Matt made to leave, but Will stopped him, "I hate to ask this, but could you possibly go check on Tim for me? I need to talk to Jack some more, but I don't want to leave him alone up there for too long."

Matt, without hesitation, nodded, "I'll try not to whack him upside the head for you."

He headed out the back door before Will could respond, so instead he turned to Jack, the only one left downstairs, "Do you need anything?"

Jack reached in his mouth, finally dislodging the last bit of broken tooth stuck in his gums. Spitting once again in the sink, he leaned on the counter, holding a piece of ice in his mouth, "I'm okay."

Wincing, "You sure you don't need to go with your mom?"

"I'm fine. It's just another tooth. I've got 30 more or something like that."

Realizing he would get nowhere, he moved on, "Then you need to tell me, every detail, every issue, everything, from the beginning. Do not mince words and do not gloss over. I need to know."

With a broken heart and aching body, Jack spoke.

◆ ◆ ◆

Faster than they thought possible, everyone was back home, stitched, bandaged and casted, under various amounts of painkillers and numbing medication. Dave crawled in his bed without a word to anyone, Dex and Claire sacked out on the couch, Dex sitting up so he could breathe easier. Emily stood in the doorway to the kitchen while Elizabeth and Will made their way out to Tim's. Jack simply sat looking at Emily, her stitches covered with gauze, her body hunched and tired, her right eye swollen shut. They were still quiet when Matt returned to the kitchen, moving slower than he had been, hand back on his side.

Seeing both of them, he broke the silence carefully, aiming his words at Emily, "How're you doing?"

"I've had better days."

"I'll bet you have." Nodding in Jack's direction, "I'm gonna head home, I think."

Emily stopped him, running her finger down the dried blood that had finally stopped trickling from his split lip, "I'm sorry."

270

"Hey, my friends needed help and my red-haired girl needed to feel safe again. All in a day's work in my world."

As he turned to leave, Emily caught his elbow, "I'll talk to you tomorrow, okay?"

Hands on either side of her neck, thumbs on her cheeks holding her still, his mouth half an inch from her, "There's still plenty of Doctor Who to watch, nice and quiet in my room. Don't forget that, all right?" Feeling her nod slightly, he closed the distance and kissed her softly on the forehead, lingering longer than necessary before heading down the hall and out the front door.

Once he disappeared, Jack finally stood, "I'm sorry, Em. You have no idea how sorry."

"Yeah, I do, but you don't have anything to apologize for, believe me."

"I went ballistic and probably scared the hell out of you."

"You didn't." Walking over to her bedroom door, she gestured towards the handle, "I had Will put the lock on because I was scared of Tim. I've been scared of him since homecoming night. He's the one I dream about when my father isn't there." She shuddered at finally having spoken her secret, "You've never scared me, Jack."

Standing up, he wore a look of horror, "Son of a bitch! I knew you weren't telling me everything and I let it go! I fucking let it go! How the hell can I be this stupid with you?" For the first time that night, tears smarted his eyes, "I'm so fucking stupid! God, I'm sorry. I'm so sorry. I should have said something then. I should have pushed it. I should've …" Standing in front of her and about to drop to his knees in a never-ending apology, "Oh God, Em, I'm sorry."

Crying as well, she sobbed as she took him by the arms, keeping him up, "None of this was your fault. None of it. I could have told you I was scared, but like you said, it's Tim. We were all hoping things would change."

By now he held her so tightly, she could barely get in a breath, "I'm still sorry. You will never know how sorry, Em."

As he sobbed into her shoulder, the most she could do was run her hand over the back of his neck, crying along with him and praying the morning would be better.

Eventually he quieted against her, but not before he'd bled on her some more, his precariously closed cuts reopening against the material of her shirt. Pulling back to find his own space again and give her hers, he scanned her from head to toe, the guilt heavy, but manageable at the moment, "Tonight has been a complete and total God-damned disaster. I need a vacation and you need a vacation. I think I should go steal Tim's car this time and we just start driving."

"Right now?"

"Like very right now. Like left five minutes ago right now. Like no packing just put on some shoes right now."

"Like we should already be there right now?"

"Exactly."

♦ ♦ ♦

They fell asleep sitting on the front room couch. It was just after dawn when Jack woke up to the sound of a sneeze followed by a slicing curse and several groans of agony. He stood up quickly and Emily, trying to stand as well, got dizzy and had to sit back down. Leaving her, Jack stumbled into the kitchen to find his parents sitting up from where they'd fallen asleep at the kitchen table. At the sink, Dex was huddled, his face practically under the faucet, cold water running over his nose and cheek. Jack looked from him to Claire, who hadn't gotten any further than the step up to the kitchen, "What happened?"

"I think he sneezed."

They all collectively winced, even Elizabeth, who was still foggy and unsure if she was awake or not. Claire walked over to Dex and, handing him a clean towel she'd snagged from the cupboard, "How're you doing?"

272

Dex reached up to turn the faucet off, "I think I may have invented several new swear words just now."

"Awesome." Holding him steady as he stood, "You should write them down."

Still white as a sheet, "I don't think I can remember how to spell yet." Pointing towards the freezer, "More frozen whatever please."

Once things had calmed down and Dex returned to a more normal color, Jack looked at his dad and decided he didn't feel like normal morning pleasantries, "What happened with Tim?"

"Not mincing words today, are we?" Knowing not to sugar coat it, Will kept it to facts, "Tim was awake and sobering up by the time your mom and I got out there. It seems that Matt forced him to get up and walk around, made him some coffee and cranked a cold shower on him."

"Good … and … "

Will gave Jack a look and continued, "And we talked."

Jack interrupted him, turning to Elizabeth, "Where is he, Mom?"

"He's going down to your uncle Larry's, at least for the summer."

"Really?"

Emily, only ever having heard the name in passing, "Uncle Larry?"

Sitting down at the table and pulling out the chair beside him for Emily, Jack answered, "Dad's brother. He lives somewhere down in South Carolina. Why's he going there?"

Elizabeth sat quiet for a moment or two before, "After everything that happened to both him and Will, Will took to my big family and work and life in general. Larry didn't. He made it through college, but he was already an alcoholic by then. He got a semi-decent job and essentially drank his paychecks. About a year after we got married and I was pregnant with Tim, Larry was drunk and driving home and hit a car full of kids. He hurt some of them pretty badly and after he served his jail time, he dried out. He came over to our apartment the day he got out, said he was sorry, got in the car and left. He told us he drove until he hit water, which happened to be in South Carolina. He bought some rundown, one room shack, got a job and hid from the world."

Emily definitely knew about hiding, "Sounds familiar."

Elizabeth gave her a smile, "Then, after a while, he saved up his money, built himself a beautiful house right on the beach and met his wife, Calla. They've been married 12 years and she's the sweetest person you'll ever meet."

Jack finally spoke up, "But what's he doing at Larry's?"

Elizabeth continued, "Hopefully behaving. We called Larry and explained what was going on and when Tim asked if he could come down there, Larry said yes immediately, as long as Tim started going to meetings with him and doing a few other things."

"Tim asked?"

Elizabeth nodded, "He said he had to go because he didn't want to make me choose, but he wouldn't tell me what that meant exactly."

Jack moved his hand under the table to rest on Emily's thigh, "During our last, happy 'drag Tim upstairs' session, I told him that one day, he was gonna force you to choose between him or me and Emily."

Emily tensed, "Jack!?"

Dex piped in, nasally voice resonating through the kitchen, "I didn't think he even heard you. Only took him a month or so to decide to put it to the test."

Elizabeth held up a finger, "You told him what exactly?"

The shame on Jack's face was evident, "I told him you'd have to choose who stayed and who left and did he really want to do that to you?"

Elizabeth drew in a sharp breath, "Jack Andrew Callaghan!"

"Mom, you didn't see him. You didn't have to hear the things he was saying."

"Jack, I never could have chosen."

"I know that, but I guess this morning, he didn't feel like taking a chance."

Looking at her son's determined eyes, "Would you have left?"

He nodded slowly, "I only said it to scare him." With a glance at Emily, "But if he had really and truly forced me into that corner, I couldn't have risked you. Not if he kept doing what he was doing and after last night, I don't doubt he would have gotten worse."

Emily spoke up, "Why didn't you tell me any of this?"

"I like to refer to it as 'things better left unsaid'."

Elizabeth reached across the table, squeezing his hand, "That was an awful big bluff you were playing."

"I know." As his face crumpled and his chin quaked, "I'm sorry."

Getting up, she came over and leaned between Jack and Emily, wrapping her arms around both of them, and whispered, "I don't think I could bear losing the two of you."

Jack's humor surfaced for a moment, "On the bright side, you would have had two less mouths to feed."

Giving him a kiss on the forehead, she stood back up, "Never joke about that."

"Sorry."

A little voice in Emily's head told her to leave well enough alone; to not ask questions to which she probably would not enjoy the answers. She ignored the voice, and touched Elizabeth's arm with her hand, "Did he say anything else before he left?"

Wishing Emily hadn't asked, Elizabeth shook her head slowly, "No, he didn't."

Jack reacted immediately, pounding his fist to the table, making them all jump, "Fucking jackass. I should have beat an apology out of him last night."

Elizabeth whirled around, "Watch your mouth. He's still your brother."

"My brother wouldn't have put me through hell for nine months, he wouldn't have knocked my teeth out, he would have apologized for saying what he did and my brother would not have called my girlfriend a whore."

"He's not himself right now and you know it."

"Really, Mom? You're gonna give him an excuse, with Emily sitting right here, knowing damn well that any excuse is about as bad as giving him the bottle yourself?"

"Jack!"

Anger drove him to his feet, "Whatever. He was sober enough this morning to know what to do and he still didn't apologize."

Will spoke up, voice quiet, "He's sick, Jack, and it's not something to cure with chicken soup and a good night's sleep. He's trying to get help and that's more than I can say about my father," indicating towards Emily, "and definitely hers, ever did. All we can do right now is be happy he's trying."

Refusing to accept that, he turned to go when he felt Emily stop him with a hand, "I don't know if I can ever believe it, Jack, but I understand what he's saying. I've never gotten an apology from anyone for things they've done to me and I don't need one now. Tim's gone and that's what I focus on today; that … I won't be scared … today. I can't think any further than that and I'm not going to, not right now."

His rage dissipated immediately and in the silence still filling the room, he put his hands on the arms of her chair and, leaning forward, forehead meeting hers, "We won't be scared today."

"Not today."

♦♦♦

Tucker came racing down the stairs only moments later, while they were still all in the kitchen. He skidded to a stop, panic all over his face from having just seen Dave and Brian asleep, but battered and bruised. When he processed the rest of them, standing there in pieces, he did something that Emily had never seen before; he let several tears roll down his cheeks before whispering to his mom, "What happened?"

Elizabeth had him in a hug immediately, "I'm sorry. We didn't mean for you to get scared." Kissing the top of his head and continuing to hold him close, "If you can wait a few minutes until we get everyone up, I promise we will answer your questions, okay?"

In another unusual gesture, he stayed in his mom's hug, eyeing everyone over the top of Elizabeth's arm. Will was luckily already heading upstairs so Tucker didn't have to wait long for an explanation. Nate came down quietly, having decided to see what was up before asking Will why he looked so serious for 7am. Dave and Brian came in behind Nate, rubbing their eyes and yawning while Sam, on the other hand, took one look at his father and hauled downstairs, racing into Emily's room, calling her name.

"Sam. Sam. I'm out here. I'm still here, I promise."

Flying back out of her room, he stopped, relief clear on his face, until he saw her bandages and bruising. Then, his little fists balled up tight, mouth and eyebrows crinkling in anger, "Who did that?" Emily looked helplessly at Will, totally lost as for a response, but before anyone could answer, Sam stomped his foot, yelling loudly, "Who did that to you?!"

Elizabeth, turning Tucker over to Will, crouched down beside him, "It was an accident, honey. She was hit with a bottle last night."

Turning in his mother's arms, he looked from Emily to Jack to Dex to Dave to Brian, each person getting a second's scrutiny, "Where's Tim?"

Emily scooted herself down on the floor, holding out her hands to Sam, "C'mere."

Sam slipped from Elizabeth's grasp and walked over to Emily, sitting down in front of her, "Was it Tim?"

"Why do you think it was him?"

"'Cause he's not here and everyone else is and if everybody looks like that and he's not here then something happened to him or he beat everybody up and I need to know where he is so I can go hit him back for you."

Pulling him in, she hugged him tight, "I love you so much, little man, but I can't have you beating up people for me."

"Jack did."

Tightening her grip, she looked up at Elizabeth over the top of Sam's head, "We're gonna have to tell them everything."

In order to thoroughly explain things to the boys, Will had to also tell about his own growing up, which was difficult, but manageable, especially given that Nate piped in with, "We kinda figured something was up 'cause you swim in a shirt. Sam thought maybe you were a superhero with a cape under there and I was hoping, maybe, that you'd had some horribly nasty surgery and had bionic wings or something now."

Will smiled at that one, "No wings, I swear."

Tucker, deadly quiet until now, looked from his parents to the rest of them, "I hate Tim."

"No you don't, Tuck. You're just really angry right now."

"Nope. I hate him and I hope he never comes back."

"I'm feeling the same way right now." Jack stepped up behind his brother and not knowing if he was lying, but feeling obligated to say it anyways, "But I think we'll change our minds ... eventually."

He knew his brother too well apparently and with a snort, "Whatever, Jack."

Sam, however, looked at Tucker, "We can't hate him, but we don't have to like him much right now."

"This from the kid who wants to beat him up."

"But I won't hate him when I do it."

Elizabeth put up her hands in surrender, "All right, kids. Enough of that for now. I'm hungry so I'm making breakfast of whatever I want and if you don't like it, tough beans."

Dex piped up, "Am I included?"

"Yes, Dexter, you are definitely one of my kids now so find a chair and try not to sneeze. I won't pepper anything just for you."

"My nostrils appreciate it more than you know."

♦ ♦ ♦

By late afternoon, the world had settled down, everyone now in the Callaghan's backyard. Claire was attempting to teach both Dave and Brian the intricacies of modern geometry at the picnic table; Dex was in one of the deck chairs, listening to Claire and still not understanding the intricacies of modern geometry. The twins, back from their sleepover with their Aunt Jenny, were asleep just inside the sliding door, with Elizabeth listening for them from her own deck chair. The rest of the boys were playing soccer at the back of the yard with Will.

Emily and Jack sat on the edge of the deck, Jack absently swinging his feet while resting his arms on the railing in front of him, bruised hands dangling over the edge. Will had cleaned the deck earlier in the day, but there was no helping the torn up lawn, clumps of grass tossed around, looking more like a pack of wild dogs had ripped it apart instead of two brothers. Careful of the bruises she knew where blossoming on his sides, she nudged him gently with her elbow, "Hey, wanna get out of here?"

Dragging back from his formless daydream, he took a second before looking over at her, "Huh?"

"Wanna get out of here? Go to the movies? Go to the park? Go to Australia and laugh at the kangaroos?"

"No," he shook his head, "not right now."

"Or we could just get in the car and go. I recall you mentioning something about that last night."

"I'll have to buy my own car if we're gonna make a run for it," shutting his eyes, "although we should probably get through graduation first."

Emily, resting her hand on his leg, "I guess it'd be nice to get my stitches out before we tackle a road trip; be able to see out of both eyes."

With a nod, he then stifled a yawn, "Stitch-free is good, visibility even better."

The exchange held none of the light tones it should have and Emily squeezed his knee gently, whispering over to him, "You know, sleep is pretty good, too."

"Nah." Shifting so he could see most of the backyard, "I like it right here. Sleep can wait."

After kissing his elbow, she rested her chin on it, studying his profile, "Yeah, it can."

Jack turned towards her, kissing her lightly on the nose, "Will you start going to Amelia with me?"

"You mean to your sessions?"

Staring intently, "I mean will you go yourself? To your own sessions."
Trying to smile, his eyes remained somber, "I think you're gonna need
more than the twice a month that I go now and I'm still screwed up
enough to need my full hour." By now, he was lightly swinging his leg into
hers, bare foot to bare foot, "We've been waiting for you to ask for help,
but I decided that maybe you already have and none of us realized it until
now."

Choosing not to answer at the moment, she continued to look at Jack, him
gazing right back, not pushing anymore, letting her decide in silence.

A few minutes later, she moved to stand up, "Back in a bit." Nodding to
her, she turned, then found Elizabeth. Standing beside her, she held out
her hand, not saying a word.

Elizabeth, for her part, didn't say anything either as she took Emily's hand
and stood up, asking Claire if she'd mind keeping an eye on the twins for a
little while. She then followed Emily inside.

Leading Elizabeth to her bedroom, Emily shut the door behind them, then
closed the blinds and curtains. The room, now as dark as it could be at that
time of day, would have to do. Turning away from her, Emily swallowed
hard, then in a quiet voice, "Will you help me?"

**More of
The Jack and Emily Series
is coming.**

**Like us on Facebook:
https://www.facebook.com/OrangePublishing**